WAR QUEST
OUT OF THE ASHES

JOHN D. BELCASTRO

Copyright © 2021 John D. Belcastro
All rights reserved
First Edition

Fulton Books, Inc.
Meadville, PA

Published by Fulton Books 2021

ISBN 978-1-63710-939-7 (paperback)
ISBN 978-1-63710-941-0 (hardcover)
ISBN 978-1-63710-940-3 (digital)

Printed in the United States of America

To my loving wife, Nancy, who never lost faith in me, and to my loyal puppy, Princess, who never left my side.

PROLOGUE

Somewhere into the unknown, the aged fighter marched. The blistering sun directly overhead burned through red, incinerated skies, driving beads of perspiration from his grimy brow. Deep lines channeled the saline moisture from his coarse, leathery cheeks like so many canals of irrigation. The grim visage of this determined warrior, framed by a dingy white mane and soiled damp beard, presented an ominous apparition. Sharp contrast indeed to the bold, dark eyes desperately searching the horizon for reasons known only to the mysterious traveler.

The scorched dust of a barren earth danced about his heels with every stride. Tendrils of smoke from the ashen soil, clinging like vines around his tattered leggings, ascended to envelop the weary wanderer in a dusky shroud. Particles of parched filth readily adhered to the greasy film of his buckskin shirt, trousers, and black bear cape.

Despite the absence of trees or vegetation, the refreshing stimulation of a gentle breeze was impossible to find. Towering mountain ranges provided an emerald backdrop some miles to the east, the point from which the wayfarer had begun. Except for an occasional outcropping of jagged rock to disturb the congruity of the desolate landscape, the depleted expanse proved to be a veritable wasteland devoid of any living thing.

The determined legionnaire trekked unerringly toward his destination. Clouds of fine particles floated in the loner's wake, refusing to dissipate in the stagnant air. The soft patting of his bruised feet against the khaki soil was nearly obscured by the bleating of frail lungs laboring to inhale the stale atmosphere. He was trudging slowly; mastication kept time with stride. Methodically, he would extend the walking staff in his right hand in an effort to maintain equilibrium. A pronounced limp, an old battle injury from some forgotten campaign, hampered his momentum.

Undaunted, the persistent rover pressed toward his destination. His stooped posture and uncertain gait belied the truth of his years. Hard years. Desperate years. Tortured years. The once-powerful fighting man was but a shadow of his former self.

Scrutinizing the desolation that lay before him, the lone excursionist was distracted by a gleaming object partially buried in the abrasive soil. Approaching the concealed artifact, the gadabout could not comprehend the objects surviving the nuclear fulmination that ravaged the country decades past. The nomad jerked spasmodically as he bent at the waist in an effort to retrieve the gadget. Losing his balance, the wretch tumbled onto his face, his wooden staff taking flight as outstretched arms attempted to halt the unexpected descent.

Righting himself to his knees, after many unsuccessful attempts to do so, the decrepit form realized the fall and ensuing maneuver buried the article from sight. Frantically, he sifted through the sandy soil, running the stiff digits of both hands in every direction. With great delight, the poor soul closed arthritic fingers around the rigid device. A smile crept across his cracked and bleeding lips; the corners of his eyes wrinkled as he reveled in his find. Trembling, the vagabond studied the object, confused by its construction. The item, fabricated of metal if the pentagonal shape of one end was any indication, incorporated a sharpened point on the other. In fact, it was the sun's red rays reflecting off the mirrorlike blade that had attracted his attention.

Turning the bright steel contraption end for end, the aging nomad noticed one curious fact: the twelve-inch length of metal was totally devoid of rust. The smile instantly disappeared from his lips. His eyes widened in comprehension as one crucial detail became obvious.

Someone had recently traveled through no-man's-land.

Cognizant to the danger, the terrified stranger struggled to rise to fend against some unseen foe. The troubled warrior constantly looked about while groping for his staff, lest he end up on an adversary's lance. Spying the hickory rod seven feet to his right, he crawled toward the shaft as fast as his mangled legs could propel him. Frantically he strove to erect himself, perceiving some evil presence would pounce at any moment. Using the staff as an aid, he began the mad scramble up the rough, splintered stalk. He did not get far before the shaft lost its anchor in the loose soil, sending him to his knees. Panic consumed him. He knew well the horrible fate one would suffer at the hands of the cutthroats. Once more, the desperate man tried to rise, and again the shaft refused to hold its ground.

A chill ran from the back of the curmudgeon's neck to the base of his spine as steely fingers encircled the leathery folds of his throat. Crying out in anguish, the frightened elder redoubled his effort to raise himself to a defensible posture. But…alas! His withered limbs refused to respond. Arms too weak from hunger and legs ravaged by the cruel environment balked at the command.

Finding it impossible to breathe, the wheezing wretch wilted to the earth. The bastard had him. He knew from experience that he would perish in some foul manner. Those in a condition such as his were useless as slaves, worthless as barter for women, or weapons. More likely, he would be traded to the slavers, sold on the black market, to be butchered for fodder to feed the boars.

Contemplating his fate, the terrified soul began to weep. He cried for his departed wife, whose grave he would never again adorn with flowers. He cried for his children, with whom he would never share another precious moment. He cried for his fellow tribesmen who would scour the ends of the earth for him—in vain. Finally, he wept for himself as he realized his plight was but a manifestation of an old doddering mind.

Regaining his composure, the ancient traveler became aware of numbness in his left hand. Shifting from his crumpled position to examine the nature of the injury, he was surprised to find the puzzling object still in his grasp. Waiting for the feeling to return to his clenched fist, he studied the knuckles of his left hand, which had turned white from his unrelenting grip. After careful study, the purpose of the metallic object became obvious. In fact, he had employed such a tool himself. Although it had been many years since he had held such a device, he was sure it was some sort of chisel. The mushroomed head indicated that the tool had sustained much abuse. Recalling his own experiences with such an implement, he had eyes that glazed, and his face lost all expression as the cobwebs disappeared from his mind. For the first time in years, the fog had lifted. He remembered a time, long ago, when a stone chisel and ball-peen hammer were as familiar to his hands as his Ingram MAC 10.

Realizing that he was at the end of his life, the aged warrior crumpled to his knees and recited a prayer, asking if he could regain his lost youth. Recover fifty years—even if it meant reliving half a century of misery and hardship, perhaps beginning with that day on the knoll, when he first met the woman who would become his loving mate. Again, tears welled within his eyes as the thoughts of her returned. Was such a thing even possible? Was there really a God who could even grant such a request? His head bent in reverence, oblivious to all but his prayer and memories of his wife; the decrepit form was alarmed to find six inches of honed steel protruding from his chest. Making a feeble effort to remove the blade, he knew his efforts were in vain as every beat of his frail heart pumped a crimson geyser, making the object too slippery to grasp.

Plunging forward, the aged fighting man managed to roll onto his right side in an effort to see he who had slain him. Indeed, he did recognize the assassin. With what little strength remained, the ancient war hero raised his left hand and extended a crooked index finger toward the culprit. As he opened his mouth to lend voice to his accusation, the dying man found he was to far gone to speak. With his surroundings quickly turning black, the last sight the warrior held was the cloaked countenance and the hooded, grinning scowl of… the Grim Reaper.

CHAPTER 1

As quickly as the darkness came, it was gone, as was the pain in his chest. Instinctively, the six-foot-eight titan ran his powerful hands over his heavily muscled chest in an effort to assess the damage inflicted by the edged weapon. Movement of his arms required no effort. His blood was quick to coagulate, and his body was swift to heal; even he was amazed at the absence of blood. His lungs drew cool breath without labor.

The strapping warrior began to take stock of his surroundings. A whirlpool of white enveloped everything within his realm. At the limits of sight and sound, he could almost see—could almost hear—people, fading in and out as if caught in some shifting dimension. A gentle breeze was blowing, carrying what seemed to be a chorus of… singing, perhaps. His feet seemed mired in questionable ground, that his body had no real consistency. Looking down, he could not see below his knees for the swirling haze encompassing him.

The supreme fighting man was quickly unsettled. He was a man unaccustomed to being someone's fool. Whatever or whomever had him at a disadvantage would soon come to know the wrath of the Angel of Death.

"Where the hell am I?" he boomed.

"Hell? Hell? Hell can certainly be arranged," a stout voice echoed back that equaled his own. Instantaneously, some…being… materialized out of the mist before him.

Despite the confusing circumstances, Angel, as always, was quick to react. Instinctively, his right hand reached cross-draw-style for the massive .50 Desert Eagle that rarely left his hip. His left hand went for the eleven-inch survival knife sheathed on his right.

The voice exploded. "Only *you* would be so bold as to draw your weapons upon the Lord Thy God, *Angel of Death*."

At first, Angel was dismayed to find his weapons absent, until the message of the voice registered within his subconscious.

Suddenly everything became amazingly clear. Understanding consumed him. The warrior realized he was somehow in possession of the knowledge promised to Eve by the serpent in the Garden of Eden. Angel had no doubt that he was before his Creator! Intimidated for the first time in his life, the commando was in awe of the presence before him. Time and space seemed to come to a halt as the warrior studied the being that was God. It was difficult for Angel to conclude exactly what His Lord looked like. Even if he could, he was certain it held no relevance. If humankind were truly created in the image and likeness of God, then, Angel decided (how he came into possession of this knowledge he was not certain), every spirited creation in the universe would hold a likeness to this being.

"Yes, drink deeply upon the existence that is your God."

Angel was compelled to kneel but was certain the swirling fog would obscure him. He did however bow in reverence.

"No, do not kneel before me! Straighten your spine! During the course of your entire life, you have groveled before no one. Do not start now with Me. It does not become you."

Angel's mouth hung agape. He was unable to speak the words.

"Yes, yes, I know. You were never at a loss for words. Speak! You will again find your tongue."

As predicted, Angel was able to communicate, although the process did not exactly involve speech. "I take it then… I am dead?"

"Yes! Finally! After thousands of attempts on your life."

Dismayed by the obvious revelation, Angel, in typical style, wanted answers. "Lord, am I before you then, to be judged?"

"You have already been judged."

"And?"

"Yours is a complicated matter, even for one such as I, Angel Martin, or more appropriate in keeping with your cognomen, Angel of Death."

"How do you mean?"

"On one hand, while you may have broken a few of My Commandments, now and then, you have committed no mortal sin, except for the taking of 17,251 lives, of course."

Angel was visibly impressed. "That many?"

"They were all my children! Do not forget to whom you speak!" The words echoed in a thunderous blast of sound and wind.

For the second time during his existence, Angel was afraid. He felt the breath drawn from his lungs, his prodigious strength sapped. He was as much at the command of His God as a kite before a hurricane. "Lord, as you know, I have truly tried to live the life you would have me live. The lives I have taken were in self-defense and in defense of God and country. I have committed outright murder against no one."

"*Of course,* I know and understand. *However, I do not condone it!* That fact is your *only* salvation. But *no* mortal can claim that many lives without consequence."

"Then what plans do you have for me?"

"Oh yes, plans indeed! You do not merit the reward of heaven—*yet*. Nor do you deserve the punishment of hell. Your punishment, your purgatory, if you will, will be to do the work of the right hand of the Lord. Appropriately, since you have been the reaper of men, hence you shall be throughout the entire universe, *the Angel of Death!* An anomaly to be sure."

"Lord, I do not understand. If it is your will to claim a life, you would not need the help of an angel of death."

"Do you not remember your Bible? I should not have posed such a rhetorical question. You were too busy dispensing death and destruction to study the Holy Word. Understand, Angel of Death, during the time of the Great Flood, I could have claimed the lives of the unfaithful with a wave of my hand. Yet I allowed nature itself to cleanse the earth. My will alone would have spared Moses and his people—My people—from the Egyptians pursuing them, yet I enlisted the Red Sea to do my bidding. And the Philistines—do you know who killed one thousand Philistines with the jawbone of an ass?"

"Yes, it was Samson, my Lord."

"It was *you*. *You!* Single-handed, *you* destroyed those wicked, evil, blasphemous, people, as you shall see. Understand this, as determined by the plight of My people, I must sometimes send an angel of mercy. Other times I must send *the Angel of Death*."

"I do not question your wisdom, but how shall I accomplish such a task?"

"That is a strange question coming from one such as you. For you, killing has become second nature, instinctive. In the fall of the year, trees shed their leaves. When the situation warrants it, you kill. It has come to you easier than any of my other creations. To answer your question, the place and time of your particular assignment shall be provided to you beforehand. Weapons, as if any were ever really necessary, will be provided appropriate to the time and place of your mission."

"You are saying I can be deployed at any time and place in history?" Deploy. Mission. These words Angel had not heard in a long time. He became visibly excited at the prospect.

"I am saying you can and *will* be placed at any point in time. At any place in My universe. In addition, before you become too enthusiastic, Angel of Death, know this: you can, and you *will* die. At the end of every assignment. When you die, it will be a painful and miserable death just like any mortal. No leniency for you. *This* is to be your punishment. During your life, you have dispensed an inordinate amount of death. Now you will come to *know* it."

"How long will I serve in this capacity?"

"Until I decree otherwise."

"Then I accept this commission, as I must. In what campaign will I first serve?"

"And only you, my son, would be so eager. However, just before your mortal body perished, your prayer touched Me as I am forever touched by the prayers of My children. Before you are conscripted into the service of the Lord, I will grant a temporary reprieve and return you to the place where you met the woman who would become your mate. Make no mistake, this time your life will take an unfortunate turn. It will not be of its original longevity, and she whom you have taken as a mate will perish a widow. Your children are naught. Go now, back to that place and time you once knew. However, remember and understand. While the capacity of My love is limitless, My justice is sure and swift, and its name shall forever be *the Angel Of Death.*"

CHAPTER 2

"Help me! Oh God, please help me," the young woman cried as she raced up the vine-covered hillside, constantly brushing the filthy blond locks from her deep-blue eyes in an effort to negotiate the rugged terrain. Her skimpy outfit, consisting of a short green halter revealing ample cleavage, faded blue denim shorts, and dingy white sneakers, did little to protect her from the brutal environment.

Repeatedly during her mad ascent, the strange vegetation attempted to entwine itself around her long shapely legs, nearly causing her to stumble headfirst into the shoulder-high growth. As her lithe, nimble form attempted to evade the bright-orange stalks bearing shiny purple leaves, their sinewy black tendrils would react accordingly, striving to impede her passage. Several times, just when it appeared the animate underbrush would entangle her, the skimpily clad woman regained her latitude, determined to continue her quest.

Angel stood on the verdant knoll surveying the spectacle before him. His powerful muscles bulged in apprehension within the confines of his camouflage coveralls. His left hand mechanically stroked the neatly trimmed growth of dark beard, vigilant to any event that would provide insight into the girl's dilemma.

The mysterious runner displayed great agility in her endeavor to elude the encircling tentacles. Prominent cheekbones complimented her light complexion and full lips. Unfortunately, her classic features were compromised by the overwhelming expression of sheer terror emblazoned on her face. She was a strikingly beautiful woman.

Or had been.

The girl's otherwise flawless torso was covered with hideous welts and bruises. Her face bore the marks of numerous beatings. Deep scratches and scrapes disfigured her thighs and calves. What appeared to be rope burns etched her ankles and wrists. Her physical appearance was the obvious result of abuse, both physical and sexual. The revealing apparel, an ensemble intended to accomplish but one purpose, was fashioned solely to stimulate the libido of her tormentors.

Angel was well acquainted with such sadistic behavior. He recalled a time three years earlier, during the Third World War, when he observed firsthand the perverse nature of humanity and grimaced at the recollection.

It was the year 2026. The United States, weary of terrorist bombings, assassinations, and futile attempts to negotiate peace, declared war on Libya and Iran. Those two countries, claiming the declaration was just an elaborate ploy to commandeer the abundant oil reserves of the Mid-East, persuaded Egypt and Saudi Arabia to join in their solemn quest to drive the "American Devils" from their land. Later, the acronym LIES was used to describe the Mid-Eastern powers. As the political climate in Washington, DC, had turned upside down, China had become the world's power, and their demand for energy grew exponentially. China, growing resentful of the former power, sided with the LIES to help destroy their mutual enemy.

It was during his tour of duty that Angel first witnessed humankind's devious conduct. It seemed that certain men, whose lives were forfeit but for a matter of time, exchanged their humanity for every known pleasure and vice known to him. Indulging themselves while they could, they had little to lose but their soul.

It was the recollection of a more recent incident, however, that turned Angel's blood to molten lava. Permanently etched in his mind was the fact that this fiancée died a violent and sadistic death at the hands of a local lunatic. The connection to Tiffany's death and the plight of the girl before him transformed Angel's hardened visage into that of rage.

"Please, they'll kill me," the girl pleaded before stumbling onto her hands and knees. "Please," she reiterated obscured by the growth.

Upon hearing the girl's allusion to a third party, Angel's massive hands instinctively dropped to the K-BAR eleven-inch survival knife on his right hip and the absent .50-caliber Desert Eagle that rarely left his left. Searching unsuccessfully for the invisible adversary, Angel mentally debated his decision to leave all firearms behind.

The sole objective of leaving the safe confines of the mountain fortress that morning had been to reconnoiter the boundless forest surrounding the impregnable stronghold. Although their food surplus was sufficient at present, necessity dictated the survivors determine available game. Angel's decision to forego firearms in lieu of bow and arrow seemed sound at the time. Even though the danger of attack by miscreants was ever present, Angel felt the gravity of the situation precluded any other options. Until the area could be secured, the attention they might draw through the discharge of a firearm outweighed all risks. However, he had not planned on this.

Angel's dark eyes swept down the grassy hillock to the weed-choked field where the feisty female was wrestling with the corporal vegetation, past two hundred yards of barren earth to the crumbling highway below.

US Route 50 ran east to west. The four-lane thoroughfare bisected the state, linking West Virginia with Maryland at its eastern border and Ohio at its western boundary. The road, originally part of the George Washington National Highway that stretched all the way to Washington, DC, had eroded to nearly impassable conditions.

Angel searched for a sign, any sign that the woman's life might be in peril. The view from the summit provided an ideal point of observation. Opening to the South, the clearing allowed the mild afternoon sun to illuminate the picturesque semicircle of forest, transforming the rustic setting into an idyllic wonderland. The potpourri of various trees, including maple, birch, and beech, landscaped the luxuriant mound. Even the robins in the trees above chirped and sang, indicating all was well with the world.

So where were her assailants? Despite her appearance, Angel deliberated whether the girl's plight might be a manifestation of her imagination. If so, she would not be the first or the last to suffer mental collapse since the *end*. A strong constitution was required to exist in the world as it had evolved. The unfortunates who survived the corrosive fulmination had to endure a world where misery and death came in grotesque form. Or possibly, like the woman before him, lose their sanity in the process.

"Are you guys going to stand there like idiots while this stuff buries me alive or what?"

"Hero," Angel summoned, addressing a man clad in a filthy football uniform to his left. "Help the lady out of her predicament."

"Unbelievable!" Hero muttered to no one in particular. "Just because a few lousy weeds haven't eaten in a while…"

Overhearing the snide remark by the unknown individual, the distressed woman, completely engulfed in the withering foliage, became frantic.

Angel studied the appearance of the young man descending the slope. When the END came, the tribe's acronym for Earth's Nuclear Destruction, the only clothing the university quarterback had access to were those on his back. A blue jersey labeled with a gold number 12 below the word *Mountaineers*, also in gold, and gold football pants were all that protected him from the elements. "When we return home, remind me to round up some normal clothes for you."

"Bitch, bitch, bitch."

In an odd way, Angel enjoyed the senior quarterback's company. He was one of the few people who were not visibly intimidated by his size, strength, or demeanor. Although Hero was testy at times, in fact belligerent would be a better description, he was a refreshing contrast to the majority of those surviving the holocaust. Many simply could not cope; the loss of civilization and all its luxuries was too great. Angel knew he could count on the quarterback no matter what the odds to cover his back should things get rough.

Hero was in excellent physical condition, the result of proper diet, exercise, and weight training, a conditioning program for which his coach had been renowned. At twenty-one, Hero was well over six feet tall and muscular, hardly an ounce of fat on his body. His shoulder-length blond hair occasionally interfered with his vision as he jounced down the slope, requiring the use of his left hand to part it to one side. Hero sported a compound bow in his right hand and a quiver of arrows over his left shoulder.

Kicking the encircling vines out of his way, the football player slung the Whitetail bow over his right shoulder, then slid a nine-inch bowie from its sheath on his left hip, and proceeded to hack the fibrous coils entrapping the girl.

"Watch what you're doing. You almost cut me," the girl admonished. Examining her left forearm, the young woman watched as a trickle of blood ran down her elbow and dripped to the ground.

The eerie vegetation bristled in anticipation.

"Hey, you did cut me. I hope that thing is sterile."

Hero halted in his task, then straightened. "I can leave you here."

The ensnared woman glared at him with cold blue eyes.

"That's what I thought." Hero snorted, resuming the extraction.

"Lookee yonder," came a warning from Angel's rear.

Angel glanced over his left shoulder at a man several feet away in order to discern the direction the speaker was indicating. Mountain Man was standing beneath a hollow beech, his right arm extended, the index finger pointing to the Southeast. Concern was evident on his oval face.

Having survived for months in a root cellar, Mountain Man enjoyed the luxury of stored root crops, canned goods, and fruit, while he weathered the destructive nuclear storm. Waiting until he was sure it was safe, the country boy packed all his belongings into a burlap sack and migrated North in search of humanity. His moniker suited his appearance. Mountain Man was dressed in blue bib overalls, white shirt, and dark-brown hunting boots. A large, tall, black wide-rimmed hat, the style popular with mountain folk, capped his head. His six-foot frame was of average build while an unusual bone structure lent a stocky aspect to his physical appearance. The man's speech and attire conveyed the impression of a simple bumpkin, much to Hero's amusement. That, however, was where all semblance of a yokel ended. The twenty-six-year-old was intelligent, brilliant in his element, and sly as the proverbial fox. His only negative attributes were his naivete and lack of humor. To his credit, Mountain Man followed orders to the letter without question. Angel took great comfort in that.

Angel focused his attention on the object of Mountain Man's alarm. Twelve armed soldiers were crossing the highway below, beginning their charge up the barren slope, rapidly closing the distance between US 50 and the girl.

Mountain Man turned his head toward Angel, his lively green eyes reflecting his disquiet.

"Why all the concern, AD?" voiced the fourth and final member of the party, addressing the leader by his wartime cognomen. "After all, they're on our side…right?" The sight of the rushing men bearing Government-Issue Heckler and Koch MP5/10A3s, followed by the disconcerting exchange between his two companions compelled the fourth man to reiterate, "Right?"

Angel, reluctant to divert his attention from the approaching men even for an instant, turned his head slightly to the right. A sullen glare from Angel confirmed Jim's suspicion.

"How soon?" Angel called down to the man who appeared to be in as much trouble as the person whose mission it was to rescue.

"What's the rush?" Hero responded in his petulant manner.

"Trouble!"

"Trouble?" Hero bellowed, searching until he spied the advancing troopers. "You think I'm having a picnic down here. I swear these chokers are becoming more aggressive every day."

Jim started down the slope, drawing his knife from its sheath on his right hip.

Angel's lightning reflexes halted his younger brother in midstride, his bulging right arm barring Jim's advance.

"Where do you think you're going?"

"To help Hero…and the girl."

The corners of Angel's mouth turned down. "We can't afford to loose *two* of our party to the chokers. Besides, Hero is capable of taking care of himself." A barrage of colorful expletives from below contradicted the leader's assessment.

"Most of the time anyway," Angel groused. "We need to divert the soldiers' attention without inciting them."

"Hey down thar," Mountain Man shouted, exposing a crop of curly red hair as he removed his hat with his left hand. "We don't mean no harm." He began waving his cap back and forth in an effort to attract the troopers' attention.

A hail of automatic gunfire splintered the limb of a tall hickory directly overhead.

"Hey, we're peaceable folks."

Another reply in the form of ten-millimeter ball was the response.

Cleaving the last few vines imprisoning the girl, Hero was afraid the armed contingent was firing at them when he caught sight of his companion in bib overalls prancing about and waving his hat. "It figures," Hero mused, shaking his head. "I should have guessed that backwoods hayseed had something to do with this."

"Remember me?" the scantily clad woman mentioned, mischievously tugging Hero's left pant leg.

"How could I forget ya, babe?" Hero replied, running his blue eyes up and down the prone female.

"The vines!" The struggling girl indicated the constricting vegetation with a nod of her head.

"Out in a sec," the ex-quarterback stated as he severed the last tentacle. "By the way, what's your name?"

"Mackenzie," the young woman replied, rising to her knees, inspecting herself for damage.

"Hero, at your service," he divulged, helping Mackenzie to her feet.

"Okay, Hero Atyourservice, let's get the hell out of here!"

Hero led the girl back out of the strangling brush and raced up the steep slope, stopping at the edge of the woods where the trio were waiting. "Angel," Hero recited, addressing the huge man in camouflage coveralls and aggressive-style hunting boots. "I would like to introduce you to Mackenzie."

"Who are *you* guys?" Mackenzie asked defiantly, denying the leader a chance to respond, her clenched fists resting on svelte hips. Her perusal of the unlikely quartet ended with Angel studying the titan from head to toe.

Although the brash woman displayed outstanding courage in confronting the immense stranger, the brief moment their eyes embraced, Angel detected abject fear.

"We are the *guys*," Hero said, emphasizing the last word, "who pulled your cute buns out of the fire."

Mackenzie's eyes remained transfixed on the bearded hulk as if it were he who replied.

"Never mind who we are," Angel thundered, pointing in the troopers' direction. "Who the hell are they?"

"They be nary halfway up tha hill, whoever they be."

"Soldiers!" Mackenzie spat. A volley of lead that shredded the bark of a nearby maple tree punctuated the obvious revelation.

"Tell us something we don't know," Hero said emphatically.

"They're getting our range," Jim informed as another burst of gunfire perforated the ground beneath their feet.

"Could we continue this conversation elsewhere?" Mackenzie testily inquired.

"Jim!" Angel barked, turning to retrieve his bow and quiver from the limb of a birch to his right. "Take point! Find a spot just off the trail where we can regroup."

"Will do," Jim said before disappearing into the brush.

"Et looks lak them army fellers is gonna skirt them thar chokers. They must ah seed tha fix that female got herself into."

As Mountain Man departed, Angel acknowledged the revelation with a scowl. He had hoped the soldiers would unwittingly blunder into the chokers. No such luck.

The muscular fighting man deliberately hung back, directing the remainder of his troop along the game trail leading into the forest. "What did you do to these guys?" Angel inquired as Mackenzie ushered past, suffering a contemptuous glare at his inquiry.

Slinging the brown deerskin quiver over his right shoulder, and ensuring the machete secured in a drab olive sheath on his left remained undisturbed, Angel ducked behind the trunk of a wide poplar to study the column of advancing men, anticipating their reaction.

The assaulting troopers, puzzled by the lack of confrontation, perceived their vulnerability in the empty field and immediately assumed a less aggressive offense.

Hoping that the troopers' hesitation would buy some time, Angel crept from behind the tree and bounded down the path. The Stalker IVs performed flawlessly, biting deep into the loose organic soil. The lightweight hunting boots enabled Angel to evade obstacles in his path with dexterity belying his colossal proportions.

Angel concentrated on assessing the situation at hand. It was imperative that he ascertain the truth before the fiasco went any further. Was it possible this seemingly innocent refugee was guilty of some heinous crime? Could it be that martial law had been declared and the army was well within their right to hound the girl? He needed time to interrogate the young woman, confirm or refute her testimony before allowing her access to their home. Yet as harmless as the girl might be, under no circumstances could he allow the encroaching assailants to discover the location of their domain or leave with knowledge of their existence.

Angel approached a quartet of silver maple. Noting the sturdy thin vines that had attached themselves to the branches overhead, his concentration arrested by a low whistle coming from his left. Latching on to one of the descending dark coils, Angel tested the brown strand with pensive scrutiny.

Perfect.

Angel arced to the left as Jim exposed his position, motioning him to the place where his team were crouched. Angel was impressed with the site Jim had selected. A breastwork of fallen trees and large rocks formed an almost perfect circle fifteen yards to the left of the game trail. It was an ideal spot in which to make a stand. Angel entered the fortification, relieved that Jim had already taken a position behind an elm, vigilant for the first sign of the approaching troops.

At twenty-five, Jim was three years younger than his brother, Angel. He was a slightly smaller version of his brother but did not quite possess the developed musculature Angel enjoyed. However, he was nearly identical in every other respect such as build and bone structure. Jim jokingly maintained his light-gray eyes gave him a slight advantage when it came to good looks.

As America's involvement in World War III raged on, tales of Angel's fighting prowess and deadly reputation flourished. Jim was determined to enlist and had hopes of fighting alongside his brother. However, the younger sibling joined the Special Forces just two months prior to the opposition's unconditional surrender. Greatly disappointed, Jim had to content himself with a two-year stretch of peacekeeping duty before receiving an honorable discharge. Fate seemed to have a morbid sense of humor for it appeared his wish to fight beside his older brother had finally materialized.

Angel wasted no time interrogating the stranger. "Why are these soldiers after you?"

"My father is…or…was, before the nuclear attack, a scientist employed by the US government. Although we were vacationing at the time, Father wanted to visit the Tygart Dam thirty miles east of here."

"I know the place," Angel remarked. "The army occasionally conducts experiments at that facility. Many of the prototype turbine blades and bearing assemblies are torture-tested in the hydroelectric generator and monitored for durability and wear."

Sensing a disturbance in the surroundings, Mountain Man assumed a crouch and stalked toward the east for some distance, ensuring that the troopers had not outflanked their position.

"In fact, my father developed a special coating for turbine components, enhancing their longevity under—"

"The Panther!" Angel interrupted, considering the implication of what the girl was telling him.

"That name does sound familiar, but Father made it a point never to discuss military projects, even with—"

"Your father is an engineer?"

"Yes. Degrees in nuclear genetics and nuclear engineering. He's the best."

"So what about the soldiers?" the man in the blue-and-gold football uniform wanted to know. Hero, listening to the conversation while scanning the forest for sign of movement, was more concerned about the troopers' intentions.

"Aren't you a little old to be running around dressed like that?" Mackenzie responded.

Angel laughed in spite of the situation.

"What about the soldiers, *Ms. Godiva*!" Hero countered.

"When word of the impending attack came, everyone, including civilian visitors, took shelter within the dam. The lower levels are equipped as a civil defense shelter and stockpiled with provisions. After the attack, the situation remained stable, but only for a while. Occasionally, the army would—"

"How many soldiers?" Angel wanted to know.

"Thirty-eight."

"Civilians?"

"Seventeen before the escape."

"Escape? What escape?"

"Some of us managed to escape."

"There are others with you?" Angel recoiled at the revelation.

"Not exactly. After we escaped—"

"How many?"

"Ten, including myself. Evidently, soldiers have been dispatched to capture us. Last night, we made camp beneath a bridge in the town just east of here. This morning, one of our lookouts spotted them approaching. Since I was the youngest, most agile, and possessed some military experience, I volunteered to lead the troopers away from our group. None of us is armed. Obviously the soldiers are."

"This is important," Angel emphasized. "Why are they so aggressive? Is there some misunderstanding? Is it possible to reason with them? Have you done anything to provoke them?"

"Nothing!" Mackenzie spat, tears running down her cheeks. The ordeal of her captivity and perilous escape, followed by the inquisition, took its toll on her eroded constitution. "You don't understand." She sobbed. "It's what I wouldn't do. Look at me, the way they forced me to dress, the bruises…" The remainder of Mackenzie's testimony became unintelligible as she began to weep.

Angel had heard enough. Kneeling forward, he took the distraught girl into his powerful arms. "I figured as much. I'm sorry, but I had to find out if these men are friend or foe before making any decisions. It's obvious we are not going to resolve this without a fight."

Struggling to compose herself, Mackenzie pulled away from Angel's protective embrace and locked her moist blue eyes on his. "I swear to you, if it's the last thing I ever do, I'm going to make those bastards pay!"

"*They will*," Angel vowed, rising to his feet. Pulling Mackenzie after him, the commando continued for all to hear, "We cannot let these men escape with knowledge of our existence!"

Mackenzie was baffled. "But there are twelve of them and only four of you. They're armed with automatic rifles, but all you have are those." She indicated the compound bows with a sweep of her right hand.

"Don't underestimate the big guy," Hero advised. "You don't know who you're dealin' with."

"Just who am I dealing with?" Mackenzie asked, obviously puzzled.

"Who I am is not important. You see that trail?" Angel pointed to the path along which they had just retreated. "It leads to our cave about a half mile from here."

"A cave?" Mackenzie repeated skeptically.

"That's right, a cave," Angel confirmed, resting his right hand on her bare left shoulder. "Now this is what I want you to do..."

*****

The point man crept along the path; his alert green eyes examined each tree and studied every rock. The sergeant had made a wise choice sending him in first, Private Timmons decided, as he analyzed the tracks before him. His performance during war games was second to none, his stealth was unequaled, and his tracking abilities were peerless. Consequently, numerous citations and boundless gratuities were lavishly bestowed him by prominent officers in an effort to coerce his participation to their side. "Yes, sir," Timmons reasoned, "finding these backwoods morons will be a piece of cake. When I get my hands on that little blond vixen, I'm going to make up for six months of doing without...what was that?"

Private Timmons came to an abrupt halt, detecting an unusual noise directly ahead. Cautiously, he advanced three paces, stopping beside the stump of a fallen beech. A smirk slowly replaced the sullen frown on his angular face as he discerned the location of the sound—a bush of unknown variety rustling fifteen yards to the north. Timmons slung the MP5/10A3 over his right shoulder and quietly unholstered the Glock 20 on his left hip, drawing the pistol to chest height. "If that's my little playmate," Timmons reasoned, "I'm sure as hell taking the bitch alive."

At that moment, a stocky man attired in blue bib overalls darted from behind the shrub and sprinted down the path.

"Damn!" Timmons swore, disappointed in his quarry. Aligning the sights of the ten-millimeter pistol to the runner's head, the expert marksman declared with certainty, "One down! Four to go!"

Before the pistol-wielding recruit could squeeze off a shot, Angel materialized from behind the stump, the machete poised overhead. The carbon steel a silvery blur, the muscle-bound Goliath swung the heavy blade straight down, severing the gunman's extended left arm at the elbow.

As if waking to some horrific nightmare, Private Timmons turned his head and gaped in horror at his dismembered stump. Crimson fluid spurted out the ruptured end, splattering the bloody appendage lying on the ground, the pistol still tight in its grasp.

The serviceman, his eyes wide in alarm, opened his mouth to scream. The sound never escaped his lips.

Angel completed the pendulous arc of the machete. The finely honed instrument cut the air right to left, cleanly separating the trooper's head from his ravaged body. His decapitated head fell alongside the amputated arm, and his butchered torso collapsed in a disjointed heap on the cool ground. The last moments in Private Timmons's illustrious career were spent gazing up at the scowling titan in disbelief, his lips desperately forming the words, "Help me."

Angel vaulted the stump in a single bound, intending to confiscate the troopers' weapons. His play was cut short when gunfire erupted seventy-five yards to the south, followed by a searing sensation lancing his left rib cage. His plan of obtaining arms thwarted, Angel retreated along the path, his left hand clamped to his injury.

"Yer hit!" Mountain Man proclaimed, exiting his place of concealment to fall alongside Angel's right.

Ignoring the observation, Angel responded. "I hope Jim and Hero have our little surprise in place."

A burst of automatic fire pulverized a rotting oak to Mountain Man's right, showering the duo with bits of decay. Angel glanced over his left shoulder. Having thrown caution to the wind, the entire squad was clustered sixty yards back and bearing down fast.

"Ten yards," a bush to Mountain Man's right declared.

"Good luck," Angel whispered to a pin oak on his left.

As if on cue, the two joggers simultaneously vaulted an unseen obstacle and continued along the trail, which hooked to the left. Convinced they were safe from reprisal, the ragtag squad scrambled after their prey, oblivious to danger.

With Angel and Mountain Man a safe distance beyond the turn and the trooper's guard down, Jim and Hero waited until their marks were forty yards from their station, then sprung from concealment, their bows drawn. Hero was the first to release, planting the razor-sharp broadhead squarely into the chest of the lead soldier. A shriek escaped the stricken trooper as he desperately tried to remove the fiberglass rod from his punctured heart.

Jim let fly almost the same instant, his shaft striking the second GI, puncturing his left eye just below the rim of his helmet and protruding behind the right ear. Collapsing, the two lead men inadvertently became obstacles to those behind, entangling the disorganized bunch. In the confusion that followed, the two archers retreated north, wary of the taut vine they had stretched across the approach.

Rounding the bend in the route, the pair continued for some time before spying their comrades. Angel situated himself behind a large boulder on the right. Mountain Man, behind a birch on the opposite side of the drag. As Jim and Hero drew near, Angel arched his dark brows in question; Jim replied by extending his right fist, thumb up.

Jim considered the commando's plan. It was simple yet effective. The four had split into two teams. Angel, pairing with Mountain Man to compensate for the civilian's inexperience, drew the soldiers' attention while he and Hero sought a place of concealment. Taking out as many of the troopers as possible, Angel and Mountain Man would then retreat to take up a new position while he and Hero kept the GIs at bay. Rotating their positions as such, they hoped to make their way home in this fashion. Suddenly a great din echoed through the wild wood; the clatter of weapons and gear interrupted the younger brother's rumination.

The vine!

Hindered by the folly of tripping over their own dead, and afraid of losing their prey to the forest, the remaining troopers redoubled their efforts and charged blindly down the lane…only to stumble again over some invisible entrapment.

Trotting alongside Jim, Hero glanced over his shoulder, a mischievous smile contorting his lips. "What a bunch of fools," the ex-quarterback mused to himself as a barrage of shouts and curses assailed his ears.

Angel wiped the blood from his left hand on the coarse surface of the gigantic rock before him, the sticky red film staining the gray porous facade. Nearly missing its mark entirely, the ten-millimeter projectile failed to penetrate his brawny rib cage. However, the deep channel cut by the bullet's path was worse than he originally thought. Blood ran from the six-inch gash on his left side, down to his left boot, saturating every thread of material in its wake. Fighting a losing battle to stem the profuse flow, the hulking warrior had no choice but to turn his misfortune into their advantage. By all indications, the ploy he devised appeared to be working. Glancing down the approach, Angel notched another arrow and waited for the events to unfold.

Not to be fooled a second time, the recruits proceeded with caution, alert to some gimmick that might encumber their pursuit.

The sergeant's brown eyes carefully studied the footpath before him, his index finger nervously stroking the trigger of the MP5/10A3 in his right hand, a stubbed chin in his left. *These yokels may not be as dumb as I thought,* the forty-year-old NCO conjectured, angling the carbine barrel upward in order to tip the camouflage helmet further back on his head. The damp nylon straps of the sergeant's headgear caressed his hollow cheeks while lengthy black hair tumbled down his grimy forehead. The greasy mop was long overdue for a cut and bothering him immensely.

"Sergeant, Sergeant Belton!" barked a young dog-faced private who had taken point.

"What is it, Private Thomas?" Belton impatiently snapped, aggravated over the bungled campaign. Transferring the rifle to his left hand, Belton raised his right, signaling those behind him to halt. Advancing to the private's position, he found the enthusiastic GI down on one knee pointing excitedly at the ground.

"Sarge!" Thomas eagerly ventured, anxious to impress his commanding officer with his tracking prowess. "Blood. Fresh blood. It seems to be consistent with the footpath."

"Humm," Belton grunted, studying the evidence. Bright-red splotches dotted the earth, marking the trail as far around the turn as the eye could see.

"Just before the arrow struck him in the chest, Brady was bragging that he hit the *big* son of a bitch," Thomas divulged.

"Good work," Belton coddled. "Now return to point. And don't lose that trail."

"Yes, sir," Thomas recited, proudly saluting his superior before dashing back to the task.

The stupid bastards, Belton mused, motioning his men to proceed. *The careless sons-a-bitches. Whoever these guys are, they were doing a good job until they screwed up. I can't believe men of their experience are actually careless enough to leave a...* "Thomas!" Belton shouted, his eyes wide with comprehension.

"Sirrr..." Thomas cried in a wavering voice as he turned toward his sergeant. The private's eyes were unnaturally crossed, his gaze transfixed on the feathered rod jutting from his forehead.

A wave of remorse washed over the astonished sergeant as he attempted to rush forward, striving to catch the hapless private before he collapsed to the ground. Befuddled by some unknown force arresting his momentum, Belton looked down, horrified to see an arrow embedded in his chest, the camouflage shaft buried to the fletching. Dropping his weapon, he immediately grasped the dart with both hands, endeavoring to pull the rigid device from his body. The volume of blood exiting the wound made the smooth surface of the instrument impossible to retain. The terrified sergeant looked up to ascertain the identity of the fiend responsible for slaying him.

Fifteen yards to the north stood a colossus of a man, over six and one-half feet tall and fully three feet in girth at the shoulders, deftly sporting a bow in his huge left fist. So great were the mysterious archer's proportions that his bulging right arm, still cocked from the release of the bowstring, threatened to rend the confines of his garment.

Sergeant Belton wilting before them, the seven remaining soldiers raced for cover. Had they pressed their advantage, the recruits would have defeated the two archers with few casualties. Lacking such leadership and even less courage, the gaze of the frightened soldiers cast from one to another, searching for one in their ranks foolhardy enough to incur the wrath of the muscle-bound bowman.

The troopers' indecision was the reaction Angel had intended. He and Mountain Man vacated their respective positions, retreating to join Jim and Hero who were waiting fifty yards down the way.

"Well?" Jim asked.

Angel stopped to glance behind him. "We managed to stall them, but I don't know how long."

"Long enough to buy Mackenzie the time she needs, I hope," the younger brother remarked.

"Ah shore weesh we had some shootin' irons," Mountain Man ventured, contemptuously scrutinizing the bow in his callused hands.

"You and me both," Angel affirmed with regret.

"It didn't take long for those jerks to clean their shorts." Hero indicated the advancing squad with a nod of his head.

"Damn!" Angel swore. "Head for the cave!" His companions departing, the commando waited until the last possible moment before taking a hasty shot at the troopers' general direction, hoping to cower their assault. The arrow clipped the lead recruit, a tall lanky fellow sporting a red mustache, catching him in the left inner thigh and completely passing through the tender flesh. The balance of the rabble, apparently unfazed, filed past the injured member, except the last GI who stopped to lend aid to the stricken man.

Angel traveled the remaining distance to the lair without incident. Never slowing to look back, he perceived the rabid pack to be hot on his trail. The situation being what it was, the Special Forces commando praised the many virtues of their new home.

Homeless and vulnerable, his residence in town demolished by the grotesque behemoths wandering the land, Angel had little choice but to convert an old "Indian cave" he used to play in as a youngster into an invulnerable heaven, safe from the countless monstrosities stalking the remnant of mankind. He was certain it would provide superior protection with an adequately fortified entrance. And fortified he constructed it.

With the entrance facing southeast, absorbing much of the sun's light and warmth, the cave was situated near the top of a high ridge. A ten-foot overhang effectively served to make an attack from above essentially impossible, while the three-hundred-foot sheer face below the lair's mouth was virtually impossible to scale. Access to the cave was accomplished by way of a narrow, sloping, easily defensible path cut into the mountain's face that terraced onto a ledge. Sixteen feet long by six feet wide, the ledge served as a landing to the grotto's entrance.

The fortification Angel had erected consisted of heavy logs set horizontally and reinforced by stout beams set vertically on two-foot centers. The huge timbers provided the framework for a solid steel door set at the extreme north end. A steel-shuttered window hung at the southern extremity. Both portals opened outward to the left in order to provide an unobstructed view of the pathway descending from the south.

The interior of the cavern, enlarged through the use of hammer, chisel, and black powder explosives, had a rough dimension of twenty feet in width and forty feet deep, while the ceiling was a uniform nine feet throughout.

As Angel descended the slender footpath, twenty-four inches at its widest, the rock face to his left exploded, sandblasting his cheeks with bits of lead, copper, and limestone. A quick glance behind confirmed his suspicions. Thirty yards back, the troopers were trailing. He could have easily outdistanced or decoyed the squad, Angel reasoned, if such were his plans.

Negotiating the gradual decline, Angel sprinted across the rock shelf toward the doorway at the far end of the bulwark. The door immediately flew open, exposing the beautiful young girl who stepped onto the ledge cradling a heavy object in her supple arms. The tribal leader reached out with his right hand, taking hold of the apparatus in his vicelike grasp. Exchanging weapons, he thrust the bow and quiver into Mackenzie's empty hands before ordering the beautiful escapee to take shelter inside the cavern.

Angel hoped that the girl had been true to her task as the soldiers stormed within range. There was no time to double-check, no time for questions, no time to make corrections. Angel sidestepped to the left, brought the weapon to waist level, and depressed the trigger.

Hell itself broke loose!

The Ingram model M10 was the deadliest close-quarters machine gun known to man. It so happened that Angel was well versed in its application. Those most familiar with the handheld select-fire machine pistol affectionately referred to it as the MAC 10. Angel's model was fitted with a ten-inch barrel extension and drum magazine holding fifty rounds of .45-caliber, 250-grain jacketed hollow-point bullets. On full auto, it had a cyclic rate of twelve hundred rounds per minute, twenty rounds and five tons of energy per second.

It was little wonder that the first soldier, stumbling within arms length of the brawny commando, was cut in half at the sternum. His upper torso, completely severed from the lower, tumbled down his ravaged hips and over the cliff wall. For an instant, the lower half remained erect, the feet shuffling of their own volition as if debating in which direction to turn, before toppling over the ledge to suffer the same fate as its other half.

The second and third troopers, seven and ten feet behind the first, desperately tried to bring their weapons into play. Terror replaced futility on their woebegone countenances as they were ripped crotch to jugular, their bodies decimated by the hail of lead. The lifeless forms remained upright for a brief moment, a static reaction produced by the negating effect of the rain of heavy slugs countering their forward momentum. As round after round hammered the slain twosome, the duo performed a macabre imitation of some outlandish jig, the morbid dance of death.

The fourth GI died instantly, his heart pulverized by the impact of the heavy projectiles. The fifth man never knew what hit him; his head disintegrated in an explosion of blood and brains. Gray and crimson spattered the ground.

Two and one-half seconds. The open-bolt machine gun slammed on empty.

Angel rolled to his right behind the safety of the bulkhead as a burst of sub-machine-gun fire chewed away the top of the doorframe. Exposing himself once more, the muscular fighting man darted out onto the rough cavern ledge and grabbed the stout door. Wrapping his hand around the cool steel bar, the tribal leader spied the wounded serviceman hobbling toward him forty yards away. His aide, rifle smoking, was close behind.

"Trish!" Angel shouted, arresting the attention of an eighteen-year-old girl with brown hair and eyes. A blue corduroy jacket and blue denim jeans encased her trim figure. "Charge number one, on my signal." Angel threw the dead bolt on the metal door and raced to the southern end of the bulkhead, unlatching the shuttered window. Unslinging her Colt M4, the brunette sibling crossed to her brother's right and manipulated a switch mounted on the cavern wall.

"Rick! Charge number two on my command." Angel's deep voice echoed within the unadorned confines of the lair. A sickly young man of sixteen hobbled to the north end of the fortification. Every step he took was strained and deliberate. His ghostly complexion was greenish yellow, the fatal result of the lethal environment. Attired in blue jeans and a brown flannel shirt, the youngest of the remaining four family members sported a stainless Ruger GP100 .357 Magnum on his right hip.

Mackenzie was surprised that the interior of the cave was well lit and warm, despite her scant garments. She knew the temperature within most caverns remained constant year round, much like the dam in which she had been held captive for six months. Yet the temperature within the flood control facility was a cool fifty-eight degrees. Feeling slightly claustrophobic, a condition nurtured by her lengthy confinement, the newcomer folded her arms across her chest and took stock of her surroundings. When she first entered the cave to warn Trish and Rick of the danger and relay Angel's instructions, she had been cognizant to the fact that the cave was well illuminated. It did not dawn on her until now that the source of heat and light originated not from torches or lanterns as she had previously assumed but from gas. *Natural gas!*

Her perusal of the amazing compound was interrupted by the ensuing activity as Angel began issuing directives.

Sighting out the narrow gap between the shutter and frame, Angel waited until the first trooper limped into position ten yards short of the ledge floor. "Charge number one…now!"

Mackenzie watched as Trish activated a series of switches assigned her. Instantaneously, there was an explosion beyond the fortification, followed by a blood-curdling scream that quickly grew distant before ending in oblivion.

Angel bolted the shutter moments before the heavy metal was struck by gunfire. Extending the index finger of his left hand in a vertical position indicating silence, Angel crept toward the north wall, scrutinizing the wooden barrier as if it were glass. Straining his exceptional senses, the decorated war hero paced in unison with his adversary on the opposite side of the reinforcement, continuously glancing from the floor to Rick, who was waiting with bated breath.

"Ready," Angel whispered.

Rick responded to the command by raising a brass lever attached to the rock wall and locking it into its socket.

An odd metallic clicking from the other side of the fortification absorbed the titan's concentration. Suddenly, his features hardened with contempt. "Now!"

An explosion more intense than the first reverberated throughout the lair. Falling particles of rock passing through the intense gas lights were transformed into glowing red streamers. The deafening roar of the blast made the uncanny silence that followed seem surreal.

Trish deserted her position at the south wall and hastened to a wooden table in the center of the room. Lifting a large black pistol from the oak furnishing, she reverently handed the heavy weapon to her oldest brother who was waiting next to the door.

Hefting the Desert Eagle in his massive right hand, Angel beamed as he admired the powerful handgun, pleased to have it back in his possession. Ensuring the pistol was hot, he deftly retracted the slide one-half inch with his left hand. He then deactivated the safety. Rotating the steel bolt in its housing, the commando carefully opened the door as the hefty portal easily swung outward on well-oiled hinges. One-quarter of the way open, the door struck a hard object, then wedged solid. Cautiously, Angel peered around the edge of the entrance, ready to confront all threats to his tribe's safety. Looking down to discern the cause of the jam, the mighty combatant visibly tensed. Two pineapple hand grenades, lying in a shallow depression, were wedged between the ledge floor and the bottom of the door.

The tension of those within the cave mounted as Angel's trepidation radiated apprehension to all those who witnessed the event.

Relief washed over the Special Forces commando when he realized that the pins activating the high explosives were undisturbed. Disappearing behind the door, Angel returned, exhibiting the inert destructive devices in his left hand.

CHAPTER 3

The strapping combatant was seated at one end of the rectangular table, facing the wooden barricade. Hanging from his left hip crossdraw style, encased in a black cordura holster, hung the commando's Desert Eagle. Since the potentially tragic events of that afternoon, the veteran of World War III vowed never to be without his prized handgun again.

The warrior's intense gaze was transfixed on the beautiful woman to his right. Refreshed, bathed, and attired in a blue blouse and black denim jeans, the recent addition to the tribe was a remarkable sight. Engaged in idle chat with the courageous newcomer, Angel was waiting for the remainder of the tribe to assemble. Because he was well versed in survival tactics and possessing vast wartime maneuvers, the tribe invariably depended on the Special Forces veteran to make the necessary decisions pertaining to their existence. Because the outcome of this particular conference would affect their very lives, as well as the lives of others, Angel wanted all parties involved to take an active role in reaching any decisions made that evening.

At Mackenzie's urging, Angel had described the operation of the device used to clear the last two soldiers from the cavern ledge. The war hero explained that two pyrotechnic charges, similar to the black powder explosives used to excavate and enlarge the cavern, were set twelve inches into the rock face of the mountain at two different locations. One charge was placed in the pathway ten feet before it terraced onto the ledge. The second was recessed in the rock wall adjacent to the door, where the protruding mountainside jutted onto the landing. Throwing either switch sent electrical current from a small battery to an electrical devise, detonating the charge. At a moment's notice, grapeshot consisting of glass, nails, metal fragments, and rocks provided the means to sweep undesirables from the cavern's entrance.

Mackenzie listened intently as Angel explained the operation of the defense system. The deep resonate quality of his voice and his direct, assertive personality made her feel secure in the unfamiliar company of her new friends.

Having removed his blood-soaked coveralls so Trish could minister to his wound, the exceptional musculature of Angel's upper torso would ripple and swell as he pointed to various fixtures during her indoctrination. Mackenzie hoped her rescuer was oblivious to her occasional stare, her blue eyes involuntarily wandering to his impossible physique. At times, she deliberately looked away, pretending to take notice of what the handsome warrior was explaining. However, in the radiant warmth of the room, under the ambiance of subdued lighting, rejuvenated body, and fresh clothing, the influence of Angel's close proximity effected a hypnotic trance, resulting in Mackenzie's unguarded attention to refocus on the man before her. She began to experience an urgency she thought would never return. Caught up in her emotions, Mackenzie was unaware the warrior had paused, conscious only of the silence…the tranquillity…the feeling in the pit of her stomach.

"Are you feeling well?" Angel inquired.

"Huh?" Mackenzie responded, rousing to the concerned expression on Angel's face.

"I said, is everything okay? You seem distant."

"Oh! Yes. Fine," she hedged, struggling to recover from her utopia. "I was…uhh… I was just wondering…um…how you managed to…heat and light this place with natural gas."

"Don't forget the gas range and hot water tank," Angel prompted.

"How can I forget? The deer roast we ate for supper was delicious!"

"As much as I would like to take credit, the feat of providing the lair with natural gas is strictly Mountain Man's engineering."

"Mountain Man? But I thought he was…kind of…you know…"

"Never underestimate him," Angel advised. "He's a true survivalist in every sense of the word. In fact, in his own way, more so than I. He has been living off the land his entire life. He knows every trick in the book, and he knows how to make do. Take the natural gas, for example. At the base of this mountain runs a large creek. One hundred and twenty yards upstream, Mountain Man found a fracture in the bedrock where natural gas was bubbling to the surface of the water. He knew it was escaping from either underground storage or a natural well that ruptured during the nuclear bombardment. Constructing a crude dam from rocks and clay, he diverted the rushing water around the gas leak, inverted an open fifty-five-gallon oil drum over the fissure, then cemented it into place. Get this," Angel paused momentarily to effect significance. "The guy even collected the necessary raw materials to make his own cement! Clay from the creek bed, limestone from natural deposits, sand from the shallows, and so on. Of course, certain supplies had to be procured from what's left of the hardware store in town—copper tubing, brass fittings, things of that nature. It was a simple matter to obtain a few gas appliances, run the tubing down the face of the mountain, and then connect it to a fitting affixed to the top of the oil drum. Soon, our energy needs were satisfied by an inexhaustible supply of natural gas."

"Truly amazing!" Mackenzie remarked in awe. Robust laughter captured her attention. Observing the way Hero and Trish teased each other over some trivial matter, she could not help but wonder if the two were an item. Nor could she ignore the quarterback's attentiveness earlier when he assisted the brunette in treating Angel's injury. During the procedure, Hero questioned the rationale of Trish's conscription into the position of doctor. The major conflict, it seemed, was the ex-quarterback's use of terminology. He preferred the title "witch doctor," claiming the few occasions Trish had ministered to him; her bedside manner had been less than merciful.

The escapee had been equally impressed with the commando's self-discipline as he casually observed his sister stitch the laceration close with sterile sewing needle and nylon fishing line. Refusing a local anesthetic concocted by Mountain Man, who was well versed in the production and use of herbal remedies, Angel insisted a quantity of the elixir be set aside for critical injuries and the remainder used to ease Rick's suffering.

Before supper, Trish had conducted Mackenzie on a tour of the cavern, familiarizing the newest member with its design. The exploration began with the front room, a fifteen-by-twenty-foot chamber that served as kitchen, dining, and conference room. Partitions, constructed of various materials, divided the remainder of the lair into six rooms or cubicles, each one eight square feet. Four feet in width, the hallway ran east to west, connecting the front room with the six cubicles, three on each side.

The first room on the left functioned as sleeping quarters for Angel and Jim. Two cots, one against each partitioned wall, and a footlocker each, comprised the veteran brothers' spartan living decor. Not particularly spacious, the design fulfilled its purpose. Directly across the corridor were Mountain Man and Hero's room. Again, two cots occupying either side of the cubicle served as bedding. However, a burlap sack stuffed with bib overalls at the foot of one cot, and a filthy heap of blue-and-gold garments at the base of the other, identified the respective owner's bedding.

Trish led the fascinated girl to the second pair of cubicles. Mackenzie gave the left-hand chamber a cursory glance, a room that she already had become acquainted with when she changed into the brunette's surplus apparel. The decor was atypical of an eighteen-year-old girl. Instead of a dresser strewn with cosmetics, jewelry, or a pink-curtained canopy bed (Mackenzie paused to reflect upon those luxuries forever gone), the eight-by-eight was furnished with only those items necessary for survival. Two olive-green cots, one yet unfolded, hugged the makeshift walls. Out of place, however, was an exquisite cherry console separating the two bunks. Sitting atop the table were numerous medical texts and an open blue diary. An uncapped green pen inserted between the leaves suggested a recent entry. At the foot of the open cot, two black satchels overflowed with assorted medical gear, equipment scavenged over the course of many months. A dusty photograph of a man and woman in their early fifties was affixed to the wall above the doorway. The location provided ideal viewing from Trish's cot. Below it, dangling from a nail embedded in the doorframe, hung a stainless Ruger SF 101 .38 Special.

Across the passageway, Rick's quarters were abnormally sparse. A cot, bedpan, and wastebasket were the only fixtures within the cubicle's dimensions. The self-educated paramedic had explained that while green disease—the tribe's nomenclature for the youngster's affliction—was noncontagious, her brother's sole occupation of the room provided the spacious accommodations necessary to care for her afflicted sibling.

The tour concluded with the last two cubicles. The chamber on the left side of the hallway was designated the "weapons room." It housed their combined collection of firearms, ammunition, knives, and explosives. In the center of the room against the rock wall was Angel's "war chest," a large black footlocker containing the commando's personal arsenal of weapons. Having spent her entire life accompanying her father from one military base to another, Mackenzie was familiar with most of the ordnance in use just before the END. Many of the weapons she recognized at a glance. Obsolete M16s, current-issue ten-millimeter HK MF5/10A3s and MF5/10A3Ks, an HK G3, Uzi, and MAC 10. Various other rifles and handguns were leaning against the walls and hanging from pegs. These, it was explained, were weapons belonging to the other tribe members. However, there were two other firearms that belonged to Angel she did not recognize. One, her escort informed her, a large gray-and-black device similar in design to a Colt M4 but twice as massive, was known as a USAS 12, a select-fire twelve-gauge shotgun with fifty-round drum magazine. The other was a black four-barreled apparatus without an obvious magazine, although spare green plastic shoulder-stocks were in abundance. Trish explained that it was the Hellcat .22, a devastating weapon and one of Angel's own designs. And the green stocks, which were hollow, served as the magazine.

Who in the world is this guy? Mackenzie had wondered as curiosity compelled her to investigate the unusual rifle.

"Come on," Trish pestered, grasping her companion above the left elbow. "You can look at that stuff later." Mackenzie smiled at the naivete. Beyond the teenager's need for self-defense, weapons were of little interest to her.

The last cubicle of the circuit was directly across the hallway. In it was an old-fashioned cast-iron bathtub, a freestanding sink with a white five-gallon plastic bucket beneath, and a silver medicine chest above.

The doors to each of the six rooms were staggered to provide additional privacy. Much to Mountain Man's accustom, the toilet facility consisted of an outhouse seventy-five yards west of the cavern. Mackenzie was informed, according to Angel's mandate, that when the necessity arose, an armed companion, preferably a bunkmate, must accompany the other, day or night. The new member was impressed with the facilities, considering that the bulk of humanity that had managed to survive were living in sewers.

Following the tour, Trish had helped the newcomer bear water for her bath. It was then the teenager presented Mackenzie with fresh clothing. The two girls were nearly identical in size as the wardrobe of the eighteen-year-old fit the blonde quite well. Her roommate's sincerity and generosity quelled any apprehension over her new environment. She felt certain she could spend the rest of her existence in harmony with her new friends.

Almost.

Thoughts of her father's incarceration inside the cold, damp dungeon of a dam served to arouse hatred and vengeance suppressed deep within her. She knew Angel had sensed her quiescent emotions and was confident the meeting would resolve the situation.

Hero sauntered to the table and took a seat across from Angel. Leaning back into his chair, its front legs hovering several inches above the stone floor and his arms folded across his chest, the pugnacious quarterback displayed a cavalier attitude. "Well?"

"I'm giving Jim and Mountain Man a few more minutes," Angel stated.

The grating of wood scraping rock signified Trish's arrival. Dropping into a chair next to her oldest brother, she leaned against his left shoulder and mentioned in a hushed voice, "He's referring to his cut and duds."

Angel ran probing eyes over the grinning football player. Sure enough, Hero had discarded the ragged uniform he had worn his entire month-long stay. The red flannel shirt and blue jeans, acquired during one of their many excursions into town, was a welcome change. His locks neatly trimmed above the ears and tapered to the base of his neck. "You call that a haircut," the titan joked.

A frown replaced the smile on the senior quarterback's clean-shaven face. "Hey, tell it to your sister, man. She's the one who cut it. I wanted it shorter."

"I think he looks cute," Trish stated defensively.

"Someone mention my name," Rick chided, mustering a feeble grin as he approached the quartet. Standing behind his sister, he surveyed the assemblage. "Ready to start the meeting?"

"Not yet," Angel said.

"If you don't mind my asking," Mackenzie ventured, noting the sickly green, almost iridescent hue of the youngest brother's complexion. "How did Rick contract...what do you call it...green disease?"

"Right. Green disease. For lack of a better name," Trish informed.

"That's a good question," Angel stated. "One, I'm not sure I can answer. Let me bring you up-to-date. During the attack, our family gathered in the basement of our parents' home here in town. Belowground, and constructed during the late 1950s at the height of the cold war between the US and Russia, it incorporated somewhat of a bomb shelter. When the structure above us collapsed onto the lower floor, we found ourselves buried alive in the shelter under tons of rubble. But it turned out to be our salvation. The debris above added extra protection, shielding us from the intense radiation. Our mother had always made a point of stocking canned goods and preserving fruits and vegetables whenever she could. That, a good supply of bottled water, and water siphoned from the water heater kept us alive until the toxic levels subsided.

"I mention this for two reasons. First, I am certain Rick's ailment is not entirely a result of radioactivity. I have seen such victims before, and they did not display these symptoms, and as I just mentioned, all of us were protected from—or exposed to—the same levels. Second, everyone in our family ate the same food, drank the same water. And as you know, our parents…" Angel halted his digression and looked at his youngest brother.

Rick looked from Angel to Mackenzie, then to the floor. "Go on."

"As you know," Angel continued, his features sullen, "our parents were the first to contract and perish with this disease. They did not receive a quarter of the exposure to the environment that we did."

"Age?" Mackenzie ventured.

"Possibly," Angel agreed. "But they were not that old—early fifties. Rick is the youngest."

"His youth should be an advantage," Trish commented.

"It could be a disadvantage also," the newcomer reasoned.

Angel folded his powerful arms across his expansive chest. "I believe his disease is a result of something else."

Mackenzie turned to ponder Rick's appearance. "Why do you say that?"

"One of the reasons World War Three will go down as our most infamous war is the extensive use of biological toxins developed by China. I have examined the victims of that war. If anything, Rick's symptoms are more synonymous with the effects of biological poisons than radiation sickness."

"Yet we know this country fell to a nuclear attack," Mackenzie maintained.

"I have a theory," Angel disclosed.

"Wait a minute," Mackenzie interrupted, leaning forward in her seat. "Who do you think launched the attack, China?"

"Lies! With China's involvement perhaps. Same difference."

Hero shot forward, his chair striking the floor. "That's the first I've heard of this!"

"What makes you think it was the OPEC nations?" Mackenzie wanted to know.

"Retaliation," Angel stated matter-of-fact. "Against our occupation of their oil fields."

"Oil!" Mackenzie spat. "That's exactly what they've claimed World War Three was all about!"

"Control of the oil fields was not our intent when the United States was thrust into war. Rather, it was the result."

"Six of one, half dozen of the other. The fact we retained control of the oil fields after the war questions our intent."

"After their defeat, the OPEC nations threatened to halt the supply of oil to the US and her allies. The instantaneous curtailment would have meant economic disaster to the industrialized world."

Mackenzie expelled a long heavy sigh as she spoke. "So isn't that what you would call the result of all this, or worse?"

"Damned if you do and damned if you don't," Hero muttered.

"That's about the size of it," Angel admitted.

"But, Angel, you mentioned a theory," Trish mentioned, trying to ease the tension.

"As far as I can tell, an ingenious approach was used in conjunction with the atomic devices. I believe nuclear warheads were used to disperse some type of biological toxin into the atmosphere over this country."

"Are you sure?" Mackenzie uttered.

"Again, this is only speculation, but at the close of World War Three, many factions possessed very little nuclear capability. However, they did command huge quantities of biological weapons, had been stockpiling it for years. Remember your history? Offensive missiles were often laced with either nerve gas, biological toxins, or depleted uranium during many of the skirmishes that took place during the nineties. They utilized the same tactic during WWIII. The effects were very similar to the symptoms we are experiencing now."

"We?" the newcomer remarked, her eyes raking those before her.

"All of us are exhibiting symptoms to some degree," Trish disclosed.

Mackenzie fell silent for several moments, contemplating the revelation. "How ingenious. Those surviving the initial attack and ensuing radiation emerged from shelter, only to die in the toxic environment."

"Or by some mutation thereof," Hero was quick to point out.

"Mutations?" Mackenzie inquired skeptically. "Sounds like something out of a science fiction novel."

Hero nodded. "Take those chokers you were caught in—"

"Why do you call them chokers?" the blonde inquired.

"Can you think of a better name?" Hero reasoned.

"Mountain Man is responsible for their name. He was the first to document their activity. In fact, he is the one who first alerted us," Angel informed.

"Once they had me, what would they have done?"

"Nothing," Hero admitted.

"Nothing? Then what makes them so dangerous?"

"The manner in which they feed," the quarterback divulged.

"But you just said—"

"Right...nothing! Once entrapped, one rarely gets away. You were lucky. The vines wrap themselves around arms, legs, but most importantly, the neck. They choke their prey. After the victim dies, the carcass decomposes, enriching the soil. That is how the chokers feed, through absorption. I've seen really large animals ensnared in the stuff. I've come across human remains still entwined. Fortunately, we possess the best device for detecting the damned things." Hero pointed with his left index finger. "The human nose. Provided you're down wind, you'll smell the remains of the previous victim before you come within range. The odd thing is, at least according to AD here"—Hero nodded at the titan sitting across the table—"the radiation should have destroyed all plant life instead of mutating it."

"Funny you should mention that," Mackenzie remarked. "Our excursion here was a potpourri of barren plains, strange plant and animal life, and unspoiled forest like the one surrounding this cave."

The conversation was abruptly interrupted when Jim and Mountain Man entered the lair via the cavern door, their arms and shoulders laden with equipment. Angel vacated his chair to assist the duo.

"This is the last of their gear," Jim informed his older brother. "Besides the rifles, we also found grenades, ammo, several pistols, a few knives, and rations."

"There wasn't much left ah them two that got themselves blowed off'n the ledge," Mountain Man ventured.

Angel slid three rifles from Jim's right shoulder and a backpack from Mountain Man's left forearm. "Did you hide the bodies?"

"After we rounded up all their possibles an' self-shuckers, we drug 'um a good ways off 'n, then we hid 'um jest like ye told us," the woodsman affirmed.

"Good work," Angel complimented, following the two into the weapons room. "I'll show you what I want done with this ordnance."

"Ever see a snow fence?" Hero began, attempting to pique the newcomer's interest.

"I can't say that I have." The blonde was amused by such a peculiar question.

"They're common in this state, particularly in the mountainous regions. In winter, snow driven by blowing winds can deposit tons of the white stuff on highways, leaving many of the rural residents stranded for weeks at a time, a condition I'm sure Mountain Man is well familiar with…" Hero then slapped the tabletop, amused by his own joke. After a delay of several moments, the chuckling quarterback was able to continue. "Anyway, the fences, picket, or slat-like affairs bound together by braided wire are strung parallel to the roadway. Due to many variables such as angle, distance, height, and so on, a snow fence will either contain the snow or divert its point of accumulation, keeping the road relatively clear."

"So what is your point?" Mackenzie incredulously replied, trying to make sense of Hero's dissertation.

"Angel believes the mountains have served to accomplish the same effect as a snow fence, except on a much larger scale. Depending on the warheads' point of detonation, location of mountain range, distance, and air currents, certain areas are almost totally free from any bionuclear effects. Some are completely wiped out, while others are in a stage of mutation."

"Anyone who has managed to survive without the safety of a bomb shelter has been affected to some extent," Trish corroborated. "Unlike Rick who is afflicted with an advanced case, the rest of us exhibit only mild symptoms. Those so afflicted generally feel well but are subject to bouts of dizziness, nausea, blackouts, and cough up greenish phlegm. Persons experiencing an advanced stage of green disease such as Rick…suffer partial paralysis, cessation of bodily functions, and an attack on skin pigmentation that turns the complexion a curious shade of green. Hence, the name." Averting her moist eyes, Trish continued, her voice beginning to crack, "In its final stage, the disease…becomes…fatal." Tears ran freely down her burning cheeks. "I don't know how much longer I could have endured watching my mom and dad waste away."

Angel reentered the room and reclaimed his seat, cognizant to the nature of the discussion that had taken place. "That's where your father plays a part in all this."

"How do you mean?" Mackenzie wanted to know.

"You said he had degrees in nuclear genetics and nuclear engineering."

"But—"

"You said he was the best," Angel prompted.

"Yes, but—"

"Surely he would not refuse to help us," the titan declared.

"Of course not, but—"

"So what's the problem?" Angel demanded.

Mackenzie looked to her right, at Hero. Compassion consumed her. These poor people had risked their very lives for her, rescued her from a terrible fate. As far as she could ascertain, the disease was far more advanced than these people realized. Obviously, green disease affects the memory as well. The last thing she wanted to do was destroy the pride of the people before her. She had to find a tactful way to remind them of her father's predicament. She deliberated, fishing for the right words. However, they failed to materialize.

Mistaking the newcomer's hesitation as an apparent lack of enthusiasm, Angel leaned forward in his chair, impatiently gripping the edge of the table in both hands. "I thought you would be overjoyed at the prospect of your father's rescue."

Quickly turning her head toward Angel, her silken hair rushing past her shoulders, the blonde remarked, "You mean you didn't forget that he is being held captive?"

Hero roared, his open palm connecting with the table for the second time.

Genuine concern clouded Rick's features. "Are you feeling well? Perhaps Trish should—"

"You are the *ones* suffering from delusions," Mackenzie uttered in resentment. "Do *you* six people honestly think that—"

"Four," Angel corrected. "Trish will have to remain with Rick."

"*Four?*" Mackenzie recited incredulously. "Okay, okay, *four* people can defeat an army?"

"Should be even odds, eh, AD?" Hero speculated.

"Who do you people think you are?" the newcomer remonstrated.

"I told you, you don't know who you're dealing with," Hero reminded.

"Okay. Tell me. *Who in the hell are you people?*" Mackenzie demanded.

A mischievous grin crossed Hero's lips. "Should we tell her, AD?"

"AD, AD," Mackenzie rolled the letters across her tongue. "Where have I heard those initials before?" Studying Angel, she found the commando silent.

"Tell me you've never heard of the *Angel of Death!*" Hero remarked suspiciously.

Mackenzie jumped from her seat as if it were on fire, the wooden chair traveling several feet before coming to a screeching halt against the gas range. *"You? You're the Angel of Death!"* she accused, her pointed finger trembling as she spoke.

Angel frowned.

"None other," Hero boasted.

"I... I've heard stories, the...the tales, the—"

"All true," Hero confirmed.

"I was younger then," Angel defended.

"Hell of it is, the guy's as modest as he is deadly," Hero verbalized.

"You...you brought over eighty hostages to freedom from deep within Iran!" Mackenzie testified. "Single-handed."

"Eighty-seven," Hero corrected.

"You carried two injured copter pilots out of Iraq, one over each shoulder, while holding off an army, an HKMP5 in each hand!" Mackenzie expounded in awe.

Hero's eyes narrowed. "Now wait one minute. That *is* a blatant lie."

Angel turned to the quarterback and smiled.

The newest tribe member studied the expression of the football player, believing his remark to be one in a series of never-ending jokes but found sincerity instead.

"The rifles were Russian-made AN 94s, not US-issue MP5s," Hero elaborated.

The entire room resounded with laughter.

CHAPTER 4

Nightfall had come all too early for Mackenzie. Instilled with the wonder of being rescued, especially by such caring and generous people, having enjoyed a hot meal, clean clothes, and warm roof overhead, made her feel like a little girl on Christmas Eve. The prospect of freeing her father made her feel excited about what the morning would bring.

Even the cot she was laying on was a welcome change from her prior sleeping arrangements. Although the confines of the dam were safe from the bionuclear fallout, and relatively warm, it offered few sleeping accommodations. For the first two months, everyone, soldiers included, was forced to sleep directly on the cold, damp concrete floor. Later, "as a reward for their services," her and two other girls—one as young as twelve—were allowed a heavy, green wool blanket to lay on. Of course, the actual reason for their generosity was to end the painful blisters the soldiers were developing on their knees. She remembered one soldier…

"…kenzie, Mackenzie," Trish whispered from the opposite bunk.

"Oh, sorry, I was, ah, just daydreaming."

"My god, girl, you should have seen the expression on your face. If that was a daydream you were having, I'd hate to see what you look like when you're having a nightmare."

Mackenzie frowned as she looked up at the small gas lamp. Even on low, the light radiating into the gloss-white cubicle performed an outstanding job of illuminating the interior. Although the tribe was certain their supply of natural gas was inexhaustible, they had no way to gauge the storage capacity of the underground facility, so logic dictated that all the main lamps be turned off at night as a conservative measure. It was permissible, however, to utilize the cubicle's small lamp as needed.

"Just thinking about how lucky I am to be here."

"Mac, I hate to say this again, but if that expression on your face was—"

"Oh, no, not again…" Mackenzie began before both girls exploded in laughter. "No, I just meant that…you know, compared to what I've been through and all…you know…"

"Oh, I'm sorry… Care to talk about it? If you need someone, I'm here for you."

The blonde debated. She didn't know if anyone really cared about her…ordeal. Whether anyone really wanted to know the circumstances. She did not know if she should share the experience… if she *could* share the experience. On the other hand, the "tribe," as they called themselves, left her wanting for nothing. They would jeopardize their very lives to help free her father, albeit in an effort to save Rick's life as well. Mackenzie considered herself a good judge of character and was certain that Angel would have offered to help, regardless of the circumstances.

"I… I'd like to, just don't know if I should…if I can—"

"Mac, it might be good therapy if you would open up and tell someone about—"

"What? So now you *think* you're a psychologist as well as a doctor," the newcomer snapped, bolting upright in her cot.

A sorrowful expression enveloped the brunette's countenance as she cast her watering eyes downward.

Mackenzie immediately regretted her words. "Oh, Trish… I'm so sorry. I didn't mean a word of that. I studied you tonight. Your protocol was flawless as you ministered to Angel's injuries. The fact that Rick is doing as well as he is is a compliment to your abilities. Please don't hate me. It's just that…you can't imagine what I went through during the last six months. It's changed me… I can only imagine what it's done to my dad. He tried to help me. He really did, but those bastards beat him until he couldn't move. And then they just laughed."

Trish realized that Mackenzie, without realizing it, was beginning to open up to her and started to rise in an effort to comfort her.

"No! Stay there. I...will...not...cry, promised myself...that I would...not...cry anymore. Just let me finish."

Trish eased back into her cot as Mackenzie continued.

"Men! I could easily hate them all, but my dad is a man, so... no, I won't. It didn't take long before the soldiers...the men with all the weapons, the men who were in...*control*, it didn't take long before they got the itch. Bastards. Initially there were five of us girls...you know...young...pretty. God knows...if there had been a way to disfigure myself..."

Trish could easily see that Mackenzie was not in control of her emotions. The beleaguered girl was incoherent, speaking in bits and pieces. Her story had no natural progression.

"One girl, a beautiful redhead...eighteen, choked to death on her own vomit...the son of a bitch raping her...he wouldn't... wouldn't even stop. Another girl, beautiful...with blond hair...blue eyes—like me. One day...a soldier forced...forced her into performing...oral sex...on him. She played along...for a while...then tried to bite it off. Son of a bitch...grabbed her by the neck...beat her head against the cement wall...until...until she was...was comatose. Still...the bastards continued to...use her...until she died...a month after.

"Then...there was Mandy...a twelve-year-old. Poor Mandy. Beautiful dark hair...down to her waist...brown eyes...virgin. Her father and mother were there with her. Her father tried to protect her...like my daddy did...tried...to stop the soldiers...shot him dead...right in front of...wife and...poor...young... Mandy. You... you wouldn't...wouldn't have believed it. Her mother...offered herself...in place of...poor...little...virginal... Mandy. Stripped herself...completely...in front of...everybody. Groped...herself... made a...a whore of herself...rubbed herself...against the soldiers... desperately tried to...distract them from...poor Mandy. No dice... troopers thought...fortysomething...too old. Once...one time, they all had their way with...poor Mandy...over and over and...

"When they came for me…dad…you know…he was there… he fought too…too valuable to them…to kill. Instead…they beat him…over…and over. Laughed…spit in his face…made him… watch. It…was so bad… I didn't even…recognize him anymore. I did… I tried everything. I told Dad…you know…after, that it was…was okay, you know…what they were doing to me. Still…he fought…every time they came. I… I pretended to…enjoy it…pretended to want it…to convince my dad…anything…to keep them from…beating him. I… I laughed… I… I…would flirt…with them whenever they…came. Anything…all to convince… Daddy that it was…was…okay. I remember…remember feeling miserable…miserable because they were beating him…miserable because…because… he thought… I had turned into a…a tramp…miserable…

"I remember this one soldier… Vince was his name…wanted me bad. Tried and tried…couldn't get it up. Imagine…what it must have been like…for him…his buddies having…a real good… time…enjoying…whoever they wanted. Just couldn't get it up…so embarrassed…failed time after time. You know… I…actually felt… sorry…you know…for him… I even… I went out of my way… for him…tried to help…all the other soldiers…kept making fun of him…eventually…he quit trying…ended up…put his service pistol in his mouth…blew his brains out."

Realizing that Mackenzie was becoming almost catatonic, Trish tried to intervene. "Mackenzie, if you don't want to continue, I'll understand."

"Then…there was Melissa…good ol' Melissa…thank God for Melissa. If there were a whore among us…it was Melissa. Well endowed…put it mildly."

With that statement, the distraught blonde took a deep breath before expelling a great sigh. It then seemed that she managed to gain control of her emotions. "I won't…go into details…but… I truly think she enjoyed every minute with the soldiers. Thanks to her, we were able to escape. She told us in advance that she would distract the soldiers if we wanted to try it. You should have seen her. Put on quite a show. Incorporated a number of tools and plumbing supplies…very imaginative…she was. The guards who were supposed to be watching us…opened their pants…took out their… Anyway…myself and nine others managed to slip out…while the guards were…distracted…by the obscene things she was doing."

As Mackenzie came out of her trance, she realized her description was more graphic than an eighteen-year-old girl should be exposed to. "I'm sorry. I didn't mean to upset you. It's just… I relive that hell each and every night. I know there will be no closure until I kill every one of those bastards and get my father back."

"No, honey, I'm the one who's sorry. I had no idea, but I do now. Trust me, if there's anyone who can get your father out of there, it's Angel. You'll see," the brunette promised.

The two remained withdrawn for a while, the newcomer dwelling on the day's events, Trish making notes in her diary. Mackenzie had discovered that thoughts of Angel were occurring with increasing frequency. Before bedtime, Trish helped the newcomer prepare her cot and gave her something comfortable to sleep in. In typical Angel style, his cot was aligned with the opening to the room he shared with Jim, so in the event of an emergency, he would be the first to scramble into the hall. What all that meant to the blue-eyed girl was that Angel was lying down right next to her, separated only by two inches of paperboard. Those thoughts made her feel good and very special. It definitely made her feel thoroughly safe and secure.

At that moment, Trish looked up from her entry in the diary. "Look at you. Now you're grinning like the Cheshire cat. What's up now?"

Mackenzie couldn't help but be touched by her bunkmate's interest. The sly look that the brunette was giving her made her wonder if Trish also possessed some of her older brother's clairvoyant powers.

"Tell me about your brother, about Angel. What are his likes and dislikes? What kind of woman is he attracted to?"

"You weasel. Don't think I haven't noticed."

Mackenzie blushed.

"The thing you have to realize about Angel is, he is genuine. What you see is what you get. He's been that way his entire life. In that respect, the war didn't change him. It may have hardened him a little, but he has always been forceful and in command. The kind of women he's attracted to? I don't think you have anything to worry about."

Feeling a little embarrassed over asking such a question, Mackenzie quickly changed the subject. "I see you've been keeping a diary."

"I usually make entries almost every night." Trish held the spiral notebook out to the girl. "Want to read it?"

"Oh no, I couldn't," Mackenzie insisted.

"It's not really that kind of a diary, believe me. It's more of a chronicle of everything that's happened to us since the END. In fact, Mac, it will help bring you up-to-date on a lot of things you'll need to know."

Mackenzie acquiesced. "Are you sure you don't mind?"

"I'm sure," Trish assured as she passed the bound notebook to Mackenzie.

Mackenzie opened the chronicle to the first page. Aside from the written word, the notebook itself—stained and tattered—was an account of their survival. The pages reeked with the strong smell of lamp oil. Candlewax had dripped onto portions. Other entries were eroded by teardrops. The smell of woodsmoke was also evident. In fact, sooty fingerprints were in abundance throughout the manifest. The entries were quite brief, understandably. The time and resources required to undertake such a task were limited, and consequently, so were the accounts. Mackenzie had neither the time nor patience to read the entire six months' worth of events. She instead concentrated on those that seemed relevant to the tribe and local environment.

9/5/29—The day the world as we knew it came to an end. Terrible explosion. Upper stories and roof collapsed on top of us. Buried us alive. Much hysteria. Especially Mom. Angel, thank God here on leave, pillar of strength and encouragement. Brought Panther home—prototype military vehicle—safe in garage. Closed gas and water valves. Prevent explosion and contamination of water in water heater and lines. Angel taking stock of situation and inventory supplies. Jim helpful. Everyone else too much in shock. Slept on whatever we could find.

9/6/29—Mom still in shock. Dad tried to comfort, no luck. Angel instructs how to care for her. Angel coordinates effort to ensure survival. Smart. Take mind off troubles. Cleanup and organization of home shelter. Inventory and sort supplies. Food, water, candles, lanterns, fuel, flashlights and batteries, etc. 120-gallon water heater and lines intact for drinking. No bathing. We'll smell really bad shortly. Makeshift bathroom, makeshift toilet in area farthest away from living area, smells bad.

9/7/29—Mom almost better. Thank God for Mom. Good supply of stored and preserved food. Ate food in freezer first before spoiled. Good to forty-eight-plus hours after loss of power. Angel rationed food to coincide with water supply. Says both should last two months. Radiation. Stay longer down here—better.

9/17/29—Mom all better. All getting used to living like this. Explosion severe. Lucky to be alive. Thank God for makeshift bomb shelter! Collapse of roof and floors above—protect us from radioactivity. Wonder if anyone else survives. Great urge to dig out through pile of debris barricading garage doors. Angel says not yet. Wait until one week left to food and water supply.

10/19/29—Strange, loud noises outside. Scary, like monster or dinosaur. Cool in evenings. Angel says safe now to use fireplace for heat. Good supply of firewood in garage. Rick and Dad clear debris from chimney. Dad almost killed by falling bricks but okay. First warm meal, heat food over fire while keeping warm. Something bothering Angel. Goes to Panther parked in garage. Sifts through "war chest." Checks and loads weapons. Says he is just getting ready for when we dig out. *Too early!* Something else on mind. Won't say.

10/31/29—Halloween. We dig out through garage. All in shock, even Angel, *that* worries me. Angel says to wait another day before venturing out. All too much in shock. Much destruction. Much. Everyone in terrible shock. Even Angel.

11/2/29—Many bodies. Most perished in nuclear explosion. Jim calls it END—Earth's Nuclear Destruction. Angel says nearest impact ten to fifteen miles northwest. Some died from exposure to radiation and maybe something else. Came across skeletons, some partially consumed by something. Angel again worried. Made sure all well armed. Said Mom, Dad, and I had to stay in basement to protect it—from what, no one knows. Angel won't say. I think he's afraid for us to be out there. No food to be found. Most all other homes and buildings destroyed.

11/3/29—Wants to conserve Panther. Used Dad's partially damaged car to explore. Roads almost impossible to travel. Found food and bottled water in demolished grocery. Loaded salvageable. Older brothers attacked by very large and aggressive rats. Tough battle. Barely got away with lives. Plan to unearth concrete sections of driveway immediately in front of garage doors to use as barricade against attack from man or beast.

11/5/29—Using parking brake cables and fan belt pulleys from destroyed vehicles and gears and chains from bicycles, made device to lower and raise driveway sections against brick face of exposed garage. Much safer. Just in time. Huge rats smell us out. Attack. Try to get in. Can't. Rats begin attacking and eating one another. Safe for now.

11/7/29—Angel ventures out to search for Tiffany. Finds her still alive in municipal complex shelter. Something bad happened. Changed him. Returned hurt and wounded. No Tiffany. Refuses to speak of it. Not pushing it. Sad. Very sad.

11/26/29—Thanksgiving. All very thankful. Fresh fish from pond one-half mile way. Fish and water seem safe…for now. Maybe not so much after first rain. Football game using water bottle stuffed with wet paper. Lots of fun.

12/12/29—Animal resembling pterodactyl swooped down. Grabbed Jim by left arm. Luckily able to draw gun with right and bring creature down far from here. Angel, Rick, and Dad went on search. Found Jim and brought back. Beat up very bad, will be okay. Begin my role of doctor.

12/24/29—Angel worried. Found huge tracks like dinosaur / large lizard near pond. Never knew Angel worry so much. Knows more than he's telling. Used to go out with lesser weapons. Now won't venture without H&K G3 .308 and .50 Desert Eagle. Angel devised explosives using black powder and anything hollow and made of metal, doorknobs, pipe, etc.

12/25/29—Christmas. All exchanged gifts, mostly things we made. Some stuff guys came across during excursions and found useful. Mom and Dad not feeling well but happy. Dad made Christmas tree from junk lying around. All happy.

1/10/30—Huge lizards / dinosaurs roaming closer to home. Many tracks nearby. Usually made at night. Becoming increasingly dangerous to go out. Angel halts foraging for food to find safer place to live. All worried. Not much any safer than here. Mom and Dad getting sicker.

1/15/30—Mom and Dad very sick. Angel and Jim go into town. Try to find remains of drugstore. Bring back any/all drugs and related might be useful both now and in future. Attacked by huge rats on way back. Car just made it to entrance of street. It's finished.

1/25/30—Parents not responding to treatment. Skin getting greener every day. Monstrosities within forty feet of basement during night. Angel regularly speaks of cave from childhood. Takes Panther to investigate/determine if livable and defensible. Goes alone. Huge creatures return. Nearly destroy what's left of basement. Jim in charge. Very worried.

1/30/30—Fifth day without Angel. Using chainsaws from hardware store continues to make cavern livable and ready for move. Rate Mom and Dad declining, will never see our new home. Jim forages alone. Rick here for protection.

2/2/30—Angel returns. Great news. Cavern like a fortress. Says nothing can ever threaten us again.

2/3/30—Preparing to move. Angel begins transfer of necessities. Will take several trips using Panther. Rick starting to feel sick. Dear God, no. Mom passes away. God, no—before Angel returns from last trip. Much sorrow. All cry.

2/5/30—Last day here. Dad passes on. Much sorrow. Buried him next to Mom. All weep. Never saw Angel cry before. Nothing else to say.

2/6/30—Made the move. Cavern everything Angel said it was and more. Wish Mom and Dad were here to see. Would have been proud. No, were very proud of us. Died proud.

2/8/30—Rick too sick to forage with Angel and Jim. Guys ran across a strange fellow. Mountain Man. Don't yet know what to think of him. A little scary. Brothers certain he's okay. M/M has lots of stories to tell about "traipsin" here. Ran across a lot of bad people. Big news. Evidently more people survived than we thought. Unfortunately, seems most are bad news. Angel says most of who survived probably did so at expense of others. Sad.

2/12/30—M/M elixir slowing Rick's decline and easing pain. Wish Mom and Dad... M/M working to supply gas to cave. Very ingenious. Taught me how to concoct poultice from various roots. Not as weird as first thought. Just talks strange. Would trust him with life.

2/15/30—Not another one. Brothers brought home another stray. Don't know real name. Angel keeps calling him Hero, I guess 'cause he thinks he was some kind of football hero at West Virginia University. Whatever. Looks like an idiot in tattered football uniform. Kind of cute. Can tell he gets under Angel's skin at times. Could be big trouble. Think he's sweet on me.

3/10/30—Angel and guys ran into trouble with soldiers. Good news! Brought back future sister-in-law.

Mackenzie looked up to find Trish smiling ear to ear.

CHAPTER 5

In the process of maneuvering the camouflage Panther from its place of concealment just off US Route 50, Angel was never more grateful his military prototype all-wheel drive had survived. At the outset of the bionuclear conflagration, the commando had just returned to his parents' home to begin a new life following his honorable discharge. Parked in the garage beneath the two-story structure, the successor to the military's Hummer, and all its contents had remained intact, entombed beneath the rubble. Pressed into service, the Panther was engineered for such hostile environments, but even it had its limits. Buckled and eroded sections of highway made travel, even in a vehicle as rugged as the ATV, difficult at best. However, the rescue mission would have been impossible without it. Concealed under brush and tree limbs the last few weeks, the camouflage paint scheme ensured the Panther remained undetected by the human eye. Nocturnal creatures skulking the forest always left their calling card however, be it excrement on the fiberglass top, a scraped fender, or a nest under construction.

The titan frowned as he glanced at the fuel gauge. Three-quarters of a tank were all that registered on the meter. Even though the Panther was a true flex fuel vehicle in every sense of the word—meaning its turbine-powered engine could run on anything from diesel to gasoline—fuel was next to impossible to obtain. They had collected what precious fuel that did not explode, burn, or leak from the ruptured tanks of automobiles. Six gallons in the Panther's tank was all that remained. Unless more could be procured, and the commando doubted that it could, three hundred miles was as far as the four-wheel drive would roam.

"Tell me, how do you plan to free my father?"

Despite the tumultuous jolt to the vehicle and its occupants as they jounced into the median separating the east- and westbound lanes, Angel managed to locate the worried face in the rearview mirror.

Securely nestled between a pair of broad shoulders, Mackenzie nervously fumbled with the black nylon sling of the M16 angled between her legs, struggling to mask the heartfelt concern so evident on her features. Attired in green fatigues confiscated from one of the dead troopers, her hair concealed beneath a green cap and soot liberally applied to her rosy cheeks to effect a heavy growth of beard, the gender of the newest tribe member was difficult to ascertain.

In the short time he had known her, the commando had grown fond of the girl. He was certain she had feelings for him also but was unsure how far those feelings strayed from platonic. Regardless of his emotions, Angel wished he could have convinced Mackenzie to remain at the compound. Despite her surviving the brutal ordeal of imprisonment and escape, the outlands were a place that no man should venture, much less a woman. The warrior chided himself for allowing her to accompany them. However, he also realized she loved her father deeply and would have attempted his rescue without their help. Angel found she could be extremely obstinate when so inclined. If there was a bright side to her presence, it was that her vast knowledge of the dam would prove invaluable once they arrived at the facility. The combat veteran was vaguely familiar with the layout of the immense structure, having toured the flood control plant on several occasions. But the commando could not ignore Mackenzie's six-month incarceration, which rendered any knowledge he possessed about the plant inconsequential.

Angel's dark eyes strayed from the highway to a red-and-black compass watch on his left wrist. "We left home at zero seven-hundred. We should—"

"Hold it, big guy," the passenger to Angel's right protested. Hero constantly scanned the terrain for sign of trouble as he spoke. Clothed in green fatigues, as were they all, the quarterback sported an HK MP5/10A3 on his lap and a Glock 20 ten-millimeter semi-automatic holstered on his left hip. "How about cutting the military crap and speak English."

The decorated war veteran frowned. Shifting his gaze to the man occupying the bucket seat next to him, he found the senior quarterback grinning like the Cheshire cat. The man was incorrigible. He also had a valid point, for once. If they were to function effectively as a team, it was imperative they communicate on the same wavelength. Expecting civilians to understand and react to the vernacular of the military was simply asking for trouble.

Angel turned his attention to negotiating the broken pavement, about to continue his digression, when he detected movement out of the corner of his left eye. "Did anyone see that?" he asked, bringing the four-wheel drive to an abrupt stop. Scrutinizing the westbound lane, the warrior hesitated to advance until he was sure it was safe.

"Only the back of turbo tongue's head and my side of the highway," Jim remarked from the seat directly behind Angel, his grip tight about the HK's receiver, wishing it were the quarterback's throat. A Ruger ten-millimeter was secure in its holster on the younger commando's right hip.

The sibling was acutely aware that his older brother tolerated abuse from no human. Why Angel put up with Hero's constant belligerence, he would never understand. Of one thing he *was* certain: there was sure to be a day of reckoning…soon.

"Cute," Hero responded sarcastically. "I'll have to remember that one."

Dense forest and alien plant life bordered the boundaries on both sides of Route 50. The parking lots of tumbled-down businesses along the thoroughfare had become so overgrown in the six months since the END that the structures beyond were barely visible. It was as if Mother Nature was determined to reclaim her world and eradicate all evidence of mankind's domination.

"Ah, shore seen somethun'," Mountain Man responded from the opposite side of the rear seat, his green eyes glued to a clump of ferns seventy yards distant.

"Get a good look at it?" the commando probed.

"Ah, can't be fer certain. Ah, do know et was big 'n black."

Angel pondered the information. Since the END, a proliferation of mutant animal life wandered the earth. Almost overnight, it seemed that common animals were mutated into their prehistoric compliment. What were once common house cats before Armageddon had evolved into something closely resembling sabertoothed tigers. Lizards the size of dinosaurs roamed the riverbeds. Bats—before their transformation—pterodactyls now flock to the skies by the hundreds. The exception to the rule were rats. Sewer rats, feeding on millions of contaminated bodies, increased in size with every generation. Ugly, black, and menacing, the German shepherd-sized rodents were to be avoided at all cost, and the Special Forces commando wondered if it had been one of those voracious creatures that disappeared into the brush.

"One of the large rats we encounter from time to time?" Angel inquired.

Mountain Man shifted the .357 magnum pump-action Timber Wolf in his lap; a Ruger Super Blackhawk of the same caliber was holstered in a leather gun belt on his right hip. "Don't thank so. This'n here's bigger'n most I seen."

Angel leaned forward in his seat, studying a clump of purple ferns typical of the variety overrunning the landscape. Instinctively, he slid his right hand around the forearm of the Heckler and Koch G3 affixed to the dashboard next to his right knee.

The G3 with its fifty-round drum magazine of .308 NATO fastened in its special mount provided instant access to an awesome amount of firepower. Secure in its holster on his left hip was the commando's cherished .50 Desert Eagle. An eleven-inch survival knife was sheathed on his right hip, a ten-inch stiletto was concealed in his left boot, and a North American Arms mini-revolver in .22 magnum was secured around his right calf. Vowing never to be caught in the outlands again without weapons, the decorated war veteran ensured they were all heavily armed before leaving home.

"Sabertooth?" Angel ventured.

"A mite bigger."

Mackenzie swallowed perceptibly. "Larger than a saber-tooth tiger?"

Angel turned clockwise in his seat. "How big was it?"

"Big as that'n right yonder," Mountain Man rendered. Angel swiveled just in time to see the huge animal disappear into the underbrush.

"What is it?" Mackenzie uttered in alarm.

"Boar," Angel replied in fascination. "Biggest son of a bitch I've ever seen."

"Another mutation no doubt," Jim reasoned.

"Are they common around here?" the girl wanted to know.

"It would appear they are *now*," the titan testified. "Hero, stand ready to shoot that hog if it threatens to charge."

Accelerating slowly, the tribe leader hoped to avoid a confrontation if for no other reason than to conserve ammunition. While he did not get a good look at the beast, he knew it was immense and would require a great amount of firepower to bring it down. Having hunted wild boar in the southern part of the state for many years, he was aware of the difficulties involved. Because they lacked a nervous system, two to three well-placed slugs from a high-powered rifle were required to down the average boar that was slightly larger than a pig.

Angel approached a spot opposite the highway from where the boar trampled a patch of vegetation in its quest to elude detection. Just as he began to entertain hope of an uneventful departure, the huge swine burst from concealment. Once again, he brought the four-wheel drive to a halt to avoid startling the animal. The titan studied the miscreant, calling to mind everything he knew about the creature so that he might devise a course of action.

In the early eighteen hundreds, a wealthy industrialist transplanted hundreds of wild boar from Germany's Black Forest to a large ranch in Northeastern Kentucky. The feral hogs were turned loose and hunted for sport. Over the years, they eventually migrated northeast into West Virginia. No longer hunted, their numbers quickly multiplied. While the term *wild boar* was loosely applied to any wild pig, which in most cases were domestic animals that had wandered off the farm, West Virginia could boast that its species were the real McCoy. The enormous creature pawing the ground across the way was no exception.

Six feet high at the shoulder, the raging animal was the size of a large rhinoceros and just as deadly. Its entire body from corkscrew tail to cloven hooves and upturned snout were covered with coarse black bristles. Savage, red eyes glowed like burning coals behind fifteen-inch razor-sharp tusks awash with saliva and glistening in the morning sun.

"Can we outrun the critter?" Mountain Man ventured.

"The condition this road is in," Hero conjectured, "no way!"

"Surely that thing can't present much of a threat to our vehicle," Mackenzie speculated.

Jim angled the muzzle of his rifle upward and cycled the action. "That porker must weigh three tons, minimum. Considering current technology—fiberglass frame, ceramic engine, and impact-resistant plastic body—as impervious as the Panther is, that animal could easily double the weight of this transport."

"We don't have all day," Angel groused. "I'm going to try to ease past. Hero, at the first sign of trouble, open fire."

Hero responded by cycling the charging lever of the MP5/10A3 and thumbing the safety to full auto. "Three ton o'sausage—coming up!"

As if challenged by remark, the hog bolted.

Hero slid out the passenger side, stepped onto the running board, and using the roof of the Panther as a rest, opened fire on the stampeding miscreant.

"Damn!" Angel swore. Encumbered by his own size within the confines of the vehicle, and further hindered by his exit past the steering wheel with the massive rifle and attached fifty-round magazine, the commando's entry into the fray was delayed by several moments.

In that eternal instant, the interior of the vehicle turned to chaos. Shouts of alarm and the clatter of weapons were nearly obscured by the thunderous din of Hero's rifle recoiling against the cab of the vehicle. Angel managed to clear the door just as the golden arc of expended brass sailing over the hood ended. The quarterback's carbine clicked on empty.

Squatting down to give Mountain Man an unencumbered field of view, Hero fumbled to insert a fresh clip into his rifle. He was disturbed by the lack of effect the volley of ten-millimeter projectiles had against the advancing creature, which had already traversed the westbound lane and half the median.

Mountain Man had entered the fray with his pump .357 Magnum Timber Wolf rifle. While it appeared that ten-millimeter ball was either bouncing off the impossibly tough hide of the creature or failed to penetrate sufficiently, he was distressed by the lack of stopping power of his rifle's powerful cartridge.

Jim tried to enter the fight but was obscured from his target by the hulking mass of his brother. He wanted to advance several paces beyond his open door but didn't want to distract the titan by pelting him with hot brass from this rifle's ejection port. All Mackenzie could do was watch in abject fear.

The tribe leader left the retractable stock of the G3 in its collapsed state; the proximity of the assaulting animal precluded his extending the stock and sighting down the barrel. Instead, he tucked the weapon into his right side and firmly depressed the trigger. Fire belched from the muzzle of the ponderous battle rifle, the butt-stock hammering the titan's impervious rib cage. Round after round of 180 grain full metal jacket drilled into the trampling horror to no avail. Crimson clouds erupted along the boar's right front quarter, serving to track the bullets' impact as Angel directed the salvo at the creature's heart. Its right foreleg entirely blown away, the feral pig persisted in its onslaught, the storm of gunfire generating little effect. Cycling six hundred rounds per minute, the G3 functioned flawlessly in the commando's unrelenting grasp. Still the hog refused to abate its frenzied attack as volumes of dust churned up by the galloping swine's three remaining hooves swirled in its wake.

Burrowing through layers of fat, muscle, and bone, the powerful projectiles finally struck home. For the first time during its mad scramble, the beast appeared to falter. Blood flowed from the porker's snout and mouth, its heart pulverized by the heavy slugs. As the three-legged demon clamored onto the pavement of the eastbound lane, Angel emptied the remainder of the drum into its brooding face, shattering its tusks, forehead, and right eye. As quickly as the rifle snapped on empty, Angel drew the Desert Eagle from its holster.

Thumbing down the safety from a condition one carry, the strapping warrior aligned the sights, about to fire.

The six-thousand-pound brute dropped at the veteran's feet.

Panting like a steam engine pulling a grade, the boar glared up at the hulking warrior with its singular eye, expelled a shrill squeal, and then expired.

The silence was deafening.

Angel holstered the pistol, then turned toward his companions, the smoking HKG3 in his left hand. By then, Mackenzie managed to compose herself. Hero had replaced the spent magazine with a fresh clip. Jim and Mountain Man, who initially clubbed each other into oblivion in an attempt to bring their rifles into play, were now perched on the edge of their seat. The five studied one another for some sign of emotion or closure. None was offered.

The five had traveled over a mile before Angel shattered the quietude. "As I was saying," casting an eye toward Hero, "we left home at seven o'clock. I hope to rendezvous with the remainder of Mackenzie's party by nine. Allowing several hours to advise, debrief, and coordinate their march back to the cave, it will be noon before we would be able to leave for the dam. Barring any unforeseen circumstances, we should reach the installation by dusk. The rescue will definitely occur after nightfall."

"And once we reach the dam?" the girl inquired.

"We'll play it by ear. It depends largely on the situation. Before we arrive, I'll have to debrief you before devising a course of action. In the meantime, I want you to concentrate on every detail you can remember about the habits of any sentries or patrols, although that information may be outdated since the escape. There's a full moon tonight, but clouds could affect our strategy."

While eastbound US 50 was mostly free of obstacles, Main Street Bridgeport was a different story. Automobiles of every description were strewn along the roadway like so many playthings out of a child's toy box. Some were on their sides or tops, while others were stacked in tiers of twos and threes. Utility poles, snapped at their bases, were lying about like so many spilled matchsticks. Those still erect were listing at acute angles. Downed power lines snaked off in every direction.

The city had not changed much since Angel's last trek into town; possibly a few more of the ruined buildings had collapsed. The hardware store on the western edge was completely enveloped by the aggressive plant life. During the last several months, the decorated war hero had made innumerable trips to the devastated establishment to salvage what he could. Hammers, chisels, axes, saws, anything of practical value. Also ammunition. Lots and lots of ammunition. The structure also contained some firearms. Conventional arms, to be sure, if pressed into service, they would fill a variety of purposes from hunting to defense, but Angel had not found the time to retrieve them.

"Look!" Jim stated, pointing to a three-story building on the right side of the street.

Angel slowed the vehicle and looked in the direction his brother had indicated. The commando surveyed the outdated edifice. Constructed entirely of red brick except for the intact plate glass entrance and windows, the building was of a mid-eighties venture. A faded blue sign with the words "City Development Company" in white letters hung askew from a single rusted chain. A debris-strewn parking lot fronted the establishment. However, it was something within the structure that had arrested Jim's attention. Standing behind the double doors and partially obscured by the tinted glass was the vague silhouette of a human. The form disappeared in a matter of seconds.

"Is that someone from your party?" Angel inquired into the rearview mirror.

"I couldn't even determine the sex, let alone if it was one of my people," Mackenzie confided.

Hero shifted in his seat. "Why don't we first check to see if the jerks are where they're supposed to be, and if not, come back and check out this place?"

"No good," Angel stated. "Now that we've been spotted in this vehicle, they might leave, afraid we may be other soldiers looking for them. Remember, they're not expecting us."

"What do we do?" Jim inquired.

Angel gunned the engine, wheeling into the small asphalt lot in front of the structure.

Hero watched in fascination as Mackenzie removed the magazine from her M16, confirming the forty-round clip was loaded to capacity. "Where do *you* think you're going?"

Mackenzie slammed the clip home. "Inside."

"You're nuts!" the ex-football player retorted.

Angel removed the spent drum from his G3. "Mountain Man, grab two magazines for my rifle, a couple of flashlights, and some spare ammo for yourself. Jim, you remain here. I want someone with combat experience to stay with the vehicle. Hero, stay with Jim and reload this while we're gone." So saying, Angel tossed the spent drum on the quarterback's lap. He then directed his attention to the woman. "You know how to handle that weapon?"

"Competed with this type of weapon in the President's Challenge four years in a row," she responded with pride.

"You're not actually thinking about taking her inside, are you?" Hero admonished.

Angel leaned across the front seat, his Herculean build expanding to fill the dimensions of the driver's compartment. "I am going to say this only once," the hulking figure elaborated, his eyes narrow and foreboding. "*I* am running this show. *I* give the orders."

"But I was only—"

"But hell! If you don't like the status quo, you can ship back up north. Sure, we can stumble around in there, in the dark, shouting that we're friendly. Probably get killed for our trouble! We can say we are friends of the girl, but what if they think it's a ploy, think we have captured her and returned for them? It's Mackenzie who must convince them we're on *their* side." Angel deliberately paused to enforce his point. "I will not have you questioning my decisions. We don't have the time, and I don't have the patience. Do I make myself clear?"

Hero was plastered against the passenger door, vigorously shaking his head in the affirmative.

"Good," the scowling titan rasped. "If everyone is ready, let's roll."

Angel opened the door, and the three disembarked from the driver's side. After they had passed the front of the vehicle, Mountain Man handed the commando the magazines he had requested. "Do ye think ye was a mite hard on the feller?"

Angel slammed one drum into his rifle and stuffed the other into his right front cargo pocket. "I was hard. I should have been harder. I will not tolerate having every decision questioned. I'm responsible for our lives and the life of my dying brother. I'm responsible for Mackenzie's people, both here in town and those held captive at the dam. People are depending on me, and if we fail, I have only myself to blame."

"Hero's ah good man, iffen he is ah tad testy," the woodsman ventured.

"I have faith in him. The fact he's here proves that." The muscular fighting man cycled the action of his rifle. "Come on, let's see if we can locate whoever it was we saw in the window. Mackenzie, stay behind me. Mountain Man, bring up the rear."

Angel cautiously advanced toward the doorway, alert to any surprise. His skin tingled. He was uncertain if it was a sense of impending doom or the cool march breeze gently blowing from the north. He felt as though they were marooned in a ghost town—vulnerable and helpless.

The smell of the dead city was sickening. Dirt and decay were everywhere. The stench of rotting flesh was heavy on the palate. The tribal leader swiftly turned as something squeaked to his left. Afraid it might be one of the large mutated rats, he was relieved to find the real estate sign swinging on its rusty mount in the light wind.

Angel motioned for those behind him to step to the left of the entrance. Grasping the HK G3 by its forearm, the commando brought the rifle around in an arc, hooking the leather sling around the door handle. Pulling the door open wide, he waited a moment, then let it swing close. Several seconds passed before he repeated the procedure, this time propping the door open with a fallen brick.

"Wait for my cue," the veteran instructed. Dashing through the doorway, he bolted to the right, then squatted, his back to the front wall. Waiting for his eyes to adjust to the dim light, the combatant took stock.

Main Street ran east to west while the building he occupied was on the south side of the avenue facing north. There would be little light within the structure. As his eyes grew accustomed to the tenebrous conditions, Angel became aware of his surroundings. He appeared to be in a lobby or foyer at the head of a long corridor. Perhaps ten or twelve offices branched off in either direction along the hallway, which intersected a staircase at the rear. The lobby and entire office complex was in absolute disarray. Not one item of furniture was intact. A desk to his right was lying on its side while several vending machines to his left were completely destroyed, no trace of their contents anywhere. Ceiling tile, fluorescent light fixtures, covers, and bulbs lay broken and scattered about the floor.

Deeming the vestibule secure, the titan motioned for his two companions to enter. "Mackenzie," he whispered, "keep a close eye on the hall and adjoining rooms. You won't be able to see it until your eyes adjust, but there's a stairway in the back. Mountain Man, did you…say, there has to be another name you answer to, your Christian name perhaps?"

"Shore is, that'n gived to me at birth."

"Great, what is it?"

"Zechariah."

"Zechariah?"

"That be rat. Named after one ah the books of the Ol' Testament."

"Oh…okay, great. Say, did you bring the flashlights?"

"Rat here en ma back pocket." With the .357 magnum Timber Wolf carefully cradled in his left arm, Mountain Man reached into his right rear pocket of his camo coveralls and extracted two red-and-white flashlights.

"You any good with that shootin' iron?" Angel inquired, using lingo his friend understood.

"Shoot the eye out'n a turkey at ah hun'ert yards."

"That's great, Zech…uh, Mountain Man, now help me bring this overturned soda machine over to the hallway."

Quietly as possible, the two men carried the vending machine to the head of the hall, laying it horizontally on its face.

"What is that for?" Mackenzie whispered.

"Insurance," the Special Forces commando disclosed. "Eyes accustomed to the light?"

"What light?" she complained.

Helping the girl over the mechanical obstacle Angel playfully admonished. "You know, you're beginning to sound like Hero."

Mackenzie mumbled unintelligibly under her breath.

"Hold the flashlight out from your body at arm's length," the titan advised. "If these people are armed and hostile, your flashlight will become the target—instead of you. Mountain Man, check the rooms on the left side of the hall. I'll take those on the right. Observe the way I secure a room before you try it on your own. Mackenzie, stay close behind me, no talking."

Both nodded in agreement as Angel motioned to proceed. Every door on either side of the corridor was closed, giving rise to suspicion and fear. As Angel approached the first door, he stopped a few feet short of the entrance. His weapon clutched firmly in his right hand, he slowly twisted the knob with his left until the latch cleared the jamb, then pushed the wooden portal slightly ajar. Extracting the flashlight from his left rear pocket, the war vet eased the door open with the barrel of his rifle, hugging the wall as he did so. With that accomplished, the commando extended the flashlight and aimed the beam against the opposite interior wall. Working the beam clockwise, Angel was careful to study all within the room, paying particular attention to any object that would conceal an assailant from view.

When the room was deemed safe, he cautiously entered the office, finding it in as much disarray as the lounge. The room was twenty-four feet deep and sixteen feet wide. White walls supported an eight-foot ceiling, the same white, suspended tile they had encountered in the foyer. A gray desk sat against the west wall while several olive-green file cabinets, their contents unceremoniously strewn about the floor, stood in the far-left corner. A green telephone and gray all-in-one computer monitor lay in a hundred pieces amid several office chairs, one upright and one on its back. It was obvious someone, at some time, had occupied the building.

Mountain Man meticulously followed the commando's example of securing the building. Room by room the trio advanced, finding every office on the floor nearly identical in size and furnishing. All were in similar chaos. Oddly, the structure contained no windows to illuminate the trio's passage. Each made certain to close every door as they reconnoitered their way toward the stairwell, the procedure providing a small measure of warning in the event they had overlooked a hiding place in one of the rooms.

Standing at the base of the staircase, Angel was apprehensive. Having led his troop deep inside the bowels of the shadowy complex, they found themselves at the mercy of an inky crossroads. Retreat was out of the question. Proceeding into the unknown entailed great risk. There were two rooms, lavatories, one on either side of the stairway that had yet to be explored.

"Mountain Man, investigate the women's room. I'll examine the men's. Mackenzie, stay close and keep it low." Angel used the beam of his flashlight to direct their movement.

Had the situation not been what it was, Angel would have been amused at Mountain Man's apparent hesitation to enter the women's facilities. Approaching the door to the men's room, the commando pushed the portal wide with the barrel of his HK. Completing his search, the tribal leader found the washroom innocuous. For whatever reason, whoever had ransacked the other offices ignored the men's facilities as everything appeared in order. Exiting the latrine, the titan was bothered by an awkward thought. Perhaps the inhabitant of the complex was a woman who had been as uncomfortable entering the privy of the opposite sex as Mountain Man had been.

The warrior returned to the hallway, cognizant to the fact that Mackenzie had not moved from the spot. Instead, she had remained behind, alone in the gloomy corridor. "I thought I told you to stay close?" he whispered to his female companion.

"I can't go in there. That's the men's room!"

The veteran of WWIII frowned in despair. There was much to be learned about human behavior. "Then why didn't you accompany Mountain Man?"

"You told me to stick with you. Remember?"

Angel's broad shoulders slumped. "Speaking of Mountain Man, where the hell is he?" The muscular commando rapidly treaded toward the ladies' room, Mackenzie in tow. His earlier premise about a woman being in the building began to haunt him. If only there were some windows, sunlight. The nocturnal environment had begun to unnerve him. Most people, and Angel claimed no exclusion, loathed the dark, the uncertainty and innuendo associated with murky surroundings, those shadowy images of things better left unspoken, which pervade the subconscious. Those "things," combined with the horrible threats the new world invariably dealt, and the premonition he experienced before entering the complex, all served to set the warrior on edge.

As Angel reached for the brass doorknob, the wooden portal suddenly flew open, startling the commando and his protégée.

"What the devil took you so long?" Angel demanded.

"Ah was a mite skittish about traipsin' 'round tha ladies' room," Mountain Man sheepishly responded.

"Let's get this over with," the titan growled, motioning toward the stairway.

The trio cautiously ascended the stairwell, ever alert to attack from above. Rounding the turn in the landing, they detected a peculiar odor permeating the air. Upon attaining the second floor, the stench was overwhelming.

"I think I'm going to be sick," Mackenzie declared, resisting the urge to gag.

"Ah know jest what ya mean, missy. Ah always spill ma taters durin' a hog renderin'."

That was all the provocation the blonde needed. Doubling over, she immediately lost the contents of her stomach.

"Thanks," Angel admonished the woodsman. Venturing several feet into the murky depths of the access, the commando flashed his light down the lengthy corridor. The reflection off the white hallway found thirteen oaken office doors closed. Consistent with the design, the second floor was identical to the first with one notable exception: an office at the end of the hall occupied the space directly above the downstairs lobby. Something did not quite add up, he deduced, assimilating everything he had experienced since entering the structure. He was debating whether to continue or call an end to the fruitless search when the girl indicated she had recovered and anxious to proceed.

To facilitate matters, Angel directed Mountain Man to the men's room at the western end of the stairs. Relieved by the change of assignment, the woodsman nodded appreciatively before stalking off. Motioning for the girl to follow, Angel cautiously approached the ladies' room, expecting the worst. It seemed as if the stench had grown stronger, if such were possible.

Angel turned to Mackenzie, who had cupped her left hand over her nose and mouth. "Want to stay here?"

"No way!" the blonde breathed, shaking her head in the negative.

"Suit yourself," the titan whispered, slowly twisting the knob.

Kicking the door wide, Angel discovered the source of the offensive odor. Despite the fact that indoor plumbing was a luxury of the past, whoever occupied the building religiously used the rest room facilities to do their business. Feces and decay overflowed the toilet. Urine and vomit covered the floor. Partially buried beneath the dung was a premature fetus. The warrior had witnessed a plethora of gruesome conditions in his travels, but without a doubt, this was the worst.

Retreating to intercept Mackenzie and spare her the encounter, the commando could not ignore the convulsive retching coming from the opposite side of the staircase. Obviously, Mountain Man had stumbled upon similar conditions. Retracing their steps to the head of the corridor, the two patiently waited for the woodsman to emerge. Wiping his mouth on his right sleeve, the woods dweller aimed a stocky left index finger at the room he had just vacated, about to elucidate.

"I know," Angel remarked, hoisting a thumb over his left shoulder. "Makes you wonder what we'll find on the third floor." Turning to the unenlightened girl, the tribe leader continued, "Any of the women who escaped with you happen to be pregnant?"

"I don't think so, not to the degree where I would have noticed. Of course, considering what those bastards did to us, anything is possible."

"If it weren't for the possibility these could be your people, I'd pull out now," the titan groused.

Angel led the team in their search of the second floor, looking for any shred of evidence that would identify the occupants of the office complex. Securing the last office on the right side of the corridor, the warrior realized he had done so routinely. The fruitless search had become mundane; his guard had dropped. Such a careless attitude would ultimately prove hazardous in such a situation. He made a deliberate attempt to redouble his efforts.

Satisfied the room was empty, Angel rejoined his companions, only to find Mountain Man with the same sick expression he had worn upon exiting the men's room. Raw intuition dictated that Angel call an end to the search, but curiosity got the better of him. "What is it?"

"In thar," Mountain Man indicated the office behind him with a nod of his head. "Thar be ah dead parson."

"Let's have a look," the tribe leader mentioned to his female companion.

"Hold et, ma'am," the woodsman began, barring the girl's passage with his right arm. "Et ain't a purdy sight."

After a moments deliberation, Angel concurred. "Wait here," then pressed into the room.

The office was an exact duplicate of all the others he had searched. The same chairs, computer hardware, file cabinets, contents strewn about the room. Was it any wonder he was becoming stale? However, in this office, lying atop the same gray seven-drawer desk was the partially consumed remains of a corpse. Angel drew to within a foot of the gruesome sight. By the beam of his flashlight, the cadaver appeared to be green. Both arms were missing, ripped cleanly from the shoulders. He spied one appendage near the east corner, bereft of tissue; the location of the other was anyone's guess.

Gleaned of flesh and internal organs from neck to crotch, the corpse's legs were intact, entrails hung from the cavity like ropes of sausage. The gender of the victim impossible to discern, its face appeared to be masculine. Angel refrained from touching the body but deemed it to be devoid of rigor mortis. The corpse had not been dead long, and Angel wondered if it had fallen prey to the huge rats.

Because carrion was so plentiful following the holocaust, the mutated vermin reproduced with abandon. As far as Angel was concerned, they were a macabre blessing, consuming the rotting remains of the slaughtered before another health crisis developed. Shortly following the END, the veteran estimated their numbers in the city alone to be into the thousands. As the victuals diminished, the huge miscreants began to fight among themselves, cannibalizing their own species. Unfortunately, not all the creatures perished but dwindled to a level commensurate with available food supply. The titan was familiar with their handiwork and was almost certain the body before him was evidence of their occupation of the structure. Perhaps the trio's arrival had somehow interrupted their meal.

Regretting his inability to drape the cadaver, Angel summoned Mackenzie to identify the corpse.

Mackenzie timidly shuffled toward the desk, her features drawn as the tribe leader placed the beam of his flashlight upon the grisly sight. "Oh, oh…augg." She gasped, covering her mouth with her left hand, the bile again rising in her throat.

Several moments passed before the sickened girl sufficiently recovered from her nausea to examine the lurid remains.

"He's…green," Mackenzie remarked, the comment sounding more like a conclusion than a statement. Looking across the table bearing the putrid cadaver, she testified into her leader's eyes. "Not one of my people."

Once again, Angel's senses began flashing red alert. "Come on, we're packing it in!" Passing the beam along the body for the final time, the war vet noticed strange depressions along the outer right thigh. Upon closer examination of the indentations, the warrior discovered that teeth had made the impressions. Human teeth!

Angel took Mackenzie's left arm in his powerful right hand, propelling her toward the door. "Everyone, outside. Now!"

"Don't ya thank we ought ah search this here room. See'n how et's the last?"

Mountain Man used the barrel of his rifle to indicate the office at the end of the corridor.

Angel spun toward the entrance, focusing his attention on the closed door and immediately realized why his keen faculties were blaring. His sixth sense detected a number of entities with hostile intent, lurking beyond the opposite side of the portal. Signaling the others to back away, the titan led the retreat one step at a time, careful not to alert the inhabitants to their actions.

Continually monitoring the room for sign of movement and confident the distance separating them from the office was sufficient, the team reached a point halfway down the length of the corridor where they turned to flee, horrified at what they saw before them. Sixty feet away, jamming the stair well above and below the landing were several dozens of the most gruesome excuses of humanity. Illuminated by flashlight and the faint glow escaping from the floor below, the creatures were cast in a ghoulish light. Green from the bane effects of the contaminated environment, they had decaying skin that possessed an eerie, almost fluorescent quality. Glassy, bloodshot eyes, hosting black dilated pupils, stared unblinkingly from dark recessed sockets. A perpetually oval sneer revealing rotting, jagged teeth and the absence of facial hair presented a ghastly apparition to the stranded survivors.

Having entertained hopes of escaping the bowels of the building without incident, the trio gaped in horror as the mindless miscreants ambled menacingly toward them.

"We don't want any trouble," Angel expounded, backing away from the oncoming rabble, striving to talk his way out. He perceived the release of a door latch somewhere behind him. "Mountain Man, cover our flank!"

No recourse but to fight, the war hero sanctioned the onslaught by firing a short burst into the masses, Mackenzie following suit. Behind him, Angel heard the woodsman enter the fray. The veteran of World War III did not know how many were bearing down on them from the rear, but if the nonstop commitment of Mountain Man's weapons were any indication, there were too many for the conventional arms the woodsman bore. "Mackenzie," the commando shouted over the din. "Behind us!"

Angel was perplexed. The slugs from his heavy machine gun had little or no effect; the bullets merely zipped through the rotting flesh. He managed to down only two of the lurching nightmares, and those had to be shred in half with a concentrated hail of lead. Two of the apparitions, their legs blown from their torsos, continued their attack, clawing and slithering across the floor.

Illuminated by the flash of gunfire, the hallway rocked with constant concussion as the thunderous explosions echoed in the narrow passage. A sickly odor assailed their nostrils as the living dead disintegrated amid the smoky corridor. The walls were awash with emerald slime, the floor littered with decomposing body parts.

His G3 clicking on a hollow chamber, Angel remanded the rifle to his left hand, drawing the Desert Eagle with his right. Mackenzie's M16 empty, a lull in the action enabled the battle-hardened vet to discern that Mountain Man had already engaged the use of his sidearm. The problem was, such a choice of weapons did not lend themselves to rapid reloading, and Angel could not carry the battle alone. The trio, fighting back to back, continued the fray, sidearms blazing; the cannibals were thirty feet and closing.

Angel, discouraged by the ineffectiveness of their weapons, employed a different approach. Discharging the .50 into the face of the nearest deviate, he was rewarded when its head exploded like a rotten melon, terminating the approach. As soon as he communicated the tactic to the others, the tide began to turn.

Twenty feet away.

The commando downed two more, and still they came.

The semiautomatic thundered four times in half as many seconds, and four ghouls ceased to exist.

One round remaining, the titan took stock of the situation.

Twenty of the walking garbage heaps were ten feet away. The woodsman's revolver snapped on a spent cartridge; five of the fiends were within reach of him and the girl. Mackenzie's Beretta had just ejected its last casing.

"This way," Angel shouted, no recourse but to take refuge in one of the many offices. Ushering his two comrades in ahead of him, the vet blasted the closest zombie before taking shelter in the room to his right. Slamming the door, the commando engaged the lock, while Mountain Man quickly barricaded the entry with a heavy metal desk. Holstering his sidearm, Angel jogged to the west wall where several steel file cabinets were arranged. Searching for just the right one, the strapping warrior flung those he found unsuitable from his path as if they were aluminum beverage cans. The oaken door rumbled and swelled as the press of the throng increased.

Finding one cabinet with its contents intact, the Special Forces Commando rested his Heckler & Koch against the nearest partition. "This should do it," he announced. Tilting the five-drawer olive-green unit away from the wall, the muscle-bound colossus grasped top and bottom corner, deftly lifting the three-hundred-pound unit over his shoulder. Angel's muscles bulged beneath his camouflage coveralls; his biceps threatened to burst the garment at its seams as the powerhouse strolled to the door and deposited the item onto the desk.

Mountain Man worked feverishly, replacing the spent cartridges in his Ruger before reloading the Timber Wolf. Mackenzie, a flashlight in each hand, provided illumination for the men as they worked. "What possible circumstances could have turned ordinary human beings into…? These people remind me of the zombies in an old movie I once saw," the blonde remarked. "I think it was made back in the sixties."

"Missy, these'uns here ain't like no people I ever seen," the woodsman countered.

Angel acknowledged the statement with a grunt. "As much as I hate to admit it, unless we find your father, we may end up just like them."

"You mean this is what green disease does to you?" Mackenzie intoned with revulsion. "I'll take my own life first."

"Their condition is highly accelerated and more acute than that of my parents. My guess is a greater level of intensity and longer exposure to the environment has served to aggravate their case. However, they do bear similar traits."

Courageous throughout the fight, Mackenzie was visibly shaken by the revelation.

Eager to change the subject, Angel continued. "You didn't happen to bring a spare magazine for your M16, did you?"

"No," the blonde admitted remorsefully. "I didn't plan on fighting a war."

Mountain Man studied the stack of office furniture. "Figure that'll hold 'em a spell?"

"I hope so," Angel remarked, retrieving his G3 from where he had deposited it. Inserting his last clip, he parked himself on the corner of the desk and cycled the action of the battle rifle. "How many rounds do you have left?"

"Lack tha lady here—"

"Please call me Mackenzie." The girl knew the woodsman was shy, especially toward members of the opposite sex. The world had become so brutal, yet he was so kind and naive. Mackenzie wondered how he had survived this long.

"Lack Ms. Mackenzie here," Mountain Man began, embellishing her name with an angelic ring, "I wern't expectin' no feud. I jest grabbed me a couple handfuls. I done loaded ma revolver full. I put all the rest, ett of 'um, in ma raffle."

"Same here," Angel revealed, a hint of remorse in his voice. "Fifty rounds in the drum and five rounds in the .22 magnum are all I have. The next time—"

Without warning, the office door exploded inward, the battering rush of the flesh-crazed zombies splintering the stout aperture. Angel spun, unloading a quarter of the magazine into the remains of the door at eye level, the retort deafening in the confines of the office. As suddenly as it had started, the offensive ceased.

Two minutes passed without redress. Then five. After ten minutes, Mackenzie became uneasy. "Maybe they figured we aren't worth the trouble."

"Don't hold your breath," Angel cautioned. The warrior was in a quandary. Where the hell were Jim and Hero? His decision to take sanctuary in the room was based on the belief that all the gunfire would have alerted the duo to their predicament. Angel was aware that his orders had specified the two remain with the Panther, but that also ensured that someone with combat experience remained in charge for just such a contingency. Too much time had elapsed. The brooding vet could not understand their failure to appear, but of *one* thing he was certain: whatever the reason, if they had not mounted a rescue by now, they were not coming.

"I will tell you this," the commando injected, hoping to distract his companions from contemplating their predicament. "Now that we've reloaded, and knowing where they're vulnerable, if we can get back into the hall, we have a fighting chance of making it out of here. I don't know what these…things are up to, and I'm not about to stick around long enough to find out."

"If 'n that's tha case, ma'am, ye best take this," the perpetually courteous woodsman exchanged his loaded revolver for Mackenzie's empty M16. "I cain't allow the notion o' them buzzards get'n their hooks in ye."

"Thank you," the blue-eyed girl replied appreciatively.

As quietly as possible, the trio cleared the doorway of debris, then entered the corridor. Angel found several bodies on the floor outside, those he had taken out with the last burst of his G3. Ensuring the hallway was devoid of movement, the commando motioned his two companions to follow.

Cautiously, they crept toward the stairwell, directing their flashlights to avoid stumbling over corpses, body parts, or sliding on slippery gore. The war vet noted Mackenzie's disdain of the carnage wreaked in the dim corridor. He also contemplated the ability of the ghouls to work in unison, despite the fact that there was no apparent leader, no communication between them—at least as far as the spoken word was concerned.

Angel came to a halt several feet short of the staircase. Leaning over the aluminum handrail, he peered as far as he could see both up and down. About to descend the stairs, the titan hesitated.

"What troubles ye?" Mountain Man whispered.

"I wish there were another way out of here."

"Might be some way a gettin' down from tha roof."

"They're probably expecting us to leave by the front entrance," Mackenzie pointed out.

Looking up over the railing again, Angel debated the possibility of making an escape from the roof. "No good. Considering everything we've been through on this floor, I'd rather not risk the third. If we were to become trapped… God only knows what's up there. Our best chance lies in going back down. Once we reach the bottom, it's only a forty-yard dash to safety. Mountain Man, take point. Mac, douse the lights. What little amount entering the front door should suffice. Besides, you'll need both hands if you're going to use that .357. I'll stay here and provide cover until you two make the next floor. Let's move it!"

Stealthily, the pair made the grueling drop one step at a time until they reached the turn in the landing, hoping their clandestine movements would not attract attention.

"Do ye reckon these here varmints gived up on us?"

Mackenzie shrugged. "I pray to God they have."

Making their final descent, their attention was arrested by shuffling sounds traveling in their direction from the second-floor lavatories.

Leaning over the handrail, Angel waved the two novices on.

The woodsman assumed the lead, trying to emulate his mentor's caution and awareness. Mackenzie was right behind him, revolver cocked. Reaching the ground floor, Mountain Man surveyed the area between himself and both restrooms, then along the dark tunnel that would take them to safety, before giving the all-clear signal.

The strapping commando instructed them to proceed to the entrance.

Realizing Angel was jeopardizing his safety for their sake, Mackenzie lowered her stiffened arms to her sides and silently mouthed the word "No." Tears began to collect in the corners of her eyes.

Angel again waved them on, a stern expression on his chiseled face. Rebounding from the distraction, the veteran of World War III found the creatures within arm's length. The abrupt discovery galvanized him into action. Using the handrail to aid his momentum, the muscular fighting man propelled himself from the top of the second floor to the landing, the heavy rifle tucked against his side. Spinning on his heels, the commando elevated the muzzle of his G3. Crouching to a point where the geometry of the staircase worked to his ballistic advantage, he depressed the trigger.

As predicted, the angle at which he fired maximized the kill as the powerful projectiles passed through the first, second, and third wave of cannibals. Chunks of flesh flew in every direction, and heads rolled as the rifle jackhammered in the combatant's grasp. Sticky green fluid began to flow down the red-tiled stairway.

The assaulting ghouls never lost momentum.

Reluctant to stray too far from the commando, the two civilians made several strides toward the front of the building, stopping to ascertain the status of the battle. That tactic proved to be unfortunate. Three green demons exited from their place of concealment beneath the hollow portion of the staircase and advanced upon the duo.

Cognizant to the danger, the pair reacted instantly, leveling their weapons and downing the gruesome trio. However, their skill was no match for the numbers that poured from the offices along the hallway. From every room came two and three hellish figures, their dark, wild eyes emblazoned with hunger. Two of the wraiths tackled the stocky Southerner, both rifles clattering to the floor. As alien limbs encircled Mackenzie's waist, she cried out in fear, swinging the revolver behind her in an attempt to smash the ogre's head. Another fiend emerged to her left and slugged the hysterical woman in the jaw. Momentarily dazed, the stunned girl let the Ruger slip from her grasp.

Enraged by the assault on Mackenzie, Mountain Man sprang into action. Pushing himself erect, he side-kicked the demon to his right and landed a haymaker to one on his left, downing both zombies. On and on he fought, punching and kicking in an attempt to clear a path to the girl. Bones and cartilage crushed under his powerful strikes, yet the mindless horde pressed on, oblivious to their injuries. In his bid to help his newfound friend, the woodsman was finally brought down and pinned to the floor by three of the relentless creatures.

Alerted by Mackenzie's screams, Angel bounded down the steps three at a stride only to find the pair enveloped by scores of the fiendish miscreants. Unable to fire his weapon for fear of hitting his partners, the war vet tripped a lever on the G3, extending the sturdy metal stock to its full length. Clutching the heavy battle rifle about the forearm and receiver, the brawny commando waded into the throng, employing the weapon as a pugil stick. Bashing heads and crushing windpipes, the conditioned fighting machine gave no quarter.

For a brief instant, Angel envisioned their escape from the hideous dungeon before the ravenous entourage pouring from the stairway brought the powerhouse down. Succumbing to sheer numbers, Angel was eventually wrestled to the floor and disarmed. Slavering in anticipation of their salubrious meal, the anxious denizens swiftly herded the trio toward their lair on the third floor.

Angel was puzzled by the abnormal strength of his captors. Considering their physical condition, the simple act of breathing should have been laborious. Yet the zombie bearing Mackenzie had effortlessly tossed her over its left shoulder, intent on carrying her up two flights of stairs. Two were all that were required to conduct Mountain Man, despite his best efforts to resist.

Four goons, two at each arm, escorted Angel toward the top floor. Somehow, their demented faculties reasoned that they were all that were required to force the warrior into compliance. He could have easily overpowered the quartet at any instant, but the time was not right. He had to wait until their guard was down, when he could ensure his companions escape as well. Although his rifle was on the first floor where it had fallen alongside those of his friends, his survival knife in its sheath on his right hip and the two weapons in his boots were still intact. The creatures may have been too far gone to think of searching for weapons or else did not care. Either way, the tribal leader would use the oversight to his advantage when the opportunity presented itself.

The farther they climbed, the more subdued the light. Any illumination provided by the glass frontage was nonexistent by the time they reached the top floor, and if the odor of the second floor was unbearable, the stench of the third floor was beyond imagination. Angel had encountered a number of miserable conditions during his tour of World War III, but those of the top floor were incomprehensible. Only by practiced discipline was he able to suppress the urge to hurl. Angel reflected upon the failure of his companions to succumb to the urge and reasoned it was probably due to shock. The subconscious denial of the harrowing ordeal, their minds simply would not accept what their senses revealed.

Angel had been unable to discern the gender of the deviates he had confronted. Sickly in appearance, green from disease, shabby clothing, and absence of hair, erased any physical attributes. Except as a source of food, the veteran doubted the deranged ghouls had much interest in members of the opposite sex. Given their state of decay, he could not imagine any body parts, let alone sexual organs, functioning normally. As evidenced by the remains in the restrooms, providing for offspring was more than the food supply could bear.

Passing door after door, it became obvious they were being led to the last office of the top floor.

Mackenzie abruptly recovered from the blow to her head and the shock of her ordeal. "Hey, let go of me you…you walking garbage pile," she exploded, hammering her fists against the back of the one bearing her.

"Et be darker 'n a tomb up here," Mountain Man ventured.

"Did you have to use the word *tomb*?" Mackenzie admonished.

"Sorry, ma'am."

At least those two are back in character, Angel surmised as he considered their fate. Were they on their way to their death or to be held for future consumption or…? Once again, he was puzzled by their lack of leadership. He had observed no spoken commands or mental activity. They seemed oblivious to pain. An instinctive, reflexive, concerted effort to obtain sustenance seemed to be their only fixation. Finally, the mob reached journey's end, stopping before the entrance of the last office. The combatant could only guess what was in store.

"Where are Jim and Hero?" Mackenzie ventured. "Surely they heard all hell breaking loose!"

"I hate to be the bearer of bad news," Angel stated as the lead goon reached out to rotate the doorknob. "I don't think they're coming."

"Swell!"

Trapped within the building for nearly half an hour, their eyes had grown accustomed to diminishing light. By contrast, the brilliant radiation that suddenly flooded the corridor as the door parted was more than their tortured retinas could endure. Unable to shield their eyes, the subsequent tears diffused the bright rays into every color of the spectrum.

The antagonists seemed unfazed.

His eyes adjusting to the light, the strapping warrior became aware of the source of illumination. The center panel was missing from the suspended ceiling, and a hole roughly the same size had been punched through the roof. The twenty-four-by-forty-eight-inch diameter of the jagged opening admitted enough light to enable the assemblage to negotiate the rank cubicle. Only one item of furniture was in the room—the ever-present gray metal desk. The fixture, a thick layer of sticky gore covering its top, was positioned directly beneath the opening. Skeletal remains lined the walls.

The ghoulish creep bearing Mackenzie deposited her on the blood-spattered table as two of the zombies, a short creature wearing flannel shirt and blue jeans, and an extremely tall one dressed in a tuxedo, shuffled up to the appurtenance. Shorty pinned the girl's arms above her head, Lurch secured her legs, while the one who had carried the resisting girl into the room, an overweight fiend in a three-piece suit, unzipped the struggling woman's camouflage garment to her navel, exposing both breasts.

Locked in their devious embrace, the bare-chested girl screamed hysterically, once again reliving her ordeal as a captive at the dam.

Mountain Man fought unsuccessfully to wrest himself free of his captors.

Angel detected the shuffle of feet scraping in the hallway as the entire fraternity assembled for the grisly ceremony. The titan returned his attention to the proceedings. What he witnessed infuriated him to the point of bestial rage. Fatso was bent over Mackenzie's naked breasts, his head turned toward Angel in blatant defiance. The miscreant was actually grinning from ear to ear. Split, bleeding lips revealed jagged rotting teeth. Salivating in anticipation of its intended meal, fetid green drool flowed from the corners of the zombie's blistered mouth, puddling in the cleavage of the traumatized girl. Turning its attention to the feast before it, the cannibalistic horror lowered its open maw to the screaming girl's bosom.

The son of a bitch was actually going to eat Mackenzie alive, beginning with her breasts. Angel's features contorted in rage. His visage alone had terrified all who witnessed the extraordinary transformation. His prodigious muscles became slabs of iron, constricting sinews taut as steel cables. His chest expanded, and his arms bulged, bursting and rending the garment that encased him. It then became obvious to those in the room who witnessed the unholy phenomenon how this man came to be known as the Angel of Death.

With little more than a shrug of his right shoulder, the two attached to his right arm were cast over the table, to collide with the three assailing the girl. His right hand free, the superhuman drove his fist into the face of the ghoul to his immediate left, splattering its countenance in a plume of green spray. The titan then grasped his remaining captor around the throat with his left hand, lifting the menace several feet into the air before slinging it against the far wall. The miscreant crumpled like a rag doll.

Mackenzie quickly took advantage of the distraction created by the fracas. Spinning to her left, she rolled off the table, fastening the top of her garment as she landed. Assuming a crouch, the blonde waited for an opportunity as she assessed the situation.

In the ensuing melee, Mountain Man had managed to wrest free and was holding his own against the four pressing him. Downing two with a couple of hard jabs, he was engaged in the act of breaking the neck of a third, when one of the denizens clamped a stranglehold about his neck.

Alert to the woodsman's plight, Angel swiftly moved to his friend's aid. Grasping the head of the assaulting zombie in his massive hands, the commando wrenched it from its body in a bone-rending snap.

A warped smile crossed the commando's lips as he grasped the hilt of the survival knife on his right hip. Whipping the eleven-inch blade clear of its sheath, the muscular fighting man then retrieved the stiletto from his left boot. Extending the weapon to its full twelve inches with the push of a button, Angel waded into the frenzied mass, honed steel gleaming in the radiant light.

Shorty and Lurch regained their footing and made the fatal mistake of charging the knife-wielding madman. Angel simultaneously plunged a blade deep into each of their hearts and lifted the duo off the floor, pitching their lifeless forms over his shoulders, extracting the blades as they sailed into oblivion. The two he had cast over the table were on their knees attempting to tackle the Herculean fighter about the thighs. Angel brought his mallet-like fists down upon their bald pates, shattering their craniums like eggshells.

Making his way to Fatso, Angel forced the drooling maniac against the wall. In a motion so swift, it defied description. The strapping commando disemboweled the wraith with the stiletto, ripping it from crotch to sternum. As its putrid entrails spilled onto the floor, Angel's right hand arced up and out, the survival knife severing the sneering cannibal's head from its wretched body.

Wasting no time, the strapping soldier rushed into the corridor, taking the fight to the unsuspecting rabble before they could react. Slashing, kicking, and punching like a man possessed, Angel decimated the hapless throng. In the constriction of the passageway, there was little escape from the unrelenting engine of death.

Having dispatched the remaining creatures that had notions of rejoining the fray, Mountain Man rushed to Mackenzie's side, ensuring her safety. Together they ventured from the chamber, following in the wake of the madman's trail of carnage. Following closely, the two civilians came to realize they were witnesses to a sight few people had lived to tell about—the fabled Angel of Death plying his trade. As the elite killing machine stormed through the ranks, the dead and dying littered the hall. Up ahead, Angel was cutting a wide swath, butchering any and all foolish enough to stand in his path.

Spying the staircase through the thinning masses, Angel redoubled his enthusiasm, decapitating and dismembering in his bid for freedom. Dropping the last of the zombies confronting him, waning light to his rear forewarned the tribal leader of impending danger. The mortally wounded who had yet to perish were starting to regroup behind them. Angel ushered his companions past in order to defend their retreat. Carefully avoiding gore and dismembered body parts so as not to stumble, the trio raced to the lower floor, Angel deliberately holding back to provide his companions a safe lead. Twice, in her obsession to escape, Mackenzie almost tumbled headlong down the dark spiral. Each time the woods dweller prevented her from doing so. They made the second floor, and the race slowed as they negotiated the corpses cluttering the landing.

"They're on our heels!" Angel called from the floor above. "Secure your weapons on the way out. And don't forget about our surprise." Wiping the blades clean as he ran, the veteran of World War III hoped the overturned soda machine would trip up the drooling idiots long enough for Jim and Hero to administer the coup de grâce. Sheathing his knives, Angel took a measured stride and bounded from the second floor to the adjacent landing in one mighty leap. Traveling the last set of steps, Angel found his comrades collecting their respective arms.

Mountain Man handed the retrieved G3 and Desert Eagle to his leader. "Ah, shore hope Jim 'n Hero is awaitin' fer us outside."

"For our sake, they damn well better be. You two go on. I'll hold them as long as I can."

Angel waited for the last of the horde to clear the bottom step, then raised the heavy battle rifle to his shoulder. With two dozen still in pursuit, the marksman thumbed the selector to semiauto, the wide-angle scope employing the abundant light behind him. Maximizing what little ammunition remained, the veteran opened fire as the throng funneled into the corridor, determined to down as many as possible with each single shot. Centering the crosshairs on their mark, Angel opened fire on the nearest foe. The .30-caliber weapon belched fire and lead as the leading creature and one behind it were knocked off their feet, their heads exploding into gray and green. Another shot, and a third went down, causing two behind it to stumble. Another stroke of the sniper-grade PSG-1 trigger assembly sent a heavy slug into the left eye of the forth, blowing much of the cannibal's face away, before exiting the cranium and entering the mouth of the fifth, taking its head off at the shoulders. The commando squeezed the trigger again, and the rifle responded with an impotent click.

Now that his eyes had adjusted to the dim conditions within the odoriferous structure, Angel was dismayed to discover yet again, he was blinded by the intensity of the light entering the frontage. Determined to escape, he successfully hurdled the vending machine, only by virtue of his involvement in positioning the obstacle.

Bursting forth from the deadly complex, Angel was stymied by his companion's obvious state of shock. Both were staring at him with defeated expressions, their languid eyes mirrored pathetic hopelessness. Opening his mouth to inquire about their lack of enthusiasm, comprehension dawned.

Their vehicle and its occupants could not be found.

CHAPTER 6

"How long you figure they been in there?" the ex-quarterback asked.

There had been little conversation between the two up to that point as both men remained alert to their surroundings. Each had been responsible for monitoring a 180-degree arc on either side of the Panther. Hero swept all points east and south, while Jim was responsible for north and west. Jim turned his head toward Hero, who was standing at the right front wheel of the camouflage Panther. "About fifteen minutes."

"You thinking what I'm thinking," Hero asked the younger commando who was positioned at the vehicle's left rear wheel.

"Yeah, I know. They've been in there too long, unless they're doing a room-by-room sweep. The thing that bothers me, you usually don't need to do that when searching for friendlies."

"Maybe it's like the big guy said, they think we're here to capture them—or worse."

"Angel gave me direct orders to stay with our transportation. But if we don't hear from him soon, I'm going in," Jim explained.

"Then I'm going in with you. Ain't no way I'm stayin' out here by myself."

Just then, Jim unslung his rifle, thumbing the fire control selector to full auto. His eyes seemed to bore right through the athlete.

Hero's blue eyes grew wide in alarm. "Hey, hold up, man. I didn't know you're as crazy as your brother."

Jim quickly brought his HK up and pressed it into his right shoulder. "No fast moves. As calmly as you can—as quiet as you can—get in the vehicle. Now!"

Hero was at a loss. He didn't think his earlier words would incite that type of response from Jim. Angel maybe, but not Jim. He knew firsthand the awesome amount of firepower inherent in the ten-millimeter machine gun and was taking no chances. As he edged toward the door, Hero was relieved that the business end of the Heckler and Koch rifle did not keep pace with his movements. Sliding into the passenger's seat, the quarterback found it odd that Jim's aim never wavered. He continued to keep his rifle trained on the exact spot that he had been standing in.

As the younger commando slowly approached the driver's door, never taking his eye off the holographic sight, Hero realized something was seriously wrong. Turning his head toward the southern exposure, the frightening reality of the evolving world struck home. Hero was terrified to see a pair of what could only be described as saber-tooth tigers stalking their way toward them. The ex-quarterback studied the two creatures. Their movements were definitely feline in nature as they prowled the lot across the street. Their coats of fur appeared to be that of house cats as one was white and gold, the other tabby. As near as Hero could tell, Angel had been correct in his speculation that common alley cats had somehow mutated into what were apparently saber-tooth tigers. However, the six-inch fangs and razor-sharp nails reinforced the notion that these creatures were not to be taken lightly.

"What now?" the alarmed quarterback asked.

"Give me a minute, good Lord. If it were a squad of enemy soldiers…the Special Forces didn't prepare me for anything like this."

"They've spotted us. Oh, hell. They're headed this way. Can they get inside this thing?"

"Maybe, maybe not. But they can certainly destroy our vehicle trying."

"Then think! What would Angel do in a situation like this!"

The tigers roared and snarled as they raced toward the Panther, jumping in leaps and bounds. Just then, the sound of gunfire erupted from somewhere inside the office complex.

"This is just great!" Hero exploded.

Jim turned his head toward the building containing his companions. "Only one thing we can do."

"What's that?" Hero asked.

"Lure them as far away as we can. If we can lose them somewhere, then we'll come back. I sure as hell don't want the team stumbling into these creatures."

"I really hope your plan works," Hero said, cycling the action of his rifle.

"Yeah? Why is that?" Jim responded as he fired up the prototype vehicle.

"Cause there's three more right behind the first two."

Jim didn't take the time to look as the pair were within thirty feet of their position. Turning the steering wheel in a tight arc, Hero floored the accelerator as the supercharger came to life. The constant metallic chatter of automatic fire coming from the building to their left all but drowned out the snarling beasts. Jim maneuvered the vehicle west onto US Route 50, heading back the way they had come.

"Good idea, man. We'll just lead them back home and let Trish and Rick worry about them."

"Boar!"

"Hey, I was just joking."

Jim turned his head toward the ex-quarterback, an incredulous expression plastered across his face. "I wasn't referring to you…this time. I'm talking about the huge boar we brought down three miles back. If I can get them to follow me there, the feast should keep them busy most of the day."

"I got to hand it to you, man, excellent thinking."

Hero entered onto the exit ramp that would allow them access to the westbound lane. Not only was the boar laying in that lane, but the eastbound route was littered with an inordinate number of demolished vehicles. Evidently, when the END came, the hysterical people must have reasoned that fleeing their home was the proper thing to do. It was if nearly all traffic was headed out of town, little had entered. The younger commando was pacing himself as he tried to keep the creatures committed while maintaining a safe distance. On undamaged and uncluttered highway, he could have easily outdistanced the cats as the Panther's top speed was close to 150 mph fully loaded. Unfortunately, twisted wreckage and erosion of the roadway prohibited nothing faster than 50 mph.

"Can't you get any more speed out of this crate? They're gaining on us."

Hero manipulated a switch on the dash. The digital instrument panel indicated that the vehicle was now in the all-wheel drive mode. AWD would not make the Panther go faster; however, it would allow the nimble vehicle to better navigate the hazardous road conditions. The pair jostled about the interior of the Panther as Jim fought to keep from damaging the valuable machine.

"Twenty-five yards and gaining," Hero expounded.

Hesitantly, Jim applied more throttle. The veteran found himself in a precarious situation. No longer was it a matter of keeping the miscreants interested in pursuing them, it now became a life-or-death race to stay ahead of the creatures, and the team were losing. Jim knew that if he lost control of the Panther, it could mean the eventual loss of all their lives.

"Fifteen yards and closing," Hero informed. Pushing a toggle on the passenger door, the quarterback lowered the bulletproof plexiglass window. "Lucky thing I'm left-handed!" Hero swiveled in his seat as he felt the vehicle accelerate even more. Fastening his seat belt and hanging out the vehicle just far enough to allow him to fire upon the determined cats, the ex-quarterback opened up on full auto.

Jim found the vehicle impossible to control as he fought the irregular road surface. At times, they were airborne in an effort to negotiate the rough and buckled roadway, at a speed that would have been ridiculous under normal circumstances.

"Don't kill it—not yet!" Jim shouted over the din.

"You kidding. The way you drive, I'll be lucky if I can scare it." With that, the football player opened fire in an effort to get the lead tabby to back off. The other four were literally on its tail.

The brute became infuriated and increased its pace.

"Five yards and closing," Hero said dejectedly as he put up the window.

"Nice going. Any more bright ideas?"

Suddenly, the Panther left the road as an unavoidable section of buckled highway sent the vehicle and its contents skyward. It seemed to the two companions that everything shifted to slow motion amid their own shouts of alarm as the contents of the vehicle sailed about them. The rearview mirror showed no sign of tabby. When the Panther came down, it landed on all fours, but a sickening explosion followed the maneuver.

"The right rear tire just blew!" Hero warned.

Jim immediately activated another toggle as he fought to maintain control of the unstable vehicle. Instantly the emergency inflate feature deployed a mixture of tire sealant and air to inflate the tire. "Where's tabby?"

"Damned if I know—or care," the blond expounded as he tried to grasp anything that would stabilize his latitude within the vehicle.

Their hearts sank as the right rear tire quickly deflated.

"Too damaged to hold," Jim informed. To his credit, the commando never eased up on the throttle, constantly fighting to compensate for the damaged tire as the vehicle swerved and slithered over the crumpled highway. The rearview mirror indicated all tigers were in close pursuit—except for the dark mottled cat. "Where's tabby?"

"Who gives a rat's ass?" the football player asserted. At that instant, razor-sharp claws punctured the fiberglass top.

"Hey, watch out!" Hero yelled as tabby began to shred the vehicle's canopy as if it were cardboard.

"Ahh, I think I found your kitty." Garnering no response, he added, "I thought the roof was supposed to be bulletproof."

As if Jim's burden wasn't enough, he now had to elude the ravaging claws assailing them and deal with Hero's antics as well. "Yeah, well, no one said anything about saber-tooth-tiger-proof. And whatever you do, don't try shooting through the top. We'll probably end up dodging bullets too."

"How much farther?" Hero shouted above the constant thump of the deflated tire.

"Should be about half a mile. At this point, I'm worried they'll continue after us instead of going for the boar."

Hero considered Jim's words. It was certainly possible that the cats were so absorbed in the pursuit they may give chase well beyond the porker. Suddenly, the thumping ceased and was replaced by a grinding sound. The ex-quarterback saw the damaged tire casing fly off the wheel, causing a jet-black tiger in the pack to stumble.

"What was that?" Jim wanted to know.

Watching the black cat roll into the path of a white Persian, tripping it up, Hero ventured, "You know how black cats are supposed to be bad luck?"

"Yeah."

"Believe it!" Hero assured.

"What was it you said? Oh, yeah. Three ton o'sausage—dead ahead. Hero, brace yourself."

"Huh?"

"I said brace yourself." So saying, the commando jammed on the brake pedal, locking the three remaining tires. The vehicle immediately slid to the right, coming to an abrupt stop.

Tabby was catapulted head over feet, tumbling until it slammed into the dead boar. The two tigers directly behind the Panther collided with the vehicle propelling it fifteen feet beyond where it had stopped. Finally disentangled, the two cats farthest back had sufficient warning to leap over the all-wheel drive before a collision occurred.

Before the creatures could react, Jim punched the throttle to the floor, the three remaining tires leaving smoke and rubber in their wake. The vehicle accelerated around the boar's carcass and continued down the highway.

"If they're still following, we're going to have to make a stand," Jim stated.

Backward in his seat, the quarterback studied the tigers, accounting for all five. "No…nope, no. They are taking the bait. Thank God!"

"Good deal. I am going back to the spot where we first pulled onto Route 50 and change that flat. Double-time. We've got to get back and rescue the guys. Lord only knows what kind of trouble they ran into."

Speaking just above a whisper, Hero speculated, "Sounded like one hell of a firefight."

Jim shook his head in anguish. "Damn it. I wish there was something I could have done."

"You did enough. More importantly, you did the right thing. No way could you have allowed our guys to fall prey to those things."

"I guess you're right," Jim admitted. "Still..." The commando knew Hero was right, but it still did not make him feel any better. He also came to realize that perhaps the cocky quarterback was not as belligerent as he would have one believe. Approaching the location he was seeking, the commando backed the Panther over a section of buckled roadway so that the right rear wheel was suspended off the ground one foot. "That'll save us some time. We shouldn't need the jack."

Jim actuated a switch on the dashboard. The result was a whining sound from the rear of the vehicle and a corresponding indicator light that flashed "SPARE" appeared on the dashboard. Exiting the Panther, he directed the football player to stand guard while he installed the new assembly. Jim lugged the spare and tools out from under the rear of the vehicle. Even having saved time in jacking the all-wheel drive, changing the flat was no easy matter. Aside from the wheel and tire combination being extremely heavy due to the modular wheel bearing and housing incorporated into the unit, one still had to contend with the emergency inflate system.

Two-thirds of the way into the replacement, Hero heard a terrifying roar coming from a place not too distant. The roar was followed by an innumerable number of snarls and growls. "You hear that?" he asked his companion.

"What?" the commando snapped.

"Roaring and growling."

"You probably heard me. This vehicle is built like a tank, but making any repair at all is a real son of a bitch."

"No, seriously, I heard something huge."

"No, seriously, I have been cursing so much I haven't heard anything. Just keep your eyes open, and don't let anything sneak up on us...again."

"Yes, sir," Hero replied. He realized he had allowed the saber-tooth tigers to sneak up on their position earlier. If it had not been for Jim monitoring both their perimeters, they would be dead right now.

With the replacement of the tire behind them, the pair traversed US 50 giving wide birth to the southbound lane via the northbound lane within one-half mile either side of the feeding sabertooths. Avoiding another conflict with the felines was of utmost importance and, more so, the rescue of their friends from their dire predicament.

*****

"What the hell?" the titan asked of no one in particular.

"There ain't nary a sign ah them other two."

"They wouldn't have deserted us, would they?"

"Not without good reason," the fighting man reassured. "What worries me is the only good reason I can come up with is there was a perceived danger that they couldn't deal with or something they were afraid we would stumble into."

Almost in unison, the three spun about in search of some unknown danger. Angel also scrutinized the hallway of the building to assess the disposition of the cannibalistic miscreants. Nearly out of ammunition, the commando chafed at the thought of being chased all over the city in order to evade the ghouls.

"You two monitor the surroundings," Angel stated as he laid down his heavy battle rifle in favor of the edged weapons. "I'll do my best to hold off these monsters!" So saying, the battle-hardened vet stepped into the doorway to constrict the assault.

For the first time since making contact with the humanoids, they appeared to cower as they approached the entrance. At first, Angel thought they lost the desire to continue the fight. After a few moments, it became apparent that they were terrified by the bright sunlight streaming through the front door and windows of the office.

Backing slowly away from the entrance, the titan was optimistic to see the rogues refused to advance. "Men, it appears we have nothing to fear from these zombies, at least until sundown." Mackenzie glared at the warrior with wide blue eyes. "And, ladies! Sheesh. And if our transport doesn't arrive soon, that just might be the case!"

"Whar should we hole up fer the night? Should we try ta find another buildin'?

Mackenzie punched the backwoodsman in the arm with her left fist.

"We're out of ammo and I…wouldn't want…to go through that…again." Angel was momentarily distracted as the blonde unzipped her coveralls to her navel and began to clean the green gruel that was between two perfect breasts and had begun running down her stomach. Using a white kerchief she had pulled out of a hip pocket, the blonde mopped up all that the rag would absorb. Nor could the commando ignore the cuts and bruises from her earlier captivity. Sensing the titan's halting speech, the beautiful woman shrugged her shoulders as if to say, "What the hell, now that you've already seen 'em!"

Mountain Man's face turned a red that matched the color of his hair as he turned to give the girl her privacy.

"Although you may have a point, Zach…uh… Mountain Man. Perhaps not a building per se but some type of defensible shelter that would—"

Before the strapping commando could finish his sentence, the air was filled with the purring of a turbine. The remainder of the team was on their way back.

Momentarily forgetting her attire, or lack of it, Mackenzie spun to watch as the Panther approached. A partial squeal left her lips as the blonde noticed the distracted driver almost colliding with an overturned car. Her task complete, she quickly tugged up the zipper and tossed the rag aside.

As the flex-fuel vehicle pulled up alongside the trio, Angel couldn't help but notice the damage. Shaking his head in the negative, he completed the survey. Hero watched as Jim took a deep breath before exiting the vehicle.

"Hang on, big brother. Before you say anything, let me explain—"

"Where the hell did you two go, and what the hell happened to the Panther?"

"Hang on, big guy…sir," Hero began as he stepped out of the all-wheel drive vehicle. "You don't know this, but we saved your lives!"

"That's right," the junior commando chimed in. "Just before we heard gunfire break out inside the building you were in, five… I don't know what you'd call 'em…saber-tooth cats…lions?…came out of nowhere and began to chase us!"

"That's right," Hero continued. "It became obvious that a fight was out of the question. We didn't want you guys to stumble out into them, so we figured the best course of action was to lead them away."

Angel listened to the remainder of their story, at times shaking his head up and down and at times right to left. The sour expression never left his face. As he and his two companions reloaded their spent weapons, Angel filled the two in on their misadventures.

"Okay, boys and girls," Angel began once they were all loaded and ready. "Main Street runs east to west. We are on the most eastern part of the city. It's three miles from one end to the other. Approximately midway is the bridge under which Mackenzie said her people were encamped. Jim, you will remember, and the others of you who are not aware, the complex where the band of cutthroats who killed Tiffany is fifty feet south of the bridge. We don't know if Mackenzie's people are still there. We don't know if the band of ruthless bastards are still entrenched in the complex. Hell, we don't even know what other threats may exist! So I'm telling you now, be alert at all times, be ready to engage, no jokes, and no bullshit. Got it?"

The war veteran waited to confirm that all understood the gravity of the mission. "Okay, Jim, hit it." Given the last encounter with a deadly animal, the veteran commando took steps to ensure he would be unencumbered should the situation warrant it. "Oh, and by the way, watch out for overturned vehicles." The strapping warrior turned and winked at the stunning blonde as he spoke.

"Just as long as no one decides to get butt naked… Ouch…" Jim reiterated before suffering a kick to the back of his seat by a size 7 combat boot.

The drive to the bridge was uneventful. As the vehicle pulled within sight of the structure, Jim slowed their approach and turned to his brother. "What now?"

"Pull to within fifty feet of the bridge, then stop. I want to get the lay of the land before we get any closer. Mac, you said your people camped beneath this bridge?"

"Yes, on this side, as close to the bridge's intersection with the ground beneath it."

"As brief as possible, tell me again how long you were here and about your experience before you ran into us," the leader asked.

"As I said, the trip here was fraught with…things…we didn't quite see or understand but knew they were out there. I don't know if the size of our numbers kept them at bay. Considering what I have seen thus far, I doubt that to be the case. Anyway, you mentioned what you call cutthroats in that building," the blonde paused to point to the complex across the way. "I can't quite put my finger on it, but as I was waiting for the soldiers to catch up to me, I sensed that someone…or something…was in that structure. It was about that time I heard the soldiers begin their march across the other side of the bridge, so I skedaddled out of there and didn't give it any more thought. How in the hell I made it to you guys without getting killed or eaten alive I'll never know!"

"Okay, Mac, I want you to search out the bridge—both sides just in case they are still encamped underneath, but be careful. Hero, I want you at the wheel. Jim and Mountain Man, you two come with me. We are going to reconnoiter…uh, that is, check out the building. Be prepared to provide cover fire if it comes down to that."

The four disembarked the safety of the vehicle to perform their respective tasks. As Angel approached the city complex, an eerie foreboding feeling washed over him. He was unable to discern if it was due to his sixth sense warning him of impending danger or if it was because his fiancée lost her life within the confines of the structure.

The veteran combatant took the lead and signaled his companions to form a single line behind him, Jim to cover their backs. Angel gauged the exterior to be as sound as he had left it. All the windows were devoid of glass. The door appeared intact, no change to the amount of debris surrounding it, as best as he could ascertain. Having been in the building some months ago, the warrior was confident of the layout. Approaching the plate glass door, Angel looked in both directions of the hallway before grasping the handle and slowly easing the door open. A shiver ran down his spine as a cold sweat bathed his entire body. It was not fear! Of that, he was sure, for he feared no man or consequence. The fact that he could not save Tiffany from the maniac who murdered her lay heavy on his mind. For all his might, for all his training, for all the special weapons in his possession, nothing could save her. Possible scenario after possible scenario played through his head. He could see the maniacal leader, Jack, laughing at him, taunting him. He could have torn down the menacing complex around them with his bare hands, but he could not help his suffering fiancée avoid the fate that destiny…

"Angel…what bothers ye?" the woodsman whispered just loud enough for his superior to hear.

The veteran of WWIII spun to confront his companion, his muscles bulging, his visage contorted in animalistic hate, Angel found himself staring into two sets of eyes betraying alarm for their friend.

"What the hell's wrong, AD? You're shaking like a freaking leaf! You haven't moved in over two minutes. What the hell," Jim demanded.

Angel's eyes locked on those of his companions for several seconds, his eyes evil and his visage set in rage. "I'll be okay, sorry! I'm taking the right side of this hallway, you two go down the left. At the end of each side of the hallway is a staircase. You will also find a door leading to the EMT garage. As quiet as possible, go down the staircase and wait at the doorway at the bottom. I'll do the same on my end. We'll give each other enough time to investigate anything suspicious and arrive at the destination before turning our flashlights on in unison. There will be another corridor. In the middle of that corridor is a heavy blast door leading to an underground bunker. If the corridor is clear, we will meet at the bunker door. The thing is, you'll see blood, a lot of it. Both of you would know if it's fresh. If it is, be extremely cautious. Got it?"

Both companions nodded in agreement. Each man struck off on his assignment. The doors leading to the stairwells were composite steel with wire-reinforced glass. The light coming through the multiple windows above them allowed enough sunlight to penetrate the composite doors and illuminate the stairwells.

Descending the staircase, the colossus was not sure what he would find as his original breach of the structure was via the opposite stairway. The stairs were littered top to bottom with a menagerie of useless objects: ruined laptop computers, eating utensils, picture frames with photos, desk lamps, coat hangers, and myriad other objects. If it held no practical purpose, it was sure to be there. Carefully avoiding the assortment, the warrior began to suspect that the complex was indeed inhabited, and the clutter served as an early warning system. Reaching the bottom of the stairway, the fighting man did so without seeing any trace of blood. Looking into the corridor, and finding it devoid of life, he waited for his companions to arrive at their destination.

As they reached the stairwell, Jim took stock of the EMT garage his brother had mentioned, finding it unoccupied and empty. Satisfied they were secure, the explorers proceeded to descend the staircase, Mountain Man holding the door open for Jim so the junior commando could enter unencumbered and ready for action. As soon as the door parted, a terrible stench assailed their nostrils. Rotting, putrid body parts of every description—some beyond description— littered the steps. Arms and legs still encased in civilian shirts and trousers. The blood. Absolutely no shortage of blood. Blood splattered on the bullet-riddled walls, blood on the stairs, blood running down the aluminum handrail. Gore and entrails everywhere. The duo squatted to examine what they had discovered. As bad as it was, the carnage did not appear to be fresh.

Mountain Man straightened and whispered to his companion. "This here's months old!"

"Did the other building reek this bad?" Jim asked of his comrade.

"Wors'en this. Lots worse! Looky down thar, thar's carcasses ah some kind."

Surreptitiously making their way to the bottom of the stairwell, repeatedly stepping on and over rotting limbs, the two men stopped at the bottom to survey the slaughter. Several bodies riddled with high-caliber wounds littered the floor, blocking the door from opening.

"We have to clear this door, but I'd hate to touch this crap," Jim complained.

Casting his eyes about, the woodsman spied a coat tree at the back of the landing. Handing his rifle to Jim, Mountain Man grasped the device at its base and used the tines of the other end as meat hooks to clear the doorway. Capturing the corpses one by one with the metal prongs, the stocky woods dweller cleared access to the metal and glass door.

Handing Mountain Man's rifle to him in exchange for the coat tree, Jim saw that his brother was waiting impatiently at his end of the passageway. Nodding his confirmation that he and his companion were both ready to proceed, Jim switched on his flashlight and entered the hallway, followed by Angel, then Mountain Man. The illumination was comforting as the light of day had grown almost nonexistent as they approached the bunker door.

The hulking warrior signaled his companions to give the opening a wide berth as he reached to open the portal. Turning the knob slowly and quietly, he could feel the bolt clear the striker plate. Easing the door open half an inch, the veteran warrior stepped back several feet and kicked the heavy blast portal wide open, resulting in a thunderous blow as it crashed into the supporting wall behind it. Before the reinforced barrier could strike the wall, the veteran of WWIII was in the shelter with his weapon ready, followed by his teammates. Angel and Jim had their weapons lights and lasers on scouring for any and all threats in the inky blackness.

Though the common area of the shelter was clear of any threat, the commando knew there were two smaller rooms, one on either side of the main area. Wasting no time in order to minimize reprisal, Jim rushed to sweep the room on the right. The junior commando did not complete his first step before a brawny arm entrapped his, arresting his momentum. "No, you and the woodsman clear the room on left. I'll check out the one on the right."

Jim did not understand his brother's reasoning; one room was just as suspect as the other. He was aware of Angel's disquiet since they entered the facility and assumed he had his motives; however, it was very unsettling to see the senior vet so spooked.

Angel stalked off toward the room on the right, quelling any debate that might have ensued. Jim held back for several seconds, providing cover in the event a fight ensued. The two watched in awe as the colossus kicked open the door without stopping to unlatch it.

"I figer he's pissed over somethun'," the woods dweller ventured in a whisper.

Jim shook his head in the affirmative and led his companion toward the door on the opposite side. The junior commando wondered if he could kick the door open in the same manner as his brother but decided not to try as a failed attempt could end in disaster if an adversary were lying in wait. Emulating Angel's maneuver, Jim slowly turned the knob until the latch cleared; the striker then kicked open the door. He and the woodsman were stunned at what they saw.

Angel jumped into the room he had chosen and flashed his weapon's light all around as he squatted to make himself as small a target as possible. Except for two large stainless steel tables and twelve metal chairs, the floor space was empty. On the right wall, a built-in refrigerator with stainless steel doors reflected his light. To the left, large stainless shelves that could have potentially held canned goods stood empty.

Angel stalked his way to the refrigerator and carefully opened it. Half expecting an adversary to be charging out of the gate with murderous intentions, he recollected the many times such a scenario had happened. Finding no danger, the warrior checked the drawers and freezer for anything that would indicate recent habitation. Again, nothing to indicate recent activity.

The two companions stood motionless five feet inside the door. The junior combatant had seen carnage to a lesser degree while the woods dweller was beyond comprehension. No less than fifteen bodies, both male and female, were sprawled on the floor before them, contorted in various poses, laying in pools of congealed blood. No other objects within the chamber except for a stainless steel table in the center of the floor; the walls were awash in the crimson liquid, high-caliber bullet holes perforating from every angle. Motioning for Mountain Man to stay alert, Jim rolled the cadavers with the barrel of his rifle in order to study their fate and make sense of the carnage. Some of the corpses were savagely butchered; some had gaping holes in them while others that displayed no obvious wounds were bent at the neck and joints in unnatural angles. The junior combatant rose from a squatting posture and shook his head as he straightened. "I swear," he whispered to no one in particular, "if I didn't know better, this looks like the work of my broth—"

"*You know whose work this is*," boomed the voice of the Angel of Death!

The woodsman had watched as the titan approached and was unfazed by the remark; however, Jim immediately spun, bringing his rifle to bear.

"Don't worry. There's no one else down here! And you're right. All of this is my work, as much as I hate to admit it."

"But how? Why? When?" the younger brother began.

The fighting man uttered just one solemn word, "Tiffany!'

The junior combatant's brown eyes arrested those of the woodsman in order to include him in the conversation. "Angel, the family knew you went in search of her. Obviously, when you returned, she wasn't with you. However, the most important thing was, and all of us understood, that conversation was going to have to wait for another day.

"Still is!"

"I understand, but let me ask you this."

The colossus glared at his brother, a subtle warning not to proceed much further.

"You deliberately avoided that staircase," Jim began, nodding his head toward the stairwell he and his companion had just descended, "and you deliberately avoided securing this room."

The fighting man nodded his head in the affirmative, his stare boring into his brother's skull.

"So, AD, why'd ya even come in here?"

Reading the hulking warrior's foul disposition, the frontiersman chimed in. "Naw et don't mean no never mind to us effin ye don't wannna say, AD."

"This is not the time! This is not the place! I'll just say this… for now," the behemoth offered. "Tiffany was tortured to near death in this room at the hands of some lunatic. I carried her poor, dying, mangled, tortured, abused body up those stairs as I fought my way back up them. I did not want to relive that. You want to know what I'm doing in this very room again? I wanted to be sure there was no sign of the fucking butcher who did that to my girl! Come on. Let's get the hell out of here before I tear this place to the ground!"

As the team exited the chamber, the Angel of Death instinctively turned left; his two companions instinctively turned right before reversing their footsteps to follow their leader. Up the stairwell and down the hallway toward the front door, the titan stopped to inspect the EMT garage. As his brother had reported, the warrior found the garage to be totally empty. Not only were the two new red-and-gold ambulances gone, but every piece of emergency equipment was missing as well. There were three types of ambulances in general use; however, the city employed type 1. They were distinguishable from the other two types through the use of heavy truck frames and suspensions as well as a box-style patient module.

The Special Forces veteran walked to the rear of the garage and lined himself up with one of the doors before squatting down to examine the floor.

"What jee lookin' fer?" the woodsman wanted to know.

"Tracks!"

"AD, are you telling me that you intend to track the whereabouts of those units?"

"Don't be preposterous, Jim, no! See for yourself. Dust all over the floor except where the tires made contact with the cement. Dust hasn't had time to settle and cover the tracks. Those bastards haven't been gone long!"

"The big 'un don't miss a trick."

"Evidently not. So now what?

"There's only two ways out of here, east or west on Route 50. I realize they could have gone either direction, but I'm willing to bet they went east. With Mackenzie's people nowhere to be found… at least not within this building… I have to assume they have been taken captive and are headed to the dam. Either these cutthroats are going to join up with the soldiers stationed at the dam or else intend on raiding them for their weapons and provisions."

"Angel, wouldn't that be biting off more than they could chew?" Jim asked in disbelief.

"Absolutely not! Their numbers are still sufficient despite my killing half of them, and these guys know how to fight. I suspect they're comprised of ex-military. Either way, they are vicious. I'm telling you both right now, *do not* let down your guard from here on out! Not for a moment!"

"We get jee, Angel O' Death!"

Once outside, the three-man team connected with Hero and Mackenzie. Both admitted to finding no trace of the escapees, not so much as an article of clothing or possession.

"Let's load up. We're burning daylight! We're heading east and," stopping to see that his watch said almost ten thirty, "while we're an hour and a half ahead of schedule, we're going to need every minute of it. Hero, you drive. Jim—"

"Why me?" the quarterback complained.

"Listen to me, college boy," the titan echoed as he approached the blonde, grasping him by the front of his flannel shirt with his beefy left hand. "I know the sport, I know the coach, I know what's expected of you." The hulking warrior lifted the football player two feet off the ground. "Until you learn to fit in and become a cohesive member of our unit, you're headed for rocky ground! Got it?"

Hero nodded rapidly in affirmative, his voice a squeaky reply. "Yes, yes, sir!"

The titan dropped him to the pavement. "Good! Now I'll tell you why. Jim, drawing upon his experience, is going to ride shotgun, keeping a lookout for possible trouble coming our way from the right. I'll be behind you doing the same from our left. If we find trouble, we may find ourselves be in one helluva a firefight. Someone is going to have to drive this crate while those with military training are going to have to do the heavy lifting."

"Yes, sir, makes sense!"

"Mountain Man, you ride behind Jim. Mac, you will be safely sandwiched between us. We all good?"

The other four members nodded in acknowledgment and loaded into the Panther.

The route east out of town was much of the same they had already witnessed. Destroyed, damaged, and intact buildings, vehicles of every size and description tossed about. Utility poles snapped off or leaning at various angles. Oddly enough, no sign of the dead. The difference between the edge of town and where the rural area began was very stark. Homes, in various stages of damage and neglect, gave way to suburban and then more secluded domiciles. The roadway was less cluttered and passable other than places where the blacktop had buckled and crumbled. The sun, ominous and red, would be in their eyes for another ninety minutes before reaching apogee.

Sandwiched between the woods dweller and the fighting man, Mackenzie sensed brooding disquiet within the warrior. After everyone had taken their seat, she gently laid her arm across his gargantuan shoulders to reassure the colossus. Angel had taken his eyes from the dismal landscape to acknowledge the action. It was the first time their eyes had locked, searching for the soul within the other. After a few moments, Angel winked at the blond-haired woman, slightly wagged his head, and returned to survey their passage.

Mackenzie had never held such a massive expanse of rigid muscle, nor had she sensed such disquiet in a human being. Shifting the rifle in her supple right arm, she pulled him slightly to her, her left arm around his neck, the girl whispered into his ear. "If you want to talk about it, I'm happy to listen."

His battle rifle in his left hand, the combatant instinctively reacted to remove the alien arm that was clinging to his neck. Sometimes, and this was such an occasion, the veteran's reflexes and temperament served him poorly. As his brawny hand grasped the girl's lithe digits to wrest them from him, Angel reconsidered his response. Moved by Mackenzie's act of kindness, the commando placed his hand over hers and patted it in place. The warrior knew he could not relate the incident to the young girl without the other passengers overhearing. He decided to make a clean break of it.

"I know I've been a son of a bitch since we arrived at the municipal complex—maybe even before," the titan began, never taking his eyes off of the countryside before him. "I suppose it's time that—"

"What the hell caused that?" Jim barked.

Hero immediately brought the Panther to a stop.

Angel studied the disturbance for several seconds. A patch of woods on the right side of the vehicle, roughly the size of a football field, had been flattened. It appeared as if a mini-tornado had touched down at the spot, ripping the trees out at the roots and splintering the wood in thousands of pieces.

"Any of you guys seen this before?" Angel wanted to know.

"Ah shore have, many ah times amongst my traipse'un!"

"Know what caused it?" Angel inquired.

"Ah cain't say fer certain but ah thank them thar monsters done it!"

"Monsters? What monsters?" Hero wanted to know.

"Ah swear, there be some mighty scary critters traipse'un around. Big'uns too! Ah shore know this much, lots ah times I'd come across sech places, I'd hear sech screamin' un hollerin' lack you ain't never hear'd b'fore. I'd mostly find carcasses of other critters sech as that hog back younder, un other big critters."

"Okay, people, let's get moving and stay frosty!" As the Panther surged forward, Angel continued his narrative. "As I was saying, I know I've been a bastard during this trip, but I think it's time that my family, well, Jim anyway, and my team know what happened at the complex." Angel stopped to take a breath and sigh. He felt a feminine hand travel up and down his back. "My fiancée, Tiffany, yes, we were engaged to wed, worked as the deputy city manager within the municipal complex. During my tour of duty, we connected every day when I wasn't on assignment. God bless her, she kept me grounded when I was close to going off the deep end. All the violence and killing… I was unstoppable…like some goddamned killing machine that—"

Again, the veteran felt Mackenzie's hand roaming over his back.

"Sorry… I hadn't been with her in months. I had just arrived home on leave when the nuclear, bionuclear, biological, whatever-the-hell attack happened. You all know pretty much what followed. As soon as I was able to ensure my family was safe and fortify our home, I set out to get Tiffany and bring her back. I knew the complex where she worked had an underground shelter. The older structure built during the Cold War of the sixties was stocked with traditional food and water in order to serve as a council and social chamber for the city.

"The trip in was pretty much uneventful. I couldn't wait to wrap my arms around the girl of my dreams. To hold her, tell her how much I loved her, to feel her…" Once again, a familiar arm ran up and down the warrior's back. "My greatest fear was that the large mutated rats would make their way inside but was reasonably sure that didn't happen.

"I pulled the Panther into the bank parking lot just west of the complex as I didn't want to draw attention to my arrival. The skylight windows were seven feet off the ground, so I was relatively certain I wouldn't be seen. When I crept up in front of the place, my heart rose in my chest. I could tell there had been activity surrounding the complex, but it was subtle. It was if those inside were trying to avoid detection. It made good sense. Didn't want trouble from the wrong element. I cautiously entered the front door just as we had earlier. I thought it was strange that it wasn't locked, but then again, I thought the key holder was away from the building when warning of the attack went out over the airwaves. After all, everyone had been urged to shelter in place.

"I unslung my G3 and quietly crept down the staircase before me. As I descended the last few steps, I heard several different voices. However, they were largely unintelligible and muted by distance and the composite steel and glass door and, as I learned later, by the blast door of the shelter." Without diverting his gaze from the mission, the combatant could sense that his teammates were waiting with bated breath for him to continue.

The Panther had traveled about four miles out of the city limits when Hero shouted, then pointed toward a place north of their position. "AD, look! About a mile to our left. Another place in the woods that has been stripped of foliage!"

Angel had noticed it about a minute prior to Hero's alarm but thought better of the admission. Indeed, the area of stripped vegetation was twice the size of the previous. "Good job, Hero! Try not to bat an eye. Out here, a lost moment can mean our lives."

"Effin' ye thank travelin' this here road in ah daytime is spooky, ye ought'a try roamin' tha woods at night! There be more afoot than them big critters, that's fer shore!"

Angel carefully considered Mountain Man's statement as he picked up his story where he had left off. "As I carefully opened the door at the bottom of the stairway, I heard raucous laughter and shouting, still largely incomprehensible. I thought it odd that, given the situation, people could still be so merry. As I approached the door to the shelter, I was in a quandary about how to approach. Men, it had been a long time since I had been this undecided as how to proceed. Do I knock? Do I announce myself? Do I kick the door open, assuming it was unlocked? That decision became moot as the door swiftly opened inward.

"I found myself face-to-face with a startled fat guy with long dark hair and long filthy beard. He had a Stainless Ruger Mini 14 slung over his left shoulder and a Colt 1911 in a holster under his right arm. His dirty and torn three-piece suit presented a peculiar contrast. Stinking of garbage, excrement, and raw meat, he was covered in grime and blood from head to toe. While in reality, I didn't expect any better from a survivor in such a situation, his appearance and the activity behind him were disturbing. The lighting from an unknown source reflecting off white dingy walls was dismal at best, but it appeared that two men were dragging someone or something right to left across the back of the room. On one hand, I didn't want to create a deadly situation for these people and myself. On the other, I didn't want to stumble into a tactical disadvantage. Instead, I chose to level my weapon and introduce myself as I shoved the door all the way open to ensure no one was lying in wait."

The combatant stopped his surveillance of what lay beyond the roadway long enough to study his companions. To their credit, they remained absorbed in their mission, all except Mackenzie whose blue eyes were like saucers as she listened to the titan recount his adventure. For some reason he could not fathom, the veteran of WWIII was having difficulty prying his gaze from the eyes of whom he considered the most caring, most beautiful girl in the world.

"Okay, everyone," the commando continued his account. "If you want to live, just chill out! I don't want to harm anyone. My name is Angel Martin, and I am looking for a young woman!"

"Aren't we all?" snickered someone on the left.

"Had I been sitting at a bar and someone gave that reply to such a question, it may have been funny to some. However, when an outsider barges through your door armed to the teeth, a fully automatic HK G3 in .308 caliber fitted with a high-capacity drum leveled at you, no one but a barbarian would think that was funny. That, combined with the suspicious activity I had just witnessed, put my senses on high alert!"

"Okay, I shouted to no one in particular, covering the mob while moving my rifle right to left. That's what I get for being Mr. Nice Guy. Everyone, drop your weapons! I'll have a look around, and if she's not here, I'll leave just as nice as I arrived."

"And what if she is?" came an unseen voice from the left.

"I was beyond disbelief! Who in the hell were these people, and how could they be so brazen? In order to make a statement, I pushed the button that activated the rifle's green laser, using it to intimidate everyone within the room as I swept the area.

"Listen up, jackasses, like I said, I want everybody to drop their weapons where they stand and line up in front of that wall on the right. To the dumb bastards who are facing me, it's the wall to your left.

"There was a clatter of weapons hitting the floor as if on cue. Someone had given a signal of some sort. As they began backing up to the wall I had indicated, I estimated the number to be a dozen or more; the largest of the brood approached me from the left. He was roughly the size and height of Jim. He wore camo fatigues and was still armed, an AK47 over his right shoulder and a stainless revolver in a black holster on his right hip.

"I'm Jack, and I run this crew! Who the fuck are you to come in here barking orders?"

"I immediately put him down with the butt of my rifle to his face. The sound of broken cartilage echoed within the chamber. 'I said drop all weapons, and that included you! Any more stupid questions? Anyone?'

"The barbarians grumbled as if they were ready to revolt! 'All of you shut up and file through that door, then close it behind you.' I indicated the portal in the right wall with a sweep of the laser."

"You son of a bitch, you broke my nose," Jack screamed as he staggered up from the floor.

"I said drop those weapons, or I swear to God I'll break more than your nose!"

"The second his armaments hit the ground, I grabbed him by the back of his uniform and ushered him toward his companions. The moment the door swung inward for them to enter, I could hear other people who were inside the room shouting, cursing, and asking questions. How many, I had no idea."

"Looky thar! Chokers," the woodsman spat, indicating his disdain for the animate tendrils. Pointing a stubby index finger to a spot seventy-five yards off the right side of the highway, he said, "An et looks lack they caught somethin'!"

"Yeah, you're right," Jim confirmed. "But what? I don't think I recognize what the heck it is."

"Could it be one of the big mutated rats you had spoken of earlier, AD," Hero queried as he stopped the vehicle to investigate.

"No, too small. Besides, we're about five miles out of town. They wouldn't stray that far from their food source," The commando replied.

Mackenzie was the next to speak up. "Could it be one of the saber-tooth cats?"

"No, it doesn't look like one. Besides, they don't stray this far from their food source either. At least not yet," Jim reasoned.

"Food source? What food source?" Mackenzie wanted to know.

"The big rats, mainly," Angel confirmed.

"Do ye thank et's one ah them thar bore hogs lacken we kilt back younder?"

"I just can't say, Zechariah," the colossus admitted.

At the mention of the woods dweller's given name, the other three occupants reacted in unison. "What?"

"Never mind," Angel responded.

The five watched in awe as the sinewy black tendrils of the bright-orange stalks and shiny purple leaves enveloped the creature. Working in concert with other stalks, the vegetation managed to ensnare and hold the creature captive. At some point, the poor animal seemed to resign itself to its fate. As Hero accelerated the Panther, the fighting man continued his narrative.

"I waited for them to file in and shut the door before advancing further. When I reached the center of the room, I heard moaning coming from the room to my left. The door was open, so I crept toward the entrance. Before I reached the chamber, I could see two bodies, or should I say corpses, on the floor near the left rear wall. Both were missing limbs. They were so mangled that I couldn't identify the sex, but one was staring right at me with wide brown eyes. To this day, I swear it might have still been alive. The cement floor was bloodstained. The walls that were visible to me were bloodstained. The stench coming from that room was indescribable. It was also obvious that the bastards had cannibalized these people.

"As the moaning continued, I heeded the sound, careful not to lose sight of the door on the opposite side of the room, alert to any indication that the cutthroats would charge. A large stainless steel table in the center of the room arrested my attention. Blood covered the table, so much so that it had stained every leg and the floor beneath it. If I were to approach the table, it meant that I would lose sight of the opposite door. Whoever was on that table was moaning and sobbing so mournfully that I was compelled to investigate.

"I walked to within five feet of the naked body lying atop it. I couldn't tell much about it. Beaten, bruised, bloody, bound hand and foot to the legs, it writhed about uncontrollably. Temporarily distracted by the find, I became alert to the distinct sound of a door latch being actuated. I sprung back to the door of the room I had just entered. Sure enough, someone was creeping through the threshold. I had seen enough! I had great contempt for those within that shelter. I leveled my weapon and fired off a short burst, killing the stalker and sending a number of slugs into the room. Spent cartridges jingled ominously on the floor. The door made a thunderous echo as it slammed shut.

"Knowing that action had purchased additional time, I went back to see if I could be of some assistance to the poor fellow on the stainless slab. The body was mangled beyond description. Upon closer examination, I was surprised to find that what I initially thought to be a man was in fact a female. Her face had been beaten bloody. Her eyes were swollen shut. Most of her hair had been ripped out. Strangle marks around her neck, her shoulders bruised and cut. Blood was flowing from her nose and mouth onto her bruised, bloody chest, breasts, and torso. Split and swollen lips revealed half of her teeth missing.

"If I hadn't been sure before, I was certain then. The poor girl had suffered horrendous sexual abuse by these bastards. Both orifices of her lower body were torn, distended, and bleeding. She was crying, but there were no tears left. She was begging for help, but the words were unintelligible. I didn't think the poor kid had a chance, but I knew by god I wasn't going to leave her there. I cut the ropes securing each limb to the four legs of the table. I thanked the Lord she wasn't shackled to it. She began thrashing and moaning as I tried to move her. Amazingly, the poor girl still had some fight in her. I quickly looked around for something to drape over her nude body, hoping something would present itself. All I could find was a torn and bloodied shirt. May have been hers. As quickly as I draped it over her, she pushed it away. In doing so, she inadvertently smeared some of the blood away from her chest. And then I saw it! Tattooed over her heart, in the shape of a heart, it read, 'Angel and Tiffany Forever.'"

CHAPTER 7

The occupants inside the Panther were tossed forward and back into their seat as the vehicle came to a screeching halt, the mandate to their assigned duty suddenly losing all significance. Jim and Mountain Man swiveled in their seats. Hero was staring at the titan through the rearview mirror, shock evident on their countenances.

"No!" Mackenzie cried as she put her right hand to her mouth, aghast at what the veteran had just disclosed. Angel turned to her, tears welling up in his eyes. "No, no, no, no, no!" the girl screamed as she began beating her fists against Angel's chest and right shoulder, reliving the nightmare of her abuse as well.

"I cried out in great anguish! How could this be, I reasoned. My Tiffany, my girl! Momentarily forgetting about the butchers, I gazed down at what used to be my beautiful fiancée. Tall, at six foot two, she weighed around one hundred fifty pounds, athletic, green eyes and red hair. My love for her had no equal. I retrieved my knives, intent on attacking the throng and ripping them to shreds just for the fun of it, a bullet being too good for them.

"Just then, Tiffany moaned, and I decided that as much as I wanted to avenge myself on them and for my poor fiancée, I realized I needed to get her out of that horrid place, to get her to safety, to get her back home where we could care for her, to Trish. My rifle cradled in my right arm, I scooped my girl up in my left and carried her out of that torture chamber. Only to come face-to-face with the rabble who were beginning to retrieve their firearms.

"Once again, I would have preferred to stay and mow down the throng but feared for Tiffany's safety as some were beginning to shoulder weapons. I stood stationary for a moment and unleashed a long burst of fully automatic fire that took down a number of assailants and cowed the rest. I raced for the main entrance backing out as I did so, firing a short burst. Running down the hallway toward the stairwell, I heard a barrage of crying, yelling, and death. The clatter of weapons, retracting bolts, and cursing were on my heels. As I made it through the steel and glass composite door, I turned to assess their distance and saw their leader at the head of the pack.

"Bounding up the steps three at a time, I was near the top when I heard a gunshot. I turned to return fire and saw Jack pointing that stainless revolver at us. As I depressed the trigger, two of the thugs brushed past Jack, absorbing the slugs. As others were beginning to file through the open door, my priority quickly changed from a firefight to a rescue mission. I had to get Tiffany out of harm's way as fast as I could. Backing out of the entrance to the complex, I did manage to send another burst of withering gunfire into those clamoring up the staircase. As I turned to flee to the safety of the Panther, my heart sank. I was facing no less than six of the ugliest oversized, mutated vermin known to man, their noses testing the air and their drooling maws agape."

The warrior's narration held his team spellbound. Hero had turned 180 degrees in his seat in order to witness such an account. All eyes were on the fighting man as he continued; the only sounds were heavy breathing and pounding hearts from those living vicariously through the combatant.

"I knew it would have been impossible to hold off those vermin, not without performing a magazine change, and there was absolutely no way that I was setting Tiffany down to do so. I did the only thing I could do. I swung the door open all the way and shielded myself behind it, hoping the rat pack would take the bait. And take the bait they did! One by one, the black beasts filed through the open doorway and down the stairs. Carnage ensued. Screaming, gunfire, cursing, moaning, it never ended. As much as I wanted to witness the cutthroats getting everything they had coming to them, I knew I had to get my fiancée home ASAP! As I slid my girl out of my embrace and onto the passenger's seat, I saw blood running down her back and over my arm. Struck near her left shoulder blade, Tiffany had suffered a gunshot by the son of a bitch that was Jack as we neared the top of the stairwell!

"As I strapped her into the seat, she looked up at me and gave me one big smile as she grabbed my arm, despite the exquisite amount of pain she had to be experiencing. I exchanged magazines in my rifle before securing it in the Panther and heading for home. I drove like a man possessed. I stopped or slowed down for nothing. As I maneuvered the vehicle around obstacles, I noticed she was getting weaker by the second. Her moans were becoming frail and less often. Three quarters of the way home, she let out a great sigh, called my name, and, was gone. I finally stopped, taking her left wrist and holding it in my right hand for several minutes, hoping for a pulse. There was none. I slid over to her seat and held her as I cried. I begged God to bring her back to me. I begged him to take us back to a time where we were deeply in love and at peace with the world, and I begged him to take my life in exchange for hers. But it never came about. Finally, I begged him that someday I might find the bastards who did this to my baby doll.

"Before coming home, I drove up and down several side streets until I found just the right place. I did not want to return home with her in that condition, nor did I want her remains uncovered by some foraging miscreant. I found a partially destroyed house, laid her down on a yellow sofa, one of the few undamaged pieces of furniture within the home, said goodbye to her after a short prayer, and torched the structure."

Angel was stunned to discover there was not a dry eye in the transport, including himself. The men turned their faces toward their assigned windows while wiping at their tears. Mackenzie broke down and began sobbing uncontrollably. Circling her arms around the colossus as far as she could reach, the young blonde buried her face into his chest.

After half a minute, Hero was the first to speak. After clearing his throat, he began, "You know, big guy, I don't know if you noticed, but the roadway—"

"Yeah, I noticed! As soon as we left the municipal building. Route 50 going east is almost totally clear of fallen timbers, utility poles, and large debris!"

"Can that be coincidence?"

"It's not!"

"It's not?" the ex-quarterback asked incredulously. "Then how do you explain—"

"Someone is traveling this road ahead of us, clearing the path as they go. And if I were a betting man, I would bet there are two ambulances somewhere up ahead!"

While everyone pondered the implication of the warrior's words, Hero and Mountain Man became aware of the fact that they may become involved in a firefight, the football player's first. Angel had preoccupied himself with tending to the distraught girl. He realized she had been through more than she could bear. From her own abuse through escape, hounded by the soldiers, nearly strangled by the chokers, worried over her father's imprisonment, mauled by the zombies, and the battle to escape them. Now to relive Tiffany's torture, rescue, and death, the titan wondered how she held up as long as she had. Angel took her into his embrace to console the troubled girl. Stroking her hair and running his hands up and down her back, the combat vet wanted to envelop her in his massive frame and keep her safe from harm.

Mackenzie, as she began to compose herself, became aware of the powerful musculature of the goliath encircling her body. The muscles in his back, still taut from recounting his experience, felt like steel bands in her clutch. The powerful arms embracing her threatened to crush her with every beat his heart. His vicelike grasp felt like a hydraulic press. Slabs of granite pushed against her breasts. The young girl's mind was clouded and confused. She struggled to break the embrace, and Angel acquiesced. However, before they parted, looking deep into each other's eyes, both consented to a deep and loving kiss.

"We just passed an old motel a mile back. Do you guys want to get a room or what?"

In a lightning-fast strike that belied his proportions, the veteran of WWIII reached forward, grabbing hold of Hero's neck, threatening to snap it like a twig while still engaged with the young girl.

"Okay, man. Just joking," the quarterback squeaked, trying to breathe through a partially collapsed trachea. "Kidding, sorry. Won't happen again. Sorry."

*****

Traveling east on US Route 50, all were alert for any sign of trouble, particularly in light of Angel's suspicions. The titan monitored the road ahead of them as he had been surreptitiously doing since they had left the municipal building.

"Mountain Man, earlier you mentioned there was more afoot…uh, more to worry about than the big crit…creatures," Angel inquired.

"Thar be traders an slavers, an other critters ah hope ah never see ah gain."

"What about the traders and slavers?" the veteran wanted to know.

"Ah tell ye, ah was grateful to git away wif ma laf. I haid ta lie to um to git clear.

"Woah, hang on, Zechariah," Angel interrupted.

"What? Who?" Some of the team members wanted to know.

Angel again dismissed the queries with a wave of his meaty hand. "Why don't you start at the beginning?"

"Ah shore will. Ah had lived in ma root celler fer about sex months but tha veg'ta'bles un fruits ah had put up were gettin' ah mite low, even tho ah had plenty uh passable spring water runnin' in. So's ah fig'erd ah ought ta seek out un find some way ta live offen civil'zation some how. Ah headed north after ah felt safe ta leave ma root celler thar in Logan County. People wuz gittin' themselfes kilt on tha highway rat un left, so's I stuck to tha back woods. It wuz safer thut way. Tha day time wuz scary enuf but nat time wuz tha worse. Tha noises en screamin' un hollerin', big critters trampin' about, ah was mighty scaret. At nat I'd shinny up tha biggest tree ah could fine, ma rafle slung over one shoulder, ma possibles, in an ol' burlap sack over tha other, an stay thar until I knowed et was safe.

"Anyway, tha further ah got along tha more people I wud spy. Ah stayed back but ah followed 'em ta see where they was a'goin'. Seems they knowed more about what they wuz ah doin' than ah did, so ah hid ma sef so as not ta be see'd. Tarns out we wuz ah comin'g up on one ah them there, what ya call, football stay'di'ums. An as poorly as ah was decked out, ah looked lak a king compare't ta them. Most ah tha captive females wuz wearin' next to nuthin effen that much. Sorry, missy," the woods dweller apologized to Mackenzie.

Mackenzie smiled to herself at the ever-courteous woodsman's remark.

Never taking his eyes from his task, the quarterback quipped, "Now where do you say this place is?"

"It's rat outside tha city ah Madison, West Virginny."

"Never mind, Zech… Mountain Man! The clown driving this rig was just being cute," Angel retorted. "Go on."

"Whal, on one side ah tha stay'di'um is where ye went effen ya had somethin' ye wanted ta trade. Ye had ta go ta tha 'cession stand un declare what ya wuz ah needin' un what ye was uh willin' ta swap ta git it. Fer zample, I wuz needin' more cart'ri'ges fer ma shootin' iron. Ah figgered ah would swap some of ma good canned vittles. Cuz ah could git way more vittles by shootin' critters, effen they not be diseased, than tha vittles I was ah swappin'. Naw let ma tell ye here un now, the folks ah runnin' the post was nothin' but low down dirty thieves. I was willin' ta part wif five cans uh green beans fer maybe ah box ah fifty bullets. Their cut from me wuz two cans, un twenty rounds from tha feller that was tradin' for em. Ah guess that feller needed tha grub as bad as ah needed tha rounds, so we swapped."

"What kept it from turning into a free-for-all?" Jim wanted to know.

"People wif guns. Place was thick as ticks on a hound wif armed guards. Un make no mistake, effun ye thank ye was goin' ta barter some whar's else and slight tha thieves outten their cut, chances are neither one of ye wuz commin' back er ever be seed again. Even wif tha guards, et was a might scary place. Some folks cum in nar dead, some would drop et your feet and git hauled offen somewhar's. Some would give ye sech a look as soon kill ye. Ah never wants ta go ta sech a place again."

Angel was oddly intrigued by Zechariah's account. "You told us what had transpired on one side of the stadium. What about the other side?" the titan wanted to know.

Mountain Man looked to the girl seated next to him. "Missy, ah jest hate to say wif a female sittin' next ta me, effen ye know what ah'm ah sayin'."

"It's okay. I've been through so much, heard so much. I doubt that what you say will shock me," the blonde assured.

"Well, missy, effen—"

"Mackenzie. It's Mackenzie. Please call me by my name."

"O'kay, Ms. Ma'kenzie."

The young girl swiveled toward the titan and winked before turning back toward the woodsman. "I guess that's an improvement, anyway. Go ahead," she encouraged.

"Ah wuz kinda wundrin' ma sef so after swappin fer ma cartridges ah headed on over thar. Thar must ah been twenty-five females ah han'cuffed ta tha back sad ah tha ble'chers. They had torn out tha wooden seats at dif'rent heights. Arount tha steel whar tha wood wuz they put manacles. Tha other end wus ah round tha females arms so they wuz stretch't out over their haids.

"Effin' they wuz ah wearin' vestments afore bein' chained, they wuz stripped clean after. They wuz of all ages un size. Ah swear missey, fer give me fer sayin'. Tha fairer of tha bunch wus sold offen for jest anythin'. Guns, knives, swords, vittles, even ah stable ah other females who warn't so fair. Ye jest name it. Tha men wuz techin' the females all over their bodies. Checkin' their privates fer disease un so on. I need ta tell ye more about this later on. Anyhow, they wuz, sorry, missy, young gals, as young as ten or twelve—some even younger. They caught one son of ah bitch ah pokin' one of the young'uns. He said he had a rat ta make shore the mer'chan'dice wuz gonna be acceptin' of him. There wuz a lot of ar'ge'un' back un forth. They had to check wif tha haid man. Since he wuz ah big cus'toe'mer, he wus allow'd to go on ah haid. After it wuz over, tha same guard asked him effen she wud work out ok. He said he thought she would git used ta him after a spell. There wuz ah nother older female three down from the young'un ah cryin' un screamin' fer tha man to stop. I'm ah thinkin' et was the child's mammy. Ah course, he paid her no mind."

As with Angel's story, the team was mesmerized by the woods dweller's recount. Mackenzie tried valiantly not to shed tears, sorry for beckoning Mountain Man to continue. The woodsman had witnessed the horror of the ordeal. The warrior brothers had been hardened by their own experiences. Mackenzie had experienced firsthand such brutalization. However, the football player realized his world had forever changed and that he would never be the same.

"Fer jest the rat price, tha females that warn't too old were let fer an hour er two. Tha way ah took et, they wuz ah hopin' ta be bought so they wouldn'ta have ta go through thut so many times a day wif diff'rent men. But effen that waren't bad enuff, what happen't to the old ones un tha ones no one wanted wuz even worse. They wuz sold as slaves un when they couldn't slave no longer, they wuz chopped up an fed ta hogs as fodder. Na here's what ah wanted ta tell ye earlier. Knowin' what'ud happen ta tha young females effin they wasn't bought right out, they per'vert'ed themselfes to git tha 'ttention of ah buyer. Ah witherin' and ah thrustin'. Speakin' lewd un ah beggin' fer it. I figger if they could'a they would ah chose ta die by thar own hand rather end up ah let out er as ah slave.

"An' let me say this here, I ain't no cow'ard. I was a'fumin' so over tha goin's on that ah wanted ta kill every last one ah them thar theiven' no account's. Even knowin' I would have got kill't ma'sef. But ah told ma'sef nothin' wud change fer tha plight ah them thar females. But ah figgered effen ah could git outten thar wif ma laf un find some body thut could help, lack the army fellers, ah could do ah lot more fer 'em sure enuff."

Angel's blood was boiling. Mackenzie turned toward the warrior with pleading, wet eyes.

"Mac, we can't save the world. Besides, we have to rescue your father, and we're not sure where he is right now."

Looking down, the blonde shook her head affirmatively. "I know. Knowing the living hell I went through, all the evil in this world, I hate to think there are so many suffering like I did."

"I understand. I'm beyond enraged when I think of poor Tiffany and the abuse she suffered. But first things first. Let's find your father, get my brother Rick some help, and then…well, we'll see. Is that okay?"

Mackenzie responded with a deep soul-searching kiss to Angel's lips. The veteran responded in kind. He was prepared to strangle Hero if his remarks repeated themselves. Luckily, for the ex-football player, they did not.

As the Panther continued along US Route 50, the hum of the turbine ever-present, the warrior reflected on the turn of events that were working to bring him and Mackenzie together. Holding hands with the young blonde as he scoured the countryside with his keen vision, Angel was beginning to experience feelings he thought would never return, an urgent stirring in a part of him that he couldn't ignore. Even though the events surrounding Tiffany's death still haunted him, the commando liked what he saw in the girl seated next to him.

"A penny for your thoughts," Mackenzie whispered in Angel's ear as she squeezed his massive hand.

The legionnaire returned the gesture. "Mac, the insanity of this world has caused the death of my fiancée, and I find myself still troubled over that. It has also brought us together. I need to know that it's more than coincidence."

The girl released her grip and slowly retracted her hand.

"No," the titan said, ever so slightly raising his voice as he redoubled his grasp of the petite hand. "Mackenzie, no. Please don't think ill of me. This is something I have to sort out on my own. I can tell you two things. Number one, ever since that first day I saw you when the soldiers were chasing you, through all that we have been through since, you have made me feel something that I haven't in a long while, and no matter what happens, I can never forget you or…stop feeling for you the way that I do. Number two, I know my feelings for you will continue to grow, and that can be a problem."

"How do you mean?" the blonde pleaded, seeking the answer in his eyes.

"Because in combat, a relationship is a liability. That is why the military not only frowns on it but also forbids it. Decisions I will inevitably make can become clouded by my affection for you. I had become concerned with Tiffany's condition, wounds, and nature of her abuse. I was in a rage. I may have gotten her out of there sooner, before she was shot. She may have survived. I could have saved her!"

The gorgeous blonde patted the warrior's wrist with her free hand. "I understand. And… I'll always be here. I'm not going anywhere. By the way, buster," the girl spoke up, "I can take care of myself!"

Both he and the girl laughed as they continued to clasp each other.

"Hero! Brakes! Now!" the titan shouted.

All but the quarterback were thrown forward as he immediately complied. "What the hell now," he demanded.

"Distractions, see what I mean!" the warrior said to Mackenzie as he leaned forward, pointing far off into the distance. "Just beyond the rise and into the next turn. Two type 1 ambulances!"

"Son of a bitch," Jim swore as he removed binoculars from forward storage and brought them to his eyes.

"Yup! Both labeled in the city's colors, about a mile away!"

"Hero, back up far enough so we can't be seen, then search for a place we can stash the Panther out of sight," the commando ordered.

"Know just the place. About one hundred yards back." So saying, the Mountaineer put the transport in reverse and negotiated the cluttered and buckled highway to the place he had mentioned. Although overgrown and in close proximity to a patch of chokers, the football player bulldozed his way into the thick brush.

"Disembark," the warrior thundered, momentarily forgetting his promise to speak only in layman's terms. "That means get the hell out of the vehicle, to those without military training. Secure your weapons and exit on the right side. The chokers are a little too close to the left side for my taste."

The five set about concealing the Panther the best they could with loose branches and scrub vegetation. The Angel of Death was again grateful for the camouflage paintwork. Mountain Man caught the sound of a small stream at the base of a hill on the opposite side of the road. Although they had plenty of water with them, his lifestyle demanded he make note of it nonetheless. As Jim was putting the final touches of concealment to the left rear of the Panther, a choker tendril coiled around his left ankle, attempting to draw him into their den. Before the junior commando was pulled off his feet and drawn into the kill zone, he unsheathed his Gerber Strong Arm knife, severing the expectant vine.

"What's with you?" Hero asked as the younger brother marched around to the passenger side of the Panther, resheathing his knife. As the junior commando spun to point out the scrape he had gotten into, the quarterback said, "Quit screwing around. Come on, we have a mission waiting." Jim just shook his head and followed.

"There's a high wall on their left side," the commando began as they began their trek. "And low bottomland on the other. We can't stay on this road and march right up to the vehicles. We can't approach from the left, so we have no option to approach from the right."

"How do you want to play this?" Jim inquired.

"Mountain Man, you've spent a lot of time in the woods. Do you think it's safe for us to enter the forest here and travel the mile to the bottomland?"

"Effen ye ain't spent much time in the timberland lait'ly et cain be ah scary place fo show. Wif all ma traipsin' I'v gotten used to et. Et should be safe providin' we don't run in ta them big'uns un watch out fer chokers."

"Okay, we'll enter here," Angel stated, indicating a likely spot with a nod of his head. "Mountain Man, you take lead! You will know better than anyone what to watch out for. We want to go deep enough and arc around, so we will exit the woods on the blind side of the vehicles. I will take second. Then Mac, Hero next. Jim, you cover our rear. Got it?"

All indicated their agreement before stalking off into the woods. The two brothers had spent considerable time in such woods hiking, hunting, and camping. But neither one was prepared for the woodlands they had just waded into. They had gotten no more than fifty yards in when their senses were arrested by some unseen entity. Almost as if the woods, trees, and brush were alive. Shadows would suddenly appear, then disappear just as quickly. It felt that things unrevealed were lurking behind every tree. What could only be described as sinister vibrations assaulted their senses. The ground itself seemed to shift under their feet.

Angel raised his clenched hand for those behind him to come to a halt. After getting the woodsman's attention, he asked, "Do you feel this?" The woods dweller shook his head in the affirmative. "Is it always like this?" Another nod confirmed it was. The titan turned back to those following him and read the same disdain for their passage as he had. He then gave them the signal to advance.

Ten minutes into their march, the creepy noises began. Growls, shrieks, cries, roars, hisses. The racket ran the gamut. The flapping of huge wings instinctively put Jim into defense mode, assuming a low squat and searching the sky with the business end of his rifle. Having been carried off by a large pterodactyl once before, he vowed never to make that mistake again. After stalking for another five minutes, the crack of a gunshot was heard somewhere in the distance.

"Ba ma estimation we should be ah closin' in on tha edge of tha woods," Mountain Man whispered to the veteran behind him.

"What do you make of that gunshot?"

"As near as ah can figger, et's them fellers we wuz trailin.'"

"Undoubtedly they've strayed from their vehicles for some reason. Look, the clearing is just up ahead. Let's stay in deep cover for as long as we can." Angel then raised his left clenched fist.

It began as the sound of flies off in the distance before increasing to the bumble of bees.

"I know I hit the son of a bitch."

"Yeah, but I told you not to kill him! We need the bastard! He's the only one left who knows anything about the dam!"

"I only meant to shoot him in the leg."

"Then where is he?"

As the group of arguing men came into view, the fighting man realized with certainty they were the cutthroats they had been tracking. It appeared there were twelve or thirteen. He gave the signal for his team to mimic his actions.

"Did the motherfucker make it into the woods?"

"Half you men search the forest. The other half come with me and search this field."

Angel silently slid behind the largest tree he could find. He was pleased to see his comrades following suit. The warrior was thankful for the turn of luck. They would avoid a possible firefight if they could quietly slay them without alerting the others. While the veteran was confident in his prowess and that of his brother, he had his doubts about the other three.

As five of the butchers stumbled to within slaying distance of the team, the commando unsheathed his KA-BAR survival knife, ready to strike. His companions did the same.

"Over here, found him! Hiding in this shallow depression."

"Thank God!" Angel's mark shouted. "These woods always give me the creeps."

The combatant's visage turned to that of the Grim Reaper. *Such foolish talk*, he thought, *for such a godless individual.* He waited until the last three that had entered the brush were transitioning from the forest to the field before giving the signal to Jim to take out the other. So doing, the Angel of Death struck with amazing speed as he cupped his hand around the man's mouth, cutting his throat, almost decapitating him. "Say hello to God for me." Jim's move was nearly identical.

The veteran of WWIII signaled for his team to converge on him. "We have to move fast before they realize they lost two of their men. Check your weapons, safeties off, on full auto. Zechariah, for right now—"

"Who? Huh?" Came more questions.

"Later," the titan groused. "I want you to swap out your pump gun for one of the HK full autos. Mac, speedily as you can, demonstrate to include a mag change."

The blonde nodded her head, leading the woods dweller to retrieve one of the two rifles. With the two engaged in instruction, the colossus crept to the edge of the clearing. Stroking his dense beard in thought, he devised a plan of action, then returned. After thirty seconds, they returned to the clearing. The woodsman had been a keen student.

"These dumb bastards are torturing the poor fellow, punishing him for trying to escape. Unfortunately for them, and fortunately for us, their backs are turned toward us. As quietly as possible, let's get as close as we can. Capture 'em if possible. Take 'em down if we have to. If it comes down to a firefight, it will be the first for you three." Looking each civilian in the eye, the combatant continued, "Keep your fingers off the trigger until you are absolutely positive you are going to shoot. You'll be under great duress, and we don't want an accidental discharge that will result in an unwanted firefight. Remember, their captive is probably one of Mackenzie's people, and we don't want harm to come to him. Also, stay cool, stay calm, stay focused. Our intent is to approach them and form not quite a semicircle but a one-hundred-fifty degree arc around them. *Stealth* is the operative word. Choose your potential targets beforehand. Look mean, look tough, and above all, remember what these people are capable of. Look like you mean business! Got it?"

The five teammates looked one another in the eye, nodding their understanding. The commando instinctively began to bark an "Oorah" but realized it would be wasted on the noncombatants. He then checked his watch and found it to be late afternoon.

"Let's roll!"

Creeping out of the brush, ensuring not to step on a twig or brush a limb, the team successfully entered the field without raising suspicions. As the titan led his outfit toward the gang of cutthroats, he analyzed the situation. Apparently, they had their captive contained in a shallow depression, fighting for his freedom. He counted ten in the party. Luckily for the rescuers, not one of the stupid sons a bitches, Angel surmised, had the sense or training to cover their backs. Several of the goons behind him obscured the butcher questioning and stomping the victim senseless. The odds were two to one against the tribe. Angel knew it would have been easy enough for them to mow down the gang, but the veteran did not like to play that way. He needed a way to distract the band without incurring immediate reprisal. The fighting man turned back to his people and mouthed the words, "On me!"

As the team found their places, completing the arc, the warrior spoke using a low intimidating growl, "No one make a move and drop your weapons." The commando felt a disturbance in the late afternoon air. An uneasiness he could not shake!

"Now how in the hell are we supposed to drop our weapons without making a move?" came the response from a tall fellow wearing corduroy trousers and jacket.

An explosion from the titan's G3 rent the air as a 180-grain hollow point took the mouthy bastard's head off at the neck.

The three teammates were taken aback by the brutality demonstrated by their leader.

"Any more stupid questions, or are you people going to continue pissing me off?"

Almost in unison, weapons hit the ground, followed by curses, shouts, and "Did you have to kill him?"

"Okay, now turn around like good little boys, hands in the air." After they had complied, the strapping commando continued, "That's fine. That's good. Have you ever seen such a sorry litter of sourpusses?" Angel asked of his men.

"More like sour pussies!" the football player observed.

"You back there, the one harassing your captive, step up here where I can see you."

The man in tan camouflage and Army boots took his time making his way to the front, having to navigate his way around two of his companions. As he sauntered to the forefront of the rabble, Angel instinctively tightened his finger on the trigger.

JACK! The murdering, raping, butchering son-of-a-bitch Jack. Dear Lord! It seemed as if he had waited all his life for this moment. "Jack, you bastard, do you know how much pain and suffering you have caused? Can you feel it in the air, Jack? Can you feel justice coming your way, JACK?" the titan spat.

"No, wait!" the leader of the mob pleaded. "You have me all wrong! The wounded guy on the ground! He was injured trying to make contact with someone from the outside world. He's from the Tygart Valley Dam. Stationed there. Look, you see those ambulances up on the road. We're trying to get him back to his people who have the means to save—"

"Jack, you are a lying piece of shit. If you told me you were drowning, I would not lend a hand."

"How can you even say that? You don't even know me! Why? We're just like you, trying to make our way in this crazy world."

"I've seen your face before, my friend." The words tasted bitter on the warrior's tongue. Then he realized, after Tiffany's death, he had grown a beard in rebellion. "But I don't know if you know *who I am*."

"What? Why? I don't know you," the leader of the rabble countered with a wry smile. "I've never seen you be—"

The gargantuan transferred his rifle to his left shoulder in order to free his right. "Well, I was there, and *I saw what you did*," the titan barked, poking Jack in the chest with his prodigious right index finger. "*I saw it with my own two eyes!* So you can wipe off the grin. I know where you've been. It's all been a pack of lies!"

Rage replaced the smile on Jack's face, telegraphing his intent to all who witnessed the exchange between the warrior and the leader of the thugs.

"Can you feel it in the air, Jack? I can. Can you feel the hand of doom, Jack? Can you not see that I've been waiting for this meeting for what seems like all of my life?"

Jack stammered for a minute trying to buy some time. "Remember me then. Remember when the bombs exploded. Remember that I gathered all the people in my building and got them into the bomb shelter, how I ensured—"

"I remember! I remember. *Don't worry.* How could I ever forget? It's the first time, the last time we ever met. But I know the reason why you keep your pretentious silence up. No, you don't fool me. The hurt doesn't show, but the pain still grows. It's no stranger to you and me. How's the nose, Jack?"

Suddenly Jack realized to whom he was speaking, realized where the two had previously met. And he realized he was a walking dead man. The dread was evident on his woebegone frown.

Jack reached his right hand into the pocket of his camo fatigues for a weapon, certain his lightning reflexes could beat the empty-handed commando to the draw. But the weapon never materialized.

Those who beheld the contest would later say that in one instant, the warrior's right index finger was still pounding the leader's chest. And the next instant the Desert Eagle .50 Magnum, which rested in his holster cross-draw style on his left hip, had materialized in his right hand, it sent a 350-grain half-inch-diameter hollow point bullet into the chest of the gang leader. The large-caliber pistol was back in its holster before the impact deposited the dead man seven feet from where he had been standing.

All hell broke loose!

The balance of the cutthroats, who had been slowly positioning themselves to their weapons, suddenly broke to retrieve them. Despite the commando's amazing reflexes, he was the last to join the fray, having to unsling his rifle from his left shoulder and bring it to bear. Witnessing the speed in which their leader had been dispatched, the merciless killers focused their revenge on the muscle-bound legionnaire. Unfortunately for the rabble, this prompted the team members to bring their weapons into play.

Being that he was in the forefront and the largest, most menacing target, Angel was expecting to feel the torment of multiple impacts as he unslung his weapon. To his surprise, the titan found Mackenzie was the first to open fire, taking out two of the remaining nine who were about to send multiple rounds into the senior veteran. The remaining seven soon came to realize there were others intent on taking their lives and swung their rifles toward them…a little too late. By then, the entire team had joined the fray, mowing down the cutthroats with abandon. Angel's G3 was severing limbs and exploding craniums as he swept the thugs with automatic gunfire left to right. Even the inexperienced woodsman was holding his own as he used his weapon as a firehose to dispense death and destruction into the treacherous ilk. Overkill would not come close to describing the depredation that ensued. Multiple hits each had torn the henchmen to pieces. Bloody limbs and entrails littered the ground, most of the cutthroats were unrecognizable, and gallons of blood splattered and tainted the ground.

When it was over, the three civilians were visibly sick. Hero was bent over at the waist, puking. After ensuring all the band were permanently out of action, the titan walked over to the ditch to attend the captive. Angel could not discern the sex of the victim due to the blood spray from the massacre, nor could he tell what injuries they sustained.

"Can you hear me? Are you okay? Can you move?"

When the victim tried to speak, only frothy blood trickled from his mouth.

"Mac, bring a wet cloth and some water. After the rest of you guys get yourselves pulled back together, reload, then collect weapons, ammo, and anything useful," the warrior directed.

"We're going to clean you up so we can assess your injuries," the strapping behemoth assured the injured man.

The injured captive could only mouth the word *no* and wave his hand to confirm the statement. Dying, pale blue eyes stared blindly into space.

Directly Mackenzie arrived on scene with the requested items. At first, they refused water but thought better of it, taking a few sips before coughing it up.

"Do you recognize who it is?" Angel wanted to know.

"I can't tell with all of the blood," the girl responded.

"Here, let's clean the blood from their face."

So doing, the pair gently moved the blood away, cleaning the wounds of dirt and debris that were embedded during the beating.

"Oh my god," the young blonde exclaimed. "Yes, I do know him! Not his name but he's one of the people who helped me escape from the dam."

Hearing the girl speak, recognition appeared to dawn on the face of the injured man.

"I'm Mackenzie. You and your wife helped me get away from my captors. I don't know your name, but I'm grateful to you both."

The retched soul tried to mouth his name, but it was unintelligible.

"Do you know what happened to the rest of our party?" the warrior asked.

Through ragged breathing, he slowly nodded his head in the affirmative.

"Sir, I…"

"Mister, my name is Angel Martin. We'll do all we can for you, but it may not be enough. For the sake of the party you were with, can you tell me of their whereabouts?"

At that inquiry, the dying man tried to rise up, his eyes wide. His mouth was opening and closing as if he were speaking, his head turning side to side. He let out a great sigh and expired.

The veteran eased the deceased man's torso back into the depression. He looked to Mackenzie and shook his head. The blonde placed her face in her hands and wept.

The strapping warrior rose to his feet to find the other three teammates surrounding him laden with weapons and gear. "We have no way to dig a grave for this brave gentleman. See if we can gather enough field stone to cover him."

"What about these'un here?" the woodsman inquired as he pointed to the dead cutthroats.

"Let the creatures of the night have them."

*****

As the team approached the pair of ambulances, their leader reminded them of their original plan and cautioned that there could be more of the murderous brood inside. Angel instructed his men to surround the second ambulance, which was twenty-five yards behind the first, and growled to anyone inside, "We have you surrounded! The rest of your men are dead! You have thirty seconds to come out with your hands up before we open fire! We do have weapons that will penetrate the cabin!"

The legionnaire allowed forty-five seconds to pass before giving the signal for Hero to throw open the back door of the patient module, the two brothers at the ready with rifles in hand. According to plan, the quarterback grabbed the handle on the left rear door and pulled it out and around, taking cover behind it as he did so. They found it was completely empty. They repeated the maneuver on the lead ambulance. It was empty as well.

"Jim, you and Hero stow the gear, then jump in the second truck and bring up the Panther, then position it in front of the two ambulances. We'll use them to transport the captives from the dam," the war vet instructed. "Zechariah, stash your gear and get these vehicles off the road as far as possible so the Panther can go around. Then set up camp. We'll bivouac…we'll stay here tonight, then set out in the morning. Mac, after you get your gear stowed, you and I need to talk. I'll be in the lead ambulance"

After all requested tasks were completed, the blonde found the titan sitting on a bench seat in the back of the patient module making notes of medical inventory. "Zechariah, is that his name?"

Angel finished writing and looked up at Mackenzie. He began to wonder if she was actually as stunningly beautiful as he believed or if it had been too long since he… "Yes, that's his given name. A book out of the Old Testament. Here, sit down." The commando moved medical gear and reference material to allow a place for the girl to sit. "Trish would love to get her hands on this stuff."

The goliath realized that this was the first time he and Mackenzie had been together and alone. There was something about this girl, he thought. She seemed so easy to fall in love with. Or was it just him? He had an overwhelming urge to take her into his arms and continue where they left off. He resisted, realizing he couldn't let his feelings for the young blonde distract him, jeopardize the mission.

"Something wrong?" Mackenzie asked, her gaze connecting with that of the titan.

"Oh, nothing, just thinking."

"I'm all out of pennies," the beautiful girl joked, her voice rising in song like a melody.

"Look, I might as well get this out of the way. I'm falling for you. I never thought I would have these feelings for anyone else again."

"Nor I," the blonde attested, confirming her feelings as well.

"It's just that it creates several problems for me. First, I can't get Tiffany out of my mind, especially having just avenged her death. We were engaged. If not for the END, we would be married now."

Mackenzie put her right arm on the legionnaire's left shoulder and mouthed the words *I know*. "Look, given the ordeal I went through in confinement"—stopping to take a deep breath, she continued,—"I thought I would never have these feelings, these… urges…ever again. Trust me, *not ever!* Honey, you're overthinking this too much. In order to heal, you have to put the past behind you and deal with the present. No one knows this better than I do."

Angel took her right hand in his left. "I know you're right. Another problem I have is your safety. This new world is not the same as the one we used to live in. Death can come at any moment, and it can be painful and grisly. Given the way Tiffany died… God help me, if it were to happen to someone else I've allowed myself to have fallen in love with. Also, if I let myself become distracted ensuring your safety, it could spell disaster for one of the others."

Grasping his left hand and placing it over her right breast, the girl continued, "Listen, I've told you before. I can take care of myself. Remember, who was the first one to pull your fat out of the fire back there? Not that you have much to begin with."

The fighting man could feel Mackenzie's nipple becoming erect under her fatigues. He was becoming aroused as well.

"Now," Mackenzie said, flirting with the hulking warrior as she looked him directly into his brown eyes, "do you, ah, have any other, um, problems I can help you with?"

Without saying a word, the veteran of WWIII took the young girl into his embrace, spinning her to the left. As he lay her down on the bench seat, he gave the eager blonde a probing kiss, his right hand caressing her left breast. She felt his hardness. He began to pull her zipper to reveal her bosom, the two warriors completely loosing themselves to their passion.

"Uhhh, ah, parked tha other truck un came ta move this'un here," Zechariah stated nervously as he stuck his head in the open back door.

Looking deep into each other's eyes, the lovers mourned the loss of the cherished intimacy.

"It's okay, Mountain Man. There's a lot to get done. The other two should be back directly."

They made camp that evening on dried venison and water. The team regretted the loss of Trish's home-cooked meals, Mackenzie in particular. During her captivity, the blonde had existed on scraps of civil defense rations and bottled water the troopers begrudgingly surrendered to their prisoners. However, once united with her new family, the meals Trish had provided tasted exceptionally satisfying by comparison.

Angel used the radio in the Panther to make contact with Trish. Even though the radio at the cave was solar-powered with a backup battery, the veteran wanted to keep all communications short. After informing his sister of their experiences to that point, Trish excitedly relayed the story of finding a lost puppy in the woods surrounding their home. She determined it to be a Pomchow, a mix of Pomeranian and Chihuahua. Being a female, Rick named it Princess. Angel groused that all they needed was another mouth to feed. Trish countered that it was potty-trained and as a watchdog would add an extra margin of safety during their excursions. Angel promised to radio in every evening, and if they did not hear from him, it meant they were probably in trouble.

As evening gave way to the darkness, it became obvious to all that nighttime in the wild should be avoided at all costs. The five took turns on guard duty, ensuring their night vision was handy, while those not assigned sheltered within the confines of the Panther. One of the main features of every Panther was plenty of storage space, and one of the things within that storage was night vision equipment and riflescopes, although none of them slept due to the disturbances that haunted their uneasy quietude. Growls, cries, and screams of unimaginable creatures of the slain shattered the night. Around 3:00 a.m., when Mackenzie was on watch, a thunderous din startled the others from their reverie. It continued to progress until the very ground itself began to shake.

The hulking warrior was the first to reach the young girl. "Mac, do you know what's going on?"

"I sure as hell don't know what's going on, but it appears to have come from the northeast."

"Zechariah," the commando barked as the woods dweller came upon him, "any ideas?"

"Ah've heard sech noises b'fer. Tha ground ah shakin', naw."

"Crap, Mountain Man, I feel like climbing up into a big tree!" Hero remarked as he joined his companions.

"Think we should check it out?" Jim ventured. The question was followed by responses by various team members: "Hell no!" "Are you out of your mind?" "Ah don't thank so." "Everyone back in the Panther. Now!"

The rest of the night remained uneventful except for the occasional cry and squeal. Jim was the first one up and out of the transport as he was intent to discover the source of the disturbance. Once he found the reason for the minor earthquake, he spun on his heel, only to slam into his brother, who was quickly coming up on his position.

"Sorry, AD," Jim apologized. "Look, whatever caused it, it was almost right on top of us!"

The war hero looked to the northeast, in the direction his brother was indicating. Just around the turn from where they were encamped, where the high wall to their left gave way to a wooded forest, was an area devoid of all plant life. "Another one of those curious patches like we've encountered yesterday."

"Shouldn't we go and check it out while it's still fresh, see if we can determine the cause?" the junior commando asked.

"Ordinarily I'd say yes, but the longer we delay, the greater risk to Mackenzie's father."

"Yeah, I guess you're right. I'll head back and get us packed up."

Pulling away from the campsite, the caravan began its arduous trek to the dam. Angel took the wheel of the Panther while Mackenzie drove the first ambulance, and Hero took control of the other. Jim rode shotgun with the warrior, and Mountain Man rode in the back behind Angel. They had only traveled one hundred yards before encountering their first obstacle, a medium-size tree and downed utility pole forming an *X* in the middle of the road.

"This here's gonna make fer some mighty slow goin'," the woodsman observed as he opened his door.

"Don't have much choice," Jim bemoaned as he stumbled out of the right front door.

"If you guys get into something the three of us can't handle, let me know, and I'll engage the winch," the titan stated.

After examining the situation, Jim jogged back to the warrior's open window. "I think the three of us can get the tree pulled aside, but we'll need the winch for the pole due to a huge tree pinning it about ten feet up from its base."

The three stout men managed to horse the tree to the left side of the road far enough to allow passage. However, the utility pole would have been impossible to move, even if all five had pitched in. Angel brought the Panther to within ten feet of the object, put the transfer case in low range, and extended the cable so that Jim could loop the cable and secure the hook. Angel put the Panther into reverse and eased the transport backward and to the right. The utility pole was no match for the power of the SUV.

"As near as I can tell, we'll travel about a quarter mile before we run into more obstruction," Jim observed. "There's been a ton of smaller debris on the highway ever since we left home, garbage that we've been able to negotiate...so far. But if we have to do this for twenty more miles, we're going to be in trouble!"

The commando acknowledged the revelation with a grimace, grateful that Mackenzie was not there to witness the feelings of doubt that began to cloud the success of the mission.

"We've been traveling at a snail's pace for the last several hours, only making what, three miles?" Jim declared. "Look, AD, I'm all for finding Mackenzie's father and saving Rick, but this is turning out to be almost impossible."

"Jim, Mountain Man! Up ahead!"

"Yeah, that's where Route 250 merges with US 50. So?" The younger commando stated.

"All be. She's clear," Mountain Man ventured.

"She, who?" Jim inquired.

"The roadway," Angel revealed. Making their way another hundred yards, the warrior was able to confirm, "Two fifty and fifty. They're both clear of debris."

"Who ye figger done thut?"

"I don't know, but we're not complaining, eh, AD?" After a few moments, Jim reiterated, "AD?"

The titan was stroking his beard in his left hand, studying the unexpected revelation. Ignoring his brother's question, the strapping veteran noticed his other two comrades approaching his window from the left side, rifles at the ready.

"The road's clear. That should let us make better time," the football player stated.

"Yeah, hopefully it stays clear all of the way. We should be at the dam by noon," Mackenzie exclaimed.

The senior commando pondered the implication of the cleared highway. "Mac, was the road clear when you fled the dam?"

"I don't know. We followed the highway but only parallel to it. Mountain Man stayed off the roads because of the danger. We stayed off for fear of being spotted."

"The problem is someone's been using this road. Could have been a onetime journey, like us," the warrior explained, "or someone is using this highway regularly. And if that's the case, we have to ask ourselves, Who?"

The other four warriors were silent as the implication of their leader's statement sank in.

"So what should we do?" Jim asked.

"Boys, here's the situation," Angel began. "If we run into trouble, we don't have enough firepower. In a running firefight, three of us driving, that leaves only two of us to provide return fire."

"Yet we need the ambulances to extract the prisoners from the dam," Mackenzie reasoned.

"Exactly!" the commando stated. "I'd like nothing better than to hide out just to see how often this roadway is used. But that could take a week or more. We may find it's used every hour or not at all.

We can take our chances only to find out we've gambled on terrible odds."

The five looked expectantly from one to another, hoping a solution would present itself. Tears began to form in the young blonde's eyes, worrying what the implication could mean. Angel found himself vulnerable to the girl's concerns. Once again, he questioned his decision to risk lives based on their developing relationship.

"The way I see it, we only have one option. We hide and observe until the sun goes down, then travel at night. The odds are in our favor that whoever else is using this road won't be doing so after dark. Also, our night vision equipment and the cover of darkness will give us an advantage."

*****

It was an hour before sundown, the vehicles parked far enough from the intersection to be nearly undetected yet close enough to allow for constant monitoring. Angel was behind the wheel in the Panther covering the highway with binoculars, Mackenzie in the passenger's seat, when Mountain Man approached the driver's window.

"AD, cain we palaver a tad?"

"Sure," the warrior agreed, never taking his eyes off the roadway. "What's on your mind?"

"I ain't sure ah should say in front ah Ms. Mackenzie here."

"Go ahead, Zechariah, its okay," the young girl assured.

"As ah done say'ed, ye should thank ah gain 'bout traipsin' tha roads at night. Et be fairly dangerous an ah lot ah spooky happenin's goin on. People has went ah missin' never ta be hear'd from ah gain."

"I haven't forgotten, Mountain Man. But we have no option. I'm thinking we should be safe within our vehicles. Besides, it appears others are using this road free from danger."

"You're ah talkin' nighttime traversin'. Ye see, am ah talkin' 'bout par'see'kles!"

"Hold on, let me get this straight," the commando intervened. 'par'see'kles?' Are you trying to say parsickles?"

"That's what ahm ah sayin'. Ye see, back when I wuz ah youngin', ma gran'pappy used ta tell us youngin's not ta wander offen too fer from tha cabin. That tha par'see'kles wud git us. Whal, we figgered they used tha fear of tha par'see'kles ta keep us in check."

"But now you're telling us you've seen them?" Mackenzie wanted to know.

"What do these parsickles look like?" Angel inquired.

"O' lordy. Ye ain't never seed sech a creation in all your born days! They're big, biggin' un ye, AD. They look lak they're half devil un half woof, un black as night. Their face is ah devil, their body is ah woof, claws lak ah woof on their forelegs, cloven hooves on their hind legs, their tail is ah devil's. Un jest as stout as ye, Ang'el."

"That sounds so crazy," Mackenzie remarked.

"Don't ah know et, missy. Ahm ah wonderin' effen tha old folks rally knowed wut they wuz ah talkin' ah bout."

"You actually saw these things?" the titan reiterated.

"Ah hopes ta tell ye! When ah would shimmy up ma tree at night et got so's ah would keep ah particular eye out fer 'em. Bein' et wuz winter an no leaves on tha bran'ches, I knowed ah could be seen. They has rally good eyesight. Whal, one night, I thank one spy'ed me. Ah wuz still as death. Et come arount tha tree ah lookin' close. As quiet as ah could, ah tried ta keep tha tree b'twixt him un me. He got to whar he looked me square en tha eye. Ah ain't never been so scarit. Ah wuz afraid he wuz gonna shimmy up after me ceptin' somethin' got his 'tention an he scampered offen."

The warrior ruminated for several moments as he and Mackenzie looked each other in the eye, attempting to make sanity of it all. That was all they needed, another threat to their existence in general and their mission in particular.

"I appreciate all that you told me," the legionnaire explained. "Share your experience with the others so they can be extra vigilant."

"Ah shore will," the woods dweller consoled.

"One more thing, Zechariah, try not to scare the hell out of them."

"Ah hears ye, jest so's ye knows ah tried ta warn ye."

"Thank ye…ah you, Zechariah! We'll be careful," the veteran assured. After the woods dweller was out of earshot, he leaned over and said to Mackenzie, "Good Lord, he even has me talking like him now!"

The blonde laughed in spite of herself, the corners of her eyes crinkling. "The dialect does seem to be contagious. Hey, look!" Mackenzie shouted, pounding on the legionnaire's left shoulder while pointing with her right index finger.

Angel was already on it. A white crew cab pickup was turning on to fifty east at the intersection three hundred yards away. "Now we know who uses this road. We have to wonder why, and we need to see if anyone else does, and when. Have you seen that truck before? Would they have business at the dam?"

"I've not seen it before but doesn't mean they don't have business there. We weren't privy to much while incarcerated. Besides, as Mountain Man pointed out about the barter town, civilization is beginning to reconnect. For good or bad."

The combatant grunted. "Huh, mostly bad would be my guess. We'll give it until midnight. If there is no other activity, we'll take our chances and see how close we can get to the dam."

"Looks like we have a few hours to kill," Mackenzie mentioned. "Any ideas?"

"Mac, don't tempt me!" the goliath countered. "We have to stay vigilant!"

"You! Tempt you? If there is one thing I do know about the Angel of Death, no one can tempt you or break your will. However, it doesn't hurt to try, sweetheart. It's just… I want you so badly."

The combatant smiled at the term of endearment and countered. "Honey, I absolutely feel the same. I can't let those feelings endanger our mission. When the time and place are right, I will show you how very much I care for you."

The girl gave the warrior a kiss on the cheek and hopped into the back seat. "I'll be right here if you change your mind," she said with a wink. "In the meantime, I'm going to dream of you while I'm catching a few zees."

"Okay, don't let the Par'see'kles bite," Angel joked, using Mountain Man's dialect. A soft binocular case to the back of the head was Mackenzie's reply. Before beginning his watch, the titan radioed home to give them an update on their journey and get any news his siblings wanted to share. As it turned out, nothing was new except for Princess. Rick was holding up as well as he could.

*****

The rest of the evening proved uneventful. As previously discussed with the team, the caravan prepared to move out at midnight.

"Okay, men, since nothing has moved since dusk, I think we can assume no one travels at night. That could work in our favor, or it can be a liability. Has Mountain Man filled you two in on the parsickles?"

"If these creatures really exist, it can be out-and-out dangerous," Jim reasoned.

"Oh, pshaw!" Hero quipped. "Stories made up to keep little kids on the straight and narrow."

"Leeson here, Meester football player," the woodsman testily burst forth. "Ye play yer sport fer fun un games. This here's laf un death. Un am ah tellin' ye, these'uns is real. An I ain't fer certain our raffles'll, bring 'em down. 'Ceptin' fer Ang'el's, poss'bly."

"Listen up, everybody. We have battle enough out there without fighting amongst ourselves. Keep your eyes open, you know what to expect. Load up, travel as we have, and let's head for the dam!"

As Angel led the team, he pondered his decision to run with lights on. In the absence of a full moon and civilization, the nights were surprisingly dark. Lights could bring unwanted attention while the lack of such would greatly impede their progress, if not make it almost impossible.

If the journey itself wasn't fraught with danger and uncertainty, the foliage that had encroached to the edge of the highway was cause enough for alarm. Erie vegetation seemed to move of its own volition. The chokers were well-known for their animation; plant life of indescribable origin was also in abundance. So thick and dense, the overhanging branches and vines transformed the highway into a veritable tunnel. The emergency lighting of the ambulances were both a blessing and a curse. The combined effect of headlights and flashing lights did a remarkable job of illuminating the dreary road; it also hinted at dangers, real and imagined.

For nearly two hours, the cabin of the Panther had been constantly bombarded with shouts of "Looky yonder" and "Angel, did you see that?" and the like. At one point, Mountain Man began stabbing his finger into the glass of the left rear door hollering, "Ah seen one! I seen a Par'see'kle!"

Angel took to the radio. "Mackenzie, Hero, pay particular attention to your left. Mountain Man swears he saw a parsickle."

The blonde was the first to chime in. "AD, I thought I saw… something. Couldn't make it out, but when I passed, something banged on the side of the truck."

The football player radioed next. "Hang on, guys. I saw something up against Mackenzie's van. I'm slowing to investigate."

"No, hell no! Do not stop. Do not slow down. Do not get separated from the column," Angel shouted into the mic.

"Hero came to a stop, AD. Should I stop too? I don't want to abandon him," came Mackenzie's warning.

"How far behind you is he?"

"About seventy-five feet. It looks…dear Lord! It looks like something has made its way onto his hood!"

"Hero! Hero?" Fifteen seconds passed with no response from the quarterback. "Mac, back up to his vehicle ASAP. We're coming in reverse. Turn on your sirens. Okay, men, check your weapons and prepare to disembark. The only siren to cut the night was that of the young girl's."

Mackenzie threw her vehicle into reverse and rapidly accelerated at an unintentional speed, almost crashing into Hero's truck. Angel was racing the one hundred feet nearly glued to her front bumper. The Panther nearly escaped, crashing into her as she rapidly came to a halt.

"Mackenzie, stay in your vehicle," the behemoth barked into the microphone. "Let's roll, boys!"

Racing to assist their comrade, the three men became unnerved by the sights and sounds of the night. Their senses assailed by strange cries, fluttering, snapping of branches, indescribable movement at the outer limits of their vision. Once again, the commando questioned the wisdom of their mission.

As they arrived at the ambulance piloted by Hero, they looked into the windshield and found him to be in a stupor, sitting behind the wheel and staring blindly into space.

"Is everything okay?" came a woman's voice from behind.

"I thought I told you to stay in the ambulance," the titan growled.

"If there's something out here, you guys can use the help. If there is a threat, well, I'm not going to die trapped and alone."

"Look at the hood!" Jim exclaimed.

The hood of the sturdy vehicle had nearly collapsed, the paint peeled and scraped to the bare metal where the creature tried to gain purchase. The imprint of cloven hooves was clearly visible.

"Ah told ye!"

"Let's get Hero out of the cab of this one and into the back of the other. We don't want to hold this conversation here," the combatant advised.

Wrestling the listless Hero out of the driver's seat and into the patient module of the other ambulance, they carefully laid him down on the bed. Still unresponsive after numerous attempts to revive the football player, Mackenzie located ammonia inhalants in one of the cabinets and administered them to the unconscious football player. Hero awoke with startling aggravation, shouting and throwing his arms in all directions. Luckily, Angel had anticipated such a reaction and quickly arrested his frenzy.

"What the hell? What in the hell? Did you see it? You had to see it! It…it…"

"Hero, yes, we all saw it. What the hell was it?" Angel demanded.

"It…it…it was just like Mountain Man described. I can't believe it!"

"Ah told ye!"

"Except, except, AD, it spoke to me. Oh, dear Lord, I think I'm losing my mind."

"What did it say?" Mackenzie asked as she ran her hands up and down the mountaineer's chest in an effort to soothe his anxiety.

"It didn't *say* anything! It…it's…more like it *communicated* with me. Like…telepathically!"

"Zechariah, do you have much knowledge of these creatures? Do they have telepathic abilities?" Angel inquired.

"Ah don't rightly know what ye mean, but when that'un wuz ah starin' me in tha eyeball, ah felt ma self gettin' swimmy haid'ed an 'bout ta pass out."

"Hero, what did it…communicate?" The veteran of WWIII wanted to know.

"It…told me 'We,' AD, 'We will kill you all!'"

The Angel of Death, slayer of untold thousands, utilizing firearms, edged weapons, and bare hands. Never cowed by any opponent of size or quantity now felt as if he had met his match. The creatures of this new world were humongous, winged, radioactive, mutated, possibly the devils themselves. And for the first time in his life, Angel was…not afraid but…intimidated.

Mackenzie noticed. She saw it in his face, his exasperated posture, his irregular breathing.

After carefully examining Hero to ensure he was sound, the titan locked eyes with the beautiful girl, who rarely strayed from his side. Returning his gaze, she snaked her hand into his.

"Don't quit on us now, big guy," Mackenzie whispered.

Like a mortar round going off within a contained environment, words suddenly exploded in his head. "You stood defiant before the Lord thy God, creator of every universe, every dimension, and everything within them, yet now you cower over the most trivial of my creations? Remember this, my son: if it bleeds, the Angel of Death can deprive it of life. Your time has not yet come!"

"…here or should we continue on," the titan became dimly aware of Jim speaking.

"What?" the titan replied.

"I said, should we circle the wagons and spend the night here, or should we continue on?" Jim repeated. "You feeling okay? All of this parsickle crap has us all spooked."

Seeing the concerned look on Mackenzie's face, the combatant arose, pulling her up after him. "No, we can't stay here! We will continue on to the dam, rescue Mackenzie's father, and return home to save Rick's life. I feel sorry for anyone or anything that gets in the way of our mission!"

"That's the man I have grown to love," the blonde confessed.

"You feeling well enough to continue?" Angel asked the football player as he pulled him up off the bed. Jim slapped his brother on the back as he did so.

"Let me at that son of a bitch," the quarterback swore as he got to his feet.

Exiting the rear of the ambulance, Jim and Zechariah made their way to the Panther, alert to any danger. Angel and Mackenzie helped Hero into the driver's seat of the second ambulance. "It's too dark here to see much," the combatant concluded. "Start it and listen for any unusual noises or poor running conditions." After a moment, the ex-football player gave the legionnaire the thumbs-up.

Escorting Mackenzie to her cab, the titan surreptitiously glanced at the spot where the creature had punched the vehicle. Careful not to let on, it was obvious that the claws of the parsickle penetrated the thick metal as if it were made of paper.

"Be safe and stay vigilant," the young blonde pleaded. "And think of me," she continued, placing his unarmed left hand upon her right breast.

"You make it difficult not to," the colossus replied with a gentle squeeze.

"Oh, you know us wily females," Mackenzie said with a smile and a wink.

The pair embraced and shared a longing kiss before departing. Once again, she could feel his eagerness.

*****

It was three twenty-five in the morning. Nothing but the occasional raccoon, deer, and other species of nocturnal animals darting out into their path. All rather mundane compared to what they had previously experienced. So much so that all but the battle hardened would have let down their guard.

"Hey, guys, help! Trouble!" It was Mackenzie's startled voice that came over the radio. "Something's on the roof trying to get inside!"

With the discovery of the claw marks still fresh on the veteran's mind, Angel threw the Panther in park and leaped out the driver's door, his trusty G3 in his right hand. Angel was stunned to find three large pterodactyls trying to breach the roof of the patient module, the red-and-white strobes of the vehicle illuminating the creatures like demons from hell. Their thin leathery wings, totaling a span of thirty feet, appeared almost translucent in the bright-white light. Generating a windstorm of debris from their nonstop beating, three-foot-long toothed beaks snapped at the air. Their cone-shaped heads, large and evil looking, were atop long thin bodies. Their tails were long and dart-shaped, coiling and uncoiling like snakes; their cries threatened to cower most men. However, these were not most men.

Hero was the first to open fire as he had seen the plight of the young woman even before she could radio her distress. The inexperienced football player sent a burst of full-auto ten-millimeter rounds into the wake of winged creatures, the unfocused barrage eliciting great cries and screams but not much damage.

The bearded hulk shouldered his rifle and focused several three-round bursts into each torso, causing the birds to falter in their attack. Jim and Mountain Man joined their leader, imitating his style, as did Hero. The belch of battle rifles sent bullets, flame, and smoke into the nighttime sky, illuminating the cover of overhanging branches like a volley of fireworks. One of the ruined miscreants managed to escape, only to crash in the brush some thirty yards away. The other two expired almost immediately, falling to either side of the ambulance.

Angel raced to Mackenzie's door to check her safety, followed by his three team members. "Mac, are you okay? Guys, keep us covered."

"I'm all right, but what the heck tried to get in, another parsickle?"

"No," the commando's lips curled down. "Just as bad, maybe worse!" With a nod of his head, he indicated the carcass of the pterodactyl sprawled on the ground on the left side of the van. "Pterodactyls! Three of them. One on the other side of the ambulance and another, dead, out in the brush."

Readjusting her position in the seat, the girl was able to see the crumpled remains in her side-view mirror. "Oh my god," she exclaimed.

The strapping commando turned his head toward his companions. "You guys notice their tails: long dart-shaped, coiling, and relaxing?"

"Yeah, ye, how can I not?"

"Well, the peculiar thing is pterosaurs, the actual name for pterodactyls, had no tail."

"What? Huh? Seriously? Really?"

"In this mixed-up, biochemical, radiated, mutated, and God only knows what else world we've inherited, I think these things are still in a stage of mutation."

"Like…into something else?" Hero questioned.

"Like…maybe some kind of…dragon." Angel speculated.

With the team dumbstruck and searching for words, the leader took the opportunity to begin issuing orders. "Men, we've either scared off every predator within ten miles or called them in for dinner by making our presence known. Get back in your respective vehicles, stay close, and stay vigilant. Let me know if anything and I mean *any…thing* looks suspicious. Got it?"

All made their agreement known.

*****

Negotiating obstacles scattered across the tarmac while keeping alert to ever-present danger, the legionnaire came to the conclusion that only large four-wheel-drive vehicles used this road as there were too many smaller trees, large branches, and debris to make travel by car possible. He realized that others had learned the hard way to stay off the road at night if sheet metal and other automotive parts strewn over the length of the highway were any indication. While the Panther itself could easily negotiate the wreckage, he had to consider the ambulance's limited ability to do the same. It made for extremely slow going. Quickly checking his watch, the warrior realized it would be sunrise soon. That also presented a problem. With daylight came the consequence of other vehicles traveling Route 50. A battle with whomever they encountered meant there was the possibility of alerting those at the dam, as by his estimate they were within five miles of the facility.

"It be lat soon," the passenger in the left rear seat mentioned.

"We should be turning off US 50 soon and on to the Tygart Valley Road. Given the overgrowth since my last visit, it's hard to say for sure," the warrior announced.

The combatant lifted the microphone from its hook. "Mac, I'm thinking we should be approaching the road to the dam soon."

"We should be close," the girl replied.

"10–4. We need to stash these vehicles and fast. Somewhere within a mile of the dam. Any ideas?"

"The best I can come up with is a metal maintenance building on the right, but it's only about half a mile or so short of the dam."

"Mac, okay, I can see the Tygart Valley Road coming within sight. It's going to have to do. Hero, keep an eye out for it. Okay, over and out."

"Got ya. Any port in a storm. Over!"

As Angel maneuvered the Panther onto the road leading to the dam, he noticed that it was much cleaner than Route 50, indicating it might be heavily in use. He realized making it to the maintenance building undetected might be a challenge. Something else began to bother the tribe leader.

"Mac, come in."

"Got ya, over."

"Get Trish or Rick on the horn. One of us would do it, but we need to stay alert as possible from here on out."

"Not a problem. How can I help? Over."

"Do not ask her, tell her—from me! Do not, under any circumstances, venture outside the cave from a half hour before dusk until a half hour past dawn. Tell her my reasons. They need to know about our experiences this night. Scare the living hell out of them, I don't care! Whatever it takes to ensure their safety. Got it?"

"10–4."

"By the way, Hero, how are you making out? I'm about to pick up the pace a bit. This road is relatively clear. Are you staying within sight of us?"

"10–4, I'm right behind Mac. Just made the turn onto this road."

"10–4. Say, after Mackenzie radios Trish, get my sister on the horn and advise her to leave her radio on this frequency. That way, they can stay abreast of our expedition without actually having to relay them directly. Besides, she may want to hear from you," Angel said with a smile on his face.

"Yessir!"

"Okay, boys, stay on your toes. Twice the speed means if trouble comes, it will come twice as fast. Here we go!"

The titan eased his foot into the pedal and was rewarded by the increased whine of the turbine engine and the feel of acceleration. Even though they were still traveling under the cover of darkness, he estimated their arrival at the building to be near daybreak. Although the road would allow a much faster pace, he confined the speed to thirty miles per hour. The veteran saw no reason to access the maintenance building in the dark or wait alongside of it too long.

"Ah thank ah seen something on ma side."

"Jim, alert the others. What did you see, Zechariah?"

"An'gel, ah swear ta ye, ah seen so many dif'rent critters in ma travels ah cain't be fer certain. Et might be one ah them thar hogs, cain't say fer sure."

"Jim, advise them not to use their firearms under any circumstances. To do otherwise would greatly endanger this mission," Angel commanded.

"Got it!"

"AD, he's ah chargin' 'kenzie."

"Jim. Give me that mic. Mackenzie, maintain your speed. No slower, no faster. Do not do anything that might antagonize him. Hero, follow Mac's lead."

"He hit me…hard," Mackenzie uttered.

"You…or the truck?"

"Both! He struck my door. I leaned as far in as I could, but I still got beat up pretty bad."

"What's the porker doing now?" the titan wanted to know.

"Slamming into Mackenzie dazed the hog a little, but now he's turned his sights on me," the ex-quarterback exclaimed.

"I don't know how fast that bore can run, or how far. Hopefully not much of either. Stick with me, you two. It's about two miles to the maintenance building. One way or another, we're going to have to outrun the son of a bitch."

As they accelerated to sixty miles per hour, Hero just did manage to outpace its angled attack and avoid a collision with the pig. The football player was as scared as he had ever been in his life to see the horrific creature just outside his window, keeping pace with the ambulance. The quarterback saw the vengeful look on the boar's face, its right eye never breaking contact with its quarry; a mix of snot, saliva, and blood sprayed out of its mouth whenever it let out a horrific squeal. Hero had no idea what to do to get out of his predicament other than to outrun the swine. "Faster, go faster," he cried into the mic.

"10-4, I'll take it to 70, but this road lays like a snake. It wasn't constructed for these speeds!"

The WVU Mountaineer was about to request another speed increase when the hog started to fall back. It could not either run any faster or keep that speed up for long. "Guys, it's beginning to flounder, but don't slow down yet."

"The maintenance building will be coming up in about a half a mile!" the young girl announced over the radio.

The colossus could not believe the turn of events. Chased by a fucking mutated boar, unable to slow down and stop or else forced to overshoot the building and probably end up in the parking lot of the dam. Could things get any crazier?

"He's done," Hero shouted over the radio. "He's given up and trampled off into the woods!"

Each teammate verbally expressed words of relief and prayers to the deity they worshipped.

Angel announced into the radio, "I can see the building coming up on the right. It's covered in vines and weeds. Could be a blessing. I just hope those vines aren't chokers. Don't appear to be, anyway."

"Coming up…coming up… Yep, that's it," the blonde announced. "During our escape, we entered the forest just this side of it. And no, no chokers. If there were, we would have been toast."

"You two, stay in your seats. That means you too, *Mackenzie*! The three of us will clear the structure."

Jim and Mountain Man led by Angel approached the structure. It was a Quonset metal hut with an open front. The half-round opening appeared to be forty feet wide, sixteen feet high, and as near as they could determine, about one hundred feet deep. As stealthily as possible, the team approached the opening from the side, the commando peering his head around the metal entrance. He waited for his eyes to adjust to the relative darkness before proceeding.

Finding no visible thereat, the legionnaire motioned his men onward, one per side. The titan crept straight down the center. As they proceeded toward the closed other end, they found the building to be mostly empty. Several large empty cardboard boxes were strewn about. The cement floor contained dark patches, presumably oil spots, indicating vehicles and equipment had been serviced at one time. As they reached the back end, there were racks of new and used parts. Stationed against the right rear were numerous toolboxes of various colors and sizes.

"Angel, over here," Jim called in a hushed volume. "Look!"

The senior veteran ambled his way to his brother who was on the left side near the parts racks. Curious to see what his brother had uncovered, Angel was surprised to find a spare tire and inflator assembly for a Panther. "Finally some good news for a change." Mountain Man joined the brothers directly. "Find anything useful?" the titan asked.

"Whal, thar be some mighty useable tools effen a feller wuz to latch on ta some of 'em."

"Okay, here's what we do," the leader began as he led his team back to the entrance. "I want the two ambulances backed in, one on either side. We may have to leave here at a moment's notice. Same way with the Panther except down the center. I want you to secure the spare assembly into the Panther. Then take only the most useful tools and put them into one of the ambulances. Mac, Hero and I are going to gather the cardboard boxes and stack them in front of the transports to hide them from prying eyes."

The two comrades nodded their approval as Angel waved the two in the vehicles to pull into the building, then whipped his raised hand in circles, indicating that they needed to back in. Jim and the woods dweller guided the duo as Angel sprinted to the Panther. Backing in his vehicle, the warrior noticed, due to the help of the additional lighting, that vines and other vegetation unsuccessfully tried to take root in several piles of dirt on the floor. There was a shallow oil drain container against the right side of the structure where a vine of some strange variety was actually thriving in the caustic fluid.

As he exited the vehicle, the colossus was pleased to see that Jim and Mountain Man were already attending to their tasks and Hero and Mackenzie were dragging the cardboard boxes into place. He silently thanked God that they were able to load and conceal the vehicles under cover of darkness. Unfortunately, they had no option but to approach the dam in broad daylight or else wait until sunset.

"What's the plan now?" Mackenzie wanted to know.

"I'm debating if we should wait until...shhhh." The fighting man suddenly put his right index finger to his lips. "Someone's driving this direction. Retrieve your weapons, everyone, and hide behind the boxes."

Within thirty seconds, the same white four-wheel drive pickup truck they spotted earlier at the intersection of 50 and 250 stopped in front of the maintenance building.

A man of around thirty years old, wearing blue jeans and a red flannel shirt, jumped out of the passenger-side door. "Sam, I'm tellin' you, some of those boxes aren't sitting in the same place since I've passed here last."

Angel motioned for his team to stay frosty.

"Butch, when's the last time you noticed them?" came Sam's reply from inside the pickup.

Butch was halfway between the truck and building, his rifle at the ready. "I don't know, a week or two ago."

The commando raised his weapon to put Butch in his crosshairs. His team followed suit.

"Jesus Christ, Butch, ever stop to think some of the guys at the dam could have been up here millin' around?"

Sam was now at the entrance, looking to see if anything was truly out of place. He slowly began to make his way into the structure.

The team found themselves tightening their trigger fingers.

"'sides, Butch," Sam continued, "ya never know when one of them big rats or cats or…worse were bumping things around lookin' for food. You sure as hell wouldn't find me pokin' around in there."

Butch appeared to consider the implication of Sam's words. "Well, I guess you're right," he responded before spinning on his heel.

The collective sound of the team expelling their breath caught Butch's ear, causing him to turn back toward the rear of the structure.

"What now?" Sam wanted to know.

"Thought I heard something!"

"Okay, Butch, go ahead. But when you're gettin' eaten alive, don't come cryin' to me. And while you're screamin' and cryin', the boss will have my sorry ass for bein' late."

Butch turned back around and headed for the truck. "Well, if it turns out someone was in there, he'll still have your sorry ass."

After a few moments, the white truck drove away.

"Okay, that cuts it then," the titan said. "We can't wait here until dark. If Butch reports the incident and they send someone to investigate, we sure don't want to be caught dead-ended in a firefight and risk damage to our transports."

"How do we play this?" Jim asked his older brother.

"Give me a minute." Angel pondered the implications. There were two obstacles to overcome. First was gaining access to the dam without arousing suspicion. Second, they could follow the tree line only so far. From his past visits, he knew that the area surrounding the entrance to the facility, given the immense parking lot and approach, was devoid of cover for several hundred yards. He looked over his team in order to assess their skills and abilities. His eyes engaged those of Mackenzie. She always radiated an eagerness that was hard to ignore, a zest for life and enjoyed living it to the fullest. More importantly, she would do anything he would ask of her, God bless her. If the situation were not what it was, he would sweep her off her feet and make passionate love to her. She was so beautiful and exciting. His brow furrowed; it was a damn shame what he had to ask of her in order to gain entrance to the dam.

"Okay, guys, listen up! Mac, give me your weapons. Take mine and put them in the front of the Panther. You three, military weapons only and make sure they are fully loaded with spare magazines. Also, get some camo war paint out of the Panther and disguise your looks as best as you can. Adjust your hats to be loose enough so you can slide them further down to cover your face."

The young blonde reappeared as the other three jogged off. "Honey, the only way we're going to be able to march to the dam unmolested and gain entrance is to pretend we are the soldiers who captured you and are bringing you back."

The ever-present smile Mackenzie had for the titan disappeared from her face.

"Honey, baby doll. It's the only way," the titan whispered. "I love you so very much. I will never let anything bad happen to you. I promise, Never! Trust me!"

The beautiful blonde looked into the commando's visage with moist eyes; her lips were pursed as she bit them close, nodding in acceptance. She embraced the veteran and pressed her head into his chest. His muscles were taut yet reassuring as he wrapped his arms around her.

"Dear, I'm so afraid," Mackenzie stated. "How do we become man and wife in such a world as this? I want to marry you! I want to be your wife! I want to bear your children!"

"Honey," the colossus began, hoping to defuse the desperation they were sharing and transform the mood into a lighter emotion. "If it's children you want, just give me thirty seconds and a secluded spot." Angel followed with a hearty laugh.

Mackenzie quipped back, laughing richly with a smile, "If that's all the longer it will take, I'm not sure I've found the right man."

The three men expectantly walked up to the titan and the girl. "What do you think?" Hero ventured, indicating the paint job.

"Mac, do you think they will have the soldiers fooled?" Angel wanted to know.

"Amazingly...hats down low, camo paint, and it's a good thing Trish gave Hero a proper haircut...yeah, yes, I think we can fool them long enough to get inside."

"One final thing, Mac. Don't hate me—"

"I could never do that."

"You might," the goliath stated as he whipped his survival knife from its sheath on his right hip. "We can't replace the clothes you were wearing when you escaped, but I *can* recreate the look." So saying, the veteran of WWII cut the fabric of the fatigues several inches below the girl's crotch, then cut the material at her shoulders.

"But now that I think about it—" Mackenzie spat resentfully.

"Sorry, sweetheart. It had to be done if we have any hope of rescuing your father. We have to make it look as if we are returning an abused girl back to her captors."

The three men were beginning to realize the two were becoming an item as they traded endearments.

"Also—" the legionnaire continued.

"There's an also," the beautiful girl expounded.

"Yes, sorry. Not now but as we get within fifty yards of the entrance to the dam, I want you to lower the zipper to your breasts. Show just a little cleavage."

"My love, do I have to? Back at the building after we escaped the zombies was one thing, given the bile and God knows what else that was running down my chest. I have come to love and respect all of you. But these miserable bastards—"

"Look, baby doll—"

"Should we leave and give you two a few minutes?" Hero groused.

One meaningful look from the Angel of Death was all it took to quiet the impertinent quarterback. "Our disguises may only go so far. When we bring you in, we want all eyes on you and you only."

"What about you?" the young girl asked of her champion. "There is absolutely no way you are going to fit in."

"I'm banking on the fact that they have no reason to expect an attack nor any reason to have a guard posted. The lead blast door to the vestibule is impossible to compromise so no need of security. I'll hide behind the bulkhead. After they have let the four of you in, I will come around, and we will quietly dispatch the soldiers with drawn knives. After that, we will carefully make our way throughout the facility and rescue your father."

"Ohh kayyy," the blonde reluctantly agreed. Smiling, she acquiesced, "I'm not beyond taking a hit for the team. Listen, buster," Mackenzie continued with menace in her words as she poked him in the chest with her right index finger, "you damn well better be there to save me!"

"I'll be there. I promise!"

CHAPTER 8

Having traveled the half mile to the dam, staying behind the cover of flora and fauna, the team was in sight of the facility. "Mac, there is a guard shack on the right before we access the road deck that spans the top of the dam to the blast doors. I'm certain the guard shack was abandoned and sealed. Would you know if they have begun using it again?"

"If that shack had been in use, I wouldn't be standing here talking to you now."

"Okay, boys," the strapping combatant stated, nodding his head toward what was left of a brown wooded sign that was almost impossible to read, "try to absorb what pertinent details you can."

Corps of Engineers US Army, Pittsburgh District, Tygart Valley Dam, Completed 1938, Purpose: Flood Control, Length 1,921 feet, Height 230 feet, Width at Bottom 207 feet, Width at Road Deck 20 feet, Elevation 1,190 feet, Dam runs east to west., equipped as civil defense shelter.

"May not hurt to memorize the dimensions of the structure."

"Ah cain see thut thar pickup is in tha parkin' lot!"

"I kind of expected that. All right, as we approach, we'll keep the guard shack between us and the blast door. Jim, with your binoculars, surveil the area from the parking lot to the entrance to the dam. Hero, Mountain Man, don't actually harm her but pretend to push Mac along with your rifles from time to time." The three acknowledged their directives. "I'm going to hang back a way just in the event that we are being watched, my size won't be as obvious. However, as we come to within fifteen feet, I'll sprint around and hide beside the bulkhead on the left-hand side. The door opens to the right."

"Anything you want me and Mountain Man to do besides poke Mackenzie?"

The young blonde spun and glared at the football player.

"With the rifles, I'm talking about."

"Don't ye go triflin' wif Ms. Mackenzie. Ah don't take kindly ta that!"

"Just trying to relieve the stress of the situation, no harm meant," Hero explained.

"I also want you three to speak at a normal tone as you approach. Zechariah, not so much. Not too loud to attract attention and not so quiet that we seem out of place, again, in the event we are observed before we arrive. I want you men to talk a little rough. Mackenzie, I want you to plead and whimper. Got it?"

Having traveled across the parking lot, the band found themselves at the guard shack with no sign of anyone at the dam. After carefully studying the interior of the shack for signs of occupancy, they pressed onto the twenty-foot-wide road deck atop the dam that led to the entrance of the facility two hundred yards away.

"See anything disturbing?" Hero asked of Jim as he nudged his captive in the back.

"No, but we need to keep an eye on the big guy in case he spots anything," Jim responded. "Come on, bitch. Keep moving," the younger brother said in a louder voice. "Sorry, Mac," he added in a whisper.

"You mess with me, and I swear to God I'll cut your nuts off," the young girl swore. "Back at you," she added in a whisper.

"We're haf way thar. No sign ah trouble yet."

At twenty-five feet from the blast door, Angel skirted his team and positioned himself on the left side of the bulkhead just behind the entrance. As he watched his team approach, he saw Mackenzie wink and, going beyond the call of duty, lower the zipper of her camo to her navel, exposing her breasts to the nipple, undisclosed to her three teammates behind her. The muscle-bound man shook his head at her disregard for his orders, even though he realized that the beautiful girl had done so in order to ensure she was the distraction he had intended.

"Open the hell up. It's us. We're tired and hungry," Jim said as he pounded on the blast door with the butt of his rifle.

After fifteen seconds, Hero added, "Hurry the hell up. There's all kinds of fucking creatures lurking about!"

The massive lead blast door opened one-half inch. "Who's out there?"

Jim looked down at the name tag on his camo fatigues. "Timmons. We've got the girl. Not in the same condition we found her in, ha ha, but she'll do in a pinch, if you know what I mean."

The warrior could tell that Mackenzie was beginning to feel uncomfortable, like a flower wilting at night. She started to reach for her zipper, possibly to raise it back up, but evidently thought better of it and retracted her hand.

Slowly, the heavy door started to open wider. The man at the door held a Glock 20 in his right hand, two soldiers bearing HK MF5/10A3s covering him. The beautiful blonde did everything within her power to squirm and move so the soldiers could see deeply into her garment. So far, the ploy was working as the men couldn't take their eyes away from the charms of the young beauty.

"This one?" the man operating the door said in surprise. "Jesus, we've fucked two women to death waiting for you guys to bring her back."

Mackenzie's face was ablaze with terror, reliving her torment of the past.

Angel resented his decision to use his girl as bait as his hands tightened into fists, about to leap into battle.

"Where are all the others that went with you in search of her?" the doorman asked.

"Dead," was Mountain Man's one-word answer.

Angel lowered his head and shook it in the negative. The last thing he wanted was for Zechariah to be engaged into a conversation.

"How?"

"I'm telling you, there are monsters out here beyond belief. Let us the hell in before we become part of the menu!" Hero ventured.

"Why is she dressed like that?" the doorman wanted to know.

"Let's just say," the quarterback detailed, "her other clothes didn't make it through the, uh, cavity search. Ha ha!"

"I can't blame ya there, but no more for you, guys. You've had enough," the sentry stated as he stepped to his left, his eyes never leaving Mackenzie's exposed breasts. "Come on in! Oh, hey, by the way, what's the password?"

"Password?" Jim asked incredulously.

"Come on, man, quit screwing around. We haven't eaten in days, just—" Hero spat.

The sentry suddenly reached out with his left hand, grabbed Mackenzie by her fatigues, and pulled her inside the bulkhead, inadvertently stripping her to the waist as he did so. "Seriously? She doesn't seem to be any worse for the wear. Who the hell are you guys?"

To Mackenzie's credit, her three companions were unable to speak, stunned by the topless girl's beauty.

Putting his pistol to the back of Mackenzie's head, the sentry barked, "Drop your weapons now, or the bitch gets it."

"Shoot the bitch, see if I care. It's your loss," Hero exclaimed.

The sentry stiffened his arm as if he were about to shoot.

The three immediately deposited their guns on the concrete.

Angel castigated himself for not anticipating a password for entry into the installation. Obviously, Mackenzie was uninformed of the requirement as well. Knowing that their ploy had failed miserably, the only card he had left was the element of surprise. Before losing his advantage, the warrior sprang into action in hopes of catching the soldiers by surprise.

Stepping back several feet in order to facilitate a lunge, he used the steel frame of the blast door to help propel him into the vestibule of the facility. Much to the soldiers' amazement, a huge musclebound colossus of a man came flying through the door feet first, bowling the three servicemen and Mackenzie off their feet. The first course of action was to disable the man who had held a pistol to the girl's head. Rising to his knees, the behemoth drove his massive right fist square into the face of the soldier, killing him instantly.

Scrambling to his feet, the fighting man grabbed the nearest trooper by the back of the head and slammed his face into the concrete bunker. The sound of breaking teeth, cartilage, and bone resounded within the tight quarters.

By then the third soldier had scrambled for his rifle and regained a crouched posture. Angel was in midflight, attempting a flying tackle when the gunman opened up on the murdering horror. Substituting expediency for accuracy, the frightened serviceman opened up on the warrior before he was in the crosshairs. Searing pain lanced Angel's right side as he caught a ten-millimeter full metal-jacketed bullet in his upper torso. Undeterred, the legionnaire approached the rifleman and swept the weapon from his grasp. The war veteran had brought the rifle back to bash the brains out of the man when the soldier dove to the floor and retrieved the doorman's pistol.

Holding the gun to Mackenzie's head, he threatened to kill the girl if the lunatic continued. Angel spun in the direction of his men to ascertain their disposition. He found they had recovered their weapons but not in time to stave off a warning by the gun-wielding trooper that if they did not drop their weapons, he would splatter the girl's brains all over the walls.

Angel's attention was quickly arrested by shouts and cries as soldiers alerted by the sounds of gunfire were scrambling up the stairwell to assist their brethren. "Get this son of a bitch!" the man holding Mackenzie screamed. "He's slaughtering us all!"

The decision was easy for a warrior of Angel's experience. If he went on attack mode, some or all of his team would die. If he allowed himself to be captured, there would be no one coming to save them, and again, all would probably die. He knew from years of deadly combat that the only option open to him was to escape and remount an attack. So concluding, the combatant raced out the door.

"Get him. Get the bastard," the gunman screamed to those who had made it to the top of the stairs.

"Get down and stay down!" Angel shouted as he sped by his men. Full automatic gunfire erupted just as they hit the ground. Undeterred, the veteran of WWIII raced for the railing at the edge of the dam as bullets grazed his arms and legs. Another bored a furrow of skin and muscle from his left butt cheek as he made a leap toward the edge of the road deck. The soldiers raced after the hulking combatant as he grasped the top rail and propelled himself into the water 120 feet below, directly into the dam's intake! Automatic gunfire never stopped from the time the hulking combatant bolted out of the vestibule onto the railing and into the chilly water. Even after the warrior hit the water, gunfire continued until there was no sign of the giants resurfacing.

By then Angel's team had followed the soldiers to the railing, Mackenzie throwing herself against the gunmen in an attempt to interfere with their aim. Crying and pleading, she offered herself to them, if only they would stop shooting, to no avail, for the soldiers laughed as they knew they had nothing to lose.

"Come on, bitch," one of the soldiers shouted. "You and your three assholes get inside. We have a special treat just for you."

"What about…what about him?" Mackenzie wept as she continued peering into the lake for signs of life.

"Don't worry about him," one of the other soldiers said. "If he's not dead already or doesn't get sucked into the intakes and drown, the lake monsters will get him! Now get that sweet ass inside."

*****

As the suction of the dam's intake system continued to pull the titan under, bullets continued to whizz around him in every direction. Many, in fact, hit the veteran, striking him in the torso and legs, but the increasing depth of the water sapped their penetrative ability. He also had to contend with the agony of the bullet that was lodged in his left side and the pain in his rump. The veteran knew if he ended up in the dam's water intake, the inescapable pressure would hold him pinned against the debris screen until he drowned. Having spent time at flood control and hydroelectric facilities, he understood the currents generated by rushing water. Due to the nature of his demolitions work, which at times brought him into contact with this kind of danger, he received training on how to escape such death.

Rather than fight the strong current, he actively swam along with it and toward one of the intake gates. With bullets still striking the water behind him, he knew, just as he had been trained, there would be only one chance to survive. To fail meant certain death. Training dictated that he needed to swim as hard and as fast as he could. He knew he must replicate the correct angle and approach. When the intake was within ten feet of him, using his legs as a rudder, Angel bent his knees in an upward angle and swam toward the surface as hard as he could. The area of water directly above the intake was subject to the least amount of suction. Dye tests had borne that out. Now that the warrior was in a safe zone, he dared not surface as he was sure troopers were still searching for him to emerge.

Because of disciplined aquatic training and huge lung capacity, Angle was able to hold his breath underwater for five minutes. This ability allowed him to refrain from swimming to the surface until he was sure the troopers had well beyond given up on him.

*****

Mackenzie wept bitterly as a trooper who bore a patch with the name Sheldon forced her down the staircase to the lower levels of the facility. She wept for her love whom she was sure, and constantly assured, she would never see again. She wept for herself, knowing the abuse she would again suffer at the hands of the vengeful military men. And finally she wept over the broken promise that Angel had made regarding her safety. Following behind her was the ever-quiet Mountain Man. It was not that the woodsman was beyond avenging himself upon his captors. He wanted to appear to be the most docile of the bunch, so when he made his move, it would be totally unexpected. As they descended, Zechariah helped the young blonde put the fatigues up over her exposed torso so she could continue with dignity.

Behind him was Jim, who had scuffled on and off with Sheldon and other captors since leaving the vestibule, to no avail. He realized that it wasn't only his life he was jeopardizing by struggling but those of his friends. Bringing up the rear was Hero, ever fighting and resisting. Constantly insulting the soldiers, he received numerous bashings to his head for his trouble.

As they descended to the first floor, Mackenzie once again began to experience the claustrophobic sensations of entrapment in the familiar but cruel surroundings. Since it was their first time within the facility, the other three were amazed to find the huge chamber well lit. Due to the fact there was no utility service, they assumed correctly that the flood control dam had incorporated some type of hydroelectric unit in one of the gates to provide power during an emergency such as a nuclear explosion or fallout catastrophe. Green civil defense drums were in abundance, identified by the CD insignia on the top and front of the containers. As the captives stepped off the last step, they saw that the bunker was equipped with electrical equipment and gauges, useless since unlimited power was a luxury that was lost to Armageddon. Hero noticed a large green-and-white sign that read, "Air Vent Gallery." He did not understand the relevance of the sign but was sure he did not care, except when he turned back around to see what was before him, something caught his eye. At the west end of the chamber, nearest the far end of the dam, he noticed that workbenches and toolboxes consumed much of the floor space.

As the soldiers forced them to make a turn onto another descending stairway, Jim noticed that there were a number of tall, gray metal lockers at the forward east end of the galley. Their captors stopped to deposit their firearms into them. The stairs took them to the second floor, which was designated inspection galley. The younger veteran did not have a clue what was inspected, or why, before the END but did notice it contained large living quarters at the eastern end, obviously the troopers'. Midway toward the west end was a smaller makeshift quarters, and at the farthest end were chains and hardware of all types.

Down another flight of stairs put them onto a floor designated as operations galley. This floor was completely different from the others they had passed. The staircase they had just descended was attached to the east end of the dam, providing a view from that end of the dam's interior to the other at the west end. The first thing that came into view were huge round cement tubes. Hundreds of gallons of water rushing through them echoed within the chamber. Greenish water leaking and dripping from cracks and fissures of the ductwork puddled on the concrete floor. Numerous attempts to correct the imperfections proved futile if the diverse patchwork was any indication. However, shouts and banging emanating from the far end of the floor caught the ears of the four teammates. Mackenzie was visibly shaken.

"That's right, bitch," Sheldon hissed as they passed the detention center on their way to the room at the farthest end where the captives were held. "Home sweet home! Bet you thought that the big dumb bastard was gonna save you from another gangbang. Surprise, surprise! Ha ha ha."

"Fuck you!" Mackenzie screamed at Sheldon.

"My plans exactly," the soldier concurred.

Hero spun around and put his fist into the joker's mouth. Mason, the trooper who was following behind Sheldon, beat the quarterback to the cold cement floor with the butt of his rifle. Jim then attacked Mason. Unfortunately, another soldier, Vidman, quickly struck Jim from behind. Mountain Man then began strangling Vidman. Full automatic gunfire erupted into the ceiling above them, sending shards of concrete, lead, and copper raining down upon them.

"That's enough!" Wooten, a short, stocky soldier screamed above the din of gunfire and ricocheting bullets, bringing the melee to a halt. Expended brass continued to make their tingling sound for a brief instant. "You motherfuckers, stop this shit before I kill you all! If the three of you sons-a-bitches weren't so valuable as slaves at barter town, I'd just as soon drop you here and now. And you, bitch, you're sure to be just as good a fuck, even with a few rounds in an arm or leg."

The four soldiers continued their escort toward the hostage room. Fifty feet from the door, two men in civilian clothes exited the room—Sam and Butch—pistols hanging at their hips.

"Hey, where'd you guys find such good slash around here?" Butch said with a sneer.

"Don't you worry about her. She's too good for you hillbillies." Wooten insisted.

"Fuck you!" Sam exclaimed. "What about these other three? Barter town?"

"Yup, same place you took that other guy last week," Wooten confirmed.

"I'm here to tell you, the bitch'll make for some good tradin' material," Butch chimed in.

"No fucking way! Young stuff is getting too hard to come by anymore. At least good stuff. Those two old broads we threw into the lake weren't worth the food it took to keep them!" Vidman chimed in.

Mackenzie visibly shuddered. If ever she felt like a slab of meat, listening to this conversation did so. The thought that she was no more than a living sex doll made her sick to her stomach. Even though the zipper to her camo fatigues was as high as possible, the young girl attempted to pull it tighter while wrapping her left arm around herself. "My love, where are you?" she whispered.

"No matter, these three clowns ought to bring almost as much as the scientist."

"What?" Mackenzie shrieked.

"Oh, that's right," Wooten chimed in. "If I remember correctly, he's your old man."

Like a smaller, more feminine version of the Angel of Death, the young blonde stormed the troopers escorting them. She cared little for herself or the fact that they were armed. Mackenzie slugged, clawed, bit, kicked, and scratched like a demon possessed. She kicked two of the troopers in the balls, dropping them to their knees as they screamed in agony.

Her three companions were tempted several times to get involved in the fray but realized it would mean certain death as there were twenty some armed soldiers plus Butch and Sam still within the confines of the facility. With the death of their leader, they knew they would have to wait until the perfect time to make an escape.

Their escorts managed to restrain the blonde hellcat after suffering a variety of injuries. Sheldon, one of the soldiers to get kicked in the groin, swore an oath that if he was able to ever get it up again, he would show her what real genital pain was like.

As the four teammates hesitantly approached the door to the makeshift hostage room, they found a foot in the small of their backs forcing them inside. The hostage room, as Mason had called it, was a piecework of office dividers attached together by nuts, bolts, bars, chains, and sheet metal from electrical panels. Despite the slipshod construction, the room seemed very stout. A conventional metal door and frame served as the portal. The teammates found themselves surrounded by five other captives. Mackenzie recognized all of them as they did her as well. Her three companions were strangers to all.

Before introducing each other, Mackenzie took stock of the captives. Most striking was Mandy, the twelve-year-old dark-haired brown-eyed preteen. In the month spanning the young blondes escape and return, what was once an angelic countenance on the beautiful child had been replaced by the look of a simple dimwit. She stank of rotten semen and dried blood. Drool ran down both corners of her mouth onto her exposed premature breasts. In fact, Mackenzie became aware that all the women were naked from the waist up.

Because Mackenzie had studied young Mandy's condition from her head down and followed the trail of the girl's saliva from her breasts to her stomach, the feminine team member recoiled in horror. Poor Mandy was obviously pregnant, viciously impregnated by her heartless captors. The little girl did not have a clue regarding the changes to her body or what would happen when the baby came to term.

Depending on what they were wearing when the attack came, the bottom halves of the females were attired in either very short makeshift dresses or shorts that once had been slacks.

Standing behind Mandy was her mother, Stacy. Stacy looked as if she had been beaten every day. She was unrecognizable except to those who suffered the daily brutality along with her. The odor was almost as strong as that of her daughter. In fact, all the women had the same stench. It permeated the room, if not the entire floor.

On the opposite side of the room stood twenty-three-year-old Melissa, wearing nothing but a smile and short shorts. Mackenzie had always taken her for a clueless sex addict, realizing that the insatiable girl did not enjoy her captivity, necessarily, but came to the conclusion long ago that if there were death and disease outside the facility, she would choose the safety of the dam even if it meant entertaining the troops on a daily basis.

The other four were men. All had a look of horror that Mackenzie had been recaptured, knowing what horrible abuse was in store for her. Their exact ages were unknown. They were all dressed in tattered and raggedy civilian clothes. All had overly long hair and beards, not having access to razors and scissors unlike their captors but guessed Steve's age was around twenty-seven and slight of build. Braiden appeared to be thirty years old with a medium build. Jason was about thirty-five and slightly heavy, although he looked a lot heavier before her escape. The final captive was Jordan, who seemed to be about forty-one. He possessed a stout build, muscular, apparently having taken very good care of himself.

All the captives rushed to reacquaint themselves with Mackenzie except for Mandy who had to be ushered forward by her mother. The young blonde introduced her team to each of the captives and acquainted her teammates with the captives.

"Honey, why in God's name did you return to his hellhole?" Melissa was the first to break the ice. "I can tell you, from the venom that came out of the soldiers' mouth when they found out you had escaped, it's going to make your first stay here look like a picnic!"

"Melissa, please, spare me the details," Mackenzie pleaded, silently saying a prayer for Angel's safety. "I came back to rescue my father but heard he isn't here. Is that true?"

Jordan spoke up. "That's true, Mac. The sons a bitches took him to some barter town somewhere and traded him for tons of food. There's two idiots who drive a white three-quarter-ton pickup truck. They are the middlemen who do the running and trading. The soldiers didn't have much use for an engineer, but evidently, someone out there does.

Stacy chimed in, "Did you four seriously think you could defeat twenty-four heavily armed soldiers?"

The beautiful blonde did not want to give away Angel's presence or who he was or even the fact that he may be dead. "Without saying too much, Stace, all I can say is that it seemed like a good idea at the time."

"What now?" Jim asked of Mackenzie.

Pulling the junior commando into a corner away from the others, the blue-eyed girl whispered into Jim's ear, "Is there a chance that Angel survived? Please be honest!"

"Mac, I've known the big guy to have gotten out of some pretty bad scrapes. But, honey"—Jim pulled the distraught girl into his chest—"given the number of bullets that were fired at him, taking a hundred and twenty foot dive into the lake, and the horrendous suction of the intake gates… Now lake monsters? I'm praying right along with you, but to be quite honest, it doesn't look good."

*****

When Angel was certain the troopers had given him up for dead and almost out of breath, he cautiously rose to the surface and took several good lungs full of air, carefully monitoring the road deck up above for signs of activity. When he was sure it was safe and after recovering his lungs, the warrior began making his way toward the east bank. He had only swam a few yards when something caught his lower right leg just above the ankle. Thinking he had become entangled in brush or tree limbs, the commando stuck his head into the water so he could extract himself from the debris.

Angel was startled to find himself face-to-face with a serpent from hell, its maw clamped tight around his leg. What the hell? He struck the demon squarely between the eyes. He may as well have kissed the horror as it had absolutely no effect on the creature. As near as he could tell, it greatly resembled the Loch Ness monster. Its head resembled that of a serpent, its long neck faded away into the dark brackish water that obscured whatever lay beyond.

In the brief instant it took to the legionnaire to assess the danger, all the pieces of the puzzle had come together. Huge lizard-like dinosaurs wandered the countryside since the END. Their tracks were in abundance surrounding his parents' home where they sheltered themselves during the nuclear-biohazardous siege. Rainfall washed the fallout into gullies, streams, rivers, and finally, lakes. It made sense that whatever was happening on a genetic level with land creatures and vegetation would also affect the aquatic life similarly. He also wondered what effect the lake water would have on his well-being.

The tribal leader wasted no more time considering the implications and burst into action. Securing his knives from their sheaths, the combatant tore into the monster, allowing no quarter. He stabbed the monster about the face and eyes, taking both of the glowing red orbs. The pressure around the titan's leg had greatly intensified. Angel hoped his heavy boots proved impervious to the creature's sharp teeth. Sightless, the denizen of the deep not only refused to back off from its attack but also dragged the pair deeper into the lake. Around and around, the duo spun as they clashed for life and death. The beast threatened to pull the juggernaut's leg out of its socket. Angel knew he was unable to hold his breath much longer, the fight consuming most of his air. The commando retracted his leg, pulling himself in as tightly to the creature as he could get. With the eleven-inch KA-BAR in his right hand, Angel stabbed the demon in the neck, then sliced downward with all his might, nearly severing the head from its body. The beast immediately released the hold it had on the titan's leg and began thrashing and making a gurgling sound as it drowned and bled out into a watery grave.

Rapidly swimming to the surface, Angel allowed himself to draw a few cool breaths of air before continuing toward the bank. As he reached the muddy soil and clambered up to dry land, the embattled warrior took stock of his wounds. He had lost a lot of blood from the bullet to his left side. His butt cheek hurt terribly despite his decision to sit down for a few minutes. His arms and legs scraped and stung from the hits both above and below the surface of the water. Peeling off his boots, he was somewhat pleased to find other than some shallow scrapes and cuts, his leg was largely unmolested, although sure to require disinfectant and bandages.

The warrior knew he had to get to the Panther, take care of himself, and obtain weapons and supplies, before returning to save his love. *There it is then*, he thought to himself. *I've finally said it! My love.* At that admission, the commando jumped up and verbalized it. "I have got to go and save the woman I love. I refuse to let you down. I made a promise not to let you down, and here I dally. I'm coming, sweetheart!"

*****

Mackenzie had been telling the other captives of the horrors that abounded outside the dam and of her exploits after she had escaped. She deliberately withheld any mention of Angel in the event that he was still alive and planning a rescue. Suddenly, the door to the facility burst open, slamming into the wall behind her.

"So, bitch! Welcome back!"

Mackenzie immediately recognized the gravelly, harsh voice. Lieutenant Hardman. She immediately spun to face him. The leader of the small platoon assigned to the dam operations was an imposing figure to say the least. He stood six foot four inches and possessed a very muscular build. Instead of the digital camo worn by his men, his camo fatigues were of the newer stealth style. They literally blended with every color and every background.

"I would tell you to go fuck off, but I don't want to give you any encouragement," the young woman explained.

Hardman walked up to Mackenzie and backhanded her across the face, drawing blood from her right cheek.

Her three comrades bristled, then steeled themselves to counterattack. A handgun that suddenly materialized in the lieutenant's hand arrested their intentions.

"Always the gentleman, I still see," the girl spat. Despite being a captive of these men before, the blue-eyed blonde could not believe her predicament. Since the holocaust, she wondered where all the good men had gone. Where was her God? Did he perish as well?

"If I want any of your lip, I'll scrape it off of my zipper! I want information from you, and I want it now before I give you a left cheek to match the right."

"You'll have to torture me first," Mackenzie assured.

"Oh, never fear. No matter the outcome, torture is certainly part of the protocol. Perhaps I might convince you by shooting one of your teammates." Hardman raised his pistol and pointed it at Mountain Man's head.

"Lucky for you, you didn't point it at the clown over there," the girl said with sarcasm, indicating the football player.

The quarterback glared at Mackenzie, mouthing the words, "What the fuck?"

"Okay, what do you want to know?"

"Where did you come across these yokels, and why did you come back?"

Mackenzie looked the lieutenant squarely in the eye. "There's a barter town north east of here."

"I know of it. We trade there occasionally. Go on."

Continuing straight-faced, the girl realized she had just gleaned valuable information from the lieutenant. "I was starving and cold when I stumbled into that encampment. I ran across these three. I explained that my father was a prisoner here and if they helped me rescue him that I would be their slave girl! That I would do anything they wanted me to do for as long as they wanted me."

"Why should they trust you?" Hardman wanted to know.

"They have the guns. What could one helpless female do against those odds?"

"Why didn't they just take you and be done with it?" the lieutenant countered.

"Because I explained to them that besides a number of potential male slaves, there were women here as well. One was a sex-addicted whore who was happy to do anything for a meal. The guy you're covering with your pistol wants her, kinky son of a bitch. The clown over there wants the twelve-year old. The sick bastard! I wouldn't repeat the things that he said he would do to her."

"What about the tall one? What is in it for him, besides you, of course?"

"Him? Ha ha." Mackenzie laughed before noticing that Hardman was becoming a hard man because of all the talk. "The big cissy is gay! He wants one of the male captives for himself."

Her three companions were staring at the young liar intensely. Zechariah could not believe the trash that was coming out of the young girl's mouth. Jim was in awe of her storytelling ability, and Hero had a hard time understanding how Mackenzie would embarrass her friends to that depth.

"Ah, so the big pussy likes men, does he? Well, we have a few here who would love to play with him. Ha ha ha, before we trade him to a special customer of ours."

"Mac!" Jim cried out.

"Enough!" Lieutenant Hardman uttered. "Guards, take this bitch out of here! Strip her, cleanse her, especially the genital areas, and dress her appropriately, if you know what I mean." As he exited the door behind his guards, Hardman turned and pointed at the three team members, adding, "So you thought you would help this useless bitch mount an attack just to rescue her father? You incompetent fools will learn the error of your ways. It will not be pretty, I might add."

The teammates looked upon one another with forlorn countenances, wondering what terrible fate awaited them.

*****

Angel made it back to the maintenance building that housed their transportation just after eleven o'clock. Normally the titan would have run the distance without stopping, but his injuries were getting the best of him. Beside the blood loss, contamination by the toxic water had infected every wound. His left leg where the beast bit him was sore and swollen. The bionuclear immersion hampered his natural recuperative ability.

Over the course of several hours and the application of the first aid supplies out of one of the ambulances, the veteran was able to clean, disinfect, and suture every cut, scratch, and bullet wound on his body. The only wound he could not stitch was that on his buttock. He used a surgical suture stapler to close that gash the best he could, then applied gauze and tape to finish the job. He discarded his wet and shredded camo coveralls for a fresh replacement.

The tribal leader then fished through the food reserves. It had been fifteen hours since he had eaten and rested. If he were going to mount a successful raid on the dam, he needed to sustain himself and get some desperately needed R&R. Angel took the opportunity to devise a plan. He would wait for the cover of darkness, on the slim chance there were lookouts on surveil, and then rappel down the back side of the facility on the western end. Once in place, a maintenance hatch that led to the electric generator bay would allow access to the inside of the dam. He would then disable production of electricity and put the facility in total darkness. Using night vision goggles, he would stand an excellent chance of freeing his friends. He was certain that night vision was not available to the soldiers.

The warrior made a meal of MREs and water. Not pleasing but nourishment just the same. He then collected his weapons and night vision from the Panther, as well as rappelling line, harness, carabineers, and other necessary equipment. He would leave while there was enough daylight to arrive at the facility. Once dark, his strategy was to cross the base to the other side of the dam, climb the embankment, then onto the road deck that was on the western side of the dam. From there he would rappel down the back face and work his way inside. The warrior knew there were some things he would have to work out once he was in the facility, and that meant there was an element of chance involved. One such example that came to mind was he had never witnessed anyone patrolling the lowest section, the grout galley, nor the generator bay during his assignments. Was it possible they remained unguarded? Yes! Was it likely? Hope so! He knew he would have to be his warrior best and strive for success.

*****

Mackenzie wanted to cry like a baby as she sat on the edge of a bed in the hostage room. But she refused to give Hardman and the rest of his ilk that satisfaction. "Angel, my love. Where are you? Did you forget your promise to me? I know you are out there."

The beautiful girl took stock of her surroundings. If she was not depressed over her captivity, she was surely disappointed over the clothing they made available to her. It was a fresh camo fatigue uniform. However, his set had been heavily modified. The legs were cut high on the hips like French bikini panties. The exception was the crotch, cut horizontally at the seam in order to make flaps that offered easy access to her female parts. In addition, it was altered short at the waist well below her navel, displaying her athletic torso. Rather than having her appear topless, a halter top cut low and scooped out so as to reveal nearly all her breasts but for the nipples. For that, the young blonde was grateful, except for the fact that the constant fifty-eight-degree temperature of the cold facility lent the appearance she was in a constant state of arousal.

During the alterations, the filthy bastards all but had their way with her as they constantly undressed and redressed her as they worked to construct the garment. Their hands roamed every square inch of her body, molesting and abusing as they pretended to make changes and adjustments to the material. When they had finished the task, they brought Hardman in for his approval. After a minute of touching, feeling, and peeking, the lieutenant swiftly grasped Mackenzie's right hand before she knew what was happening and cupped it around his erect organ. The blonde slapped him across the face with her other hand hard enough to draw blood.

"You little slut!" Hardman screamed. "All of us will have our turn with you tonight. In fact, you will probably beg us to kill you before we are done. However, don't worry. We will make sure that doesn't happen. Your life will be hell as you continue to pleasure us for a long time to come."

The female team member was deeply ashamed, being on display as she was. The first half hour after arriving in the hostage room, she kept as much of her exposed breasts draped with one arm while the other hand covered her genitalia. Her arms growing tired and unable to keep her attempt at modesty any longer, the twenty-year-old resigned her efforts to do so. Her teammates as well as the other men in the room tried to avert their eyes but found it nearly impossible. All but Mountain Man would occasionally admire her beauty as he stood facing the opposite wall.

The beautiful team member wanted out of that hellhole before anything else happened to her. She walked to the farthest end of the room where the men had conspicuously gathered at the west wall. "Look, guys, I've been thinking—"

Suddenly the door to the room burst open. Vincent, the ugliest soldier in the ranks, strode in with a look of depraved need etched on his face. Mackenzie was sure he had come for her, as did all the other captives. She remembered the pervert well. When he was not raping, he was masturbating to the rape.

In an effort to break up their gathering and make it appear random, Jordan marched over to the soldier. "What do you want? Get the hell out of here!"

Vincent drew his pistol and shoved it into Jordan's face. "Just one more word, say it, just one more, and I'll blow your fucking head off. Where is she? Where's the little bitch?"

Mackenzie, consigned to her fate, and fearing for Jordan's life, approached the trooper. "Okay, you ugly little jerk, let's get this over with."

"Not you, you fucking whore. No one is going to have you until the lieutenant does. He hates sloppy seconds. Or should I say, sloppy twenty-fourths. I'm looking for the *little* bitch."

"No, please don't." Mandy's mom, Stacy, pleaded from a bed near the north wall. Standing from her seated position on the bed, she approached the soldier and continued. "Look what you have done to my little one," pointing to the drooling youngster who was counting her fingers. "Look at her, you son of a bitch!"

Vincent slapped the grieving mother across her face with the barrel of his gun. "Shut the hell up, woman! I don't know why we even keep you around, except as backup. We ought to throw you into the lake with the other two hags and be done with you." The trooper looked at the slobbering little girl who had begun silently reciting the "piggies" on her toes. "Over here, bitch!" Pointing his weapon at the captives one at a time, "You even think about getting in the way and the *little* whore is the first to die."

Mandy got off the bed and dutifully, robotically, walked toward the officer. Jim momentarily debated attacking Vincent and snapping his neck. If the trooper got off a shot and killed poor Mandy, the junior commando debated, might she be better off? Just as Jim made the decision to act, another thought stayed his response: he did not want Stacy to see her little angel getting her head blown off right in front of her.

As Vincent and Mandy left the room walking hand in hand like a pair of lovers, Mackenzie had a complete meltdown. She wailed and cursed, questioning God, questioning why, in a facility full of men, was there not one hero in the bunch who would come to the twelve-year-old's rescue. Silently, she doubted Angel's ability to survive the lake and rescue her and the rest of the captives. Concerned for her mental state, her teammates tried to comfort and reassure the distraught girl. The other four men, Stacy, and even Melissa attempted to comfort her, but Mackenzie was inconsolable. She ran to one of the beds and flopped down face-first, covering her head with a pillow, moaning unintelligibly.

After thirty minutes, Mackenzie fell into a much-needed deep sleep. Throughout the three hours she slept, the young blonde tossed and turned, dreaming of Angel, her hero who would rescue her. Several times, she called out his name. At one point, she awoke to the sound of something falling into the bed next to her. Turning her head to the right to determine the source of the commotion, the feminine team member realized it had been Vincent returning Mandy's poor abused body to her bunk. The knowledge sent the girl into another downward spiral and into a trauma-induced slumber.

CHAPTER 9

One-half hour before nightfall, the legionnaire collected his gear and headed out. Nourished, hydrated, and rested, he felt much better, although his wounds were still painful despite the extensive triage. He kept twenty yards well into the woods to avoid detection from possible passersby. As he could see the dam in the distance, Angel corrected his trajectory to cross the spillway that would take him to the far west side of the facility. That path dictated he travel deeper into the woods and, given the waning sunlight, resulted in near-nocturnal conditions.

As Angel negotiated a thicket of trees and seemingly prehistoric fauna, he noticed the atmosphere around him suddenly went quiet. The experienced veteran took that as a bad sign. Carefully moving through the brush, his senses on high alert, Angel began to feel as if he were walking through quicksand. He remembered as a young boy he would occasionally have dreams of being unable to run from danger, as if he were in quicksand. So similar was the feeling that he had to check to ensure that it was not the case. He certainly knew he was not dreaming. Confused, he pressed on. Next, it appeared that objects were rising from the ground and floating skyward. Small stones, pieces of bark, and bits of debris seemed to be defying gravity. The tribal leader began to question his sanity or blame it on the possible contamination of his wounds by the corroded lake water, when he spied what looked like a tail protruding from the other side of a tree ten yards distant.

Angel's senses were raw as he felt compelled to investigate the phenomenon. He thought it appeared to be the tail of a devil. Wonder rather than apprehension consumed him. Trudging forward, he found it was becoming increasingly difficult to move his feet. Suddenly, jumping out from behind a large tree in front of him was what could only be described as a...parsickle!

Angel found it impossible to advance any farther. The debris rising from the ground continued to escalate. It was only then that the strapping commando realized the phenomena was associated with the arrival of the creature, and it was either a manifestation projected into the warrior's mind or the demon was in possession of some degree of mental power or telekinesis, as alluded to by Mountain Man.

Realizing he was under the spell of this apparition, which had accounted for his lack of mental acuity and fight reflex, all the veteran of WWIII could do was stare into the black demonic eyes of the creature. His rifle slid off his right shoulder and clattered uselessly to the ground.

As the veteran of WWIII was drawn into those ebony evil eyes, he saw a dark, gruesome world filled with hate, hate for its own kind and hate for its miserable existence. A world where the sun never shone, a world where life had no value, a world without hope. A godless world, a world without hope, a world without compassion.

Angel attempted to study the miscreant head to toe. However, he was unable to avert his eyes from those of the parsickle. Using his peripheral vision, the juggernaut could verify the description that both Mountain Man and Hero described. Its coat of fur was exceedingly coarse and blacker than black. It appeared to have a black mane. The creature was as large as he was. Maybe larger, maybe...more powerful? It possessed a devilish countenance. The evil smile on its face revealed sharp teeth but oddly no incisors as he had expected. From his height and proximity to the beast, Angel could not verify cloven hooves but had already witnessed its spear-tipped tail. It did indeed have claws on the upper legs; long tapered nails extended three inches from its paws.

The parsickle began communicating with Angel, although it did not involve speech, exactly. It was closer to what the titan regarded as telepathy.

"Through your folly, you slow-witted humans have destroyed the paradise given you by your creator. Now we will claim the lives of the few who survive."

Angel carefully guarded his thoughts. He did not know if a response to the creature needed to be deliberate or if it could understand mere contemplation. "Who are you?" Angel wanted to know. "What manner of creature are you? Are you of this world or elsewhere?"

"Puny human, before I take your pitiful life, I will elaborate to a small degree. I doubt you will understand as you are a dim-witted species. Your kind lives in a four-dimensional world. Height, width, depth, and time. Your species suspect there may be as many as ten. Stupid humans, there are hundreds. I am from one such domain. We are one of the very few species that are able to transcend dimensions at will. The sapient creatures of your domain were blessed with the finest dimension your creator could envision. Now though your world is dying, it is far better than that of the others, except for the dimension you refer to as heaven."

Angel fully understood what this parsickle was relating to him. He was having a difficult time accepting the fate of the human race. He needed to buy more time in order to fashion a retaliation to this being. "We have been referring to you as parsickle. What do you call yourselves?"

"You would not understand nor be able to pronounce the name of our race. Parsickle will suffice. Enough of this idle banter! Prepare to meet your maker, *human!*" The parsickle communicated the last word as if it were vulgar.

"Very well then," Angel communicated to the parsickle. "Answer a simple question for me if you will. Are you mortal? Can you bleed?"

The being exhaled an audible laugh that sounded like it came from the inside of a tomb, exposing two complete rows of sharp pointed teeth as he did so. "If you are asking me if I can die," the parsickle began, grasping the tribe leader by his coveralls in its right paw and raising him off the ground, "the answer is yes. But not at the hands of such as you!" Another laugh punctuated his statement.

As the titan engaged the parsickle, hoping the distraction would ease the creature's power over him, he began to test his muscle reflex and noticed that the debris had stopped rising but slowly falling to the ground. Angel determined that, indeed, the parsickle could not carry a conversation while holding him completely powerless at the same time.

Angel made one final attempt to distract the devilish beast. "Then before you kill me, indulge me just one more question. Are you the creature our species refers to as the devil?"

Again, the parsickle rent the air with a terrible laugh more powerful than the first.

The strapping commando took that opportunity to plunge an eleven-inch blade into the creature's chest. Oily and thick, putrid black fluid spurted out of the wound and covered the forest floor, much of it saturating Angel's overalls.

The miscreant verbally screamed what sounded like, "What?" before dropping Angel on his feet. Before the parsickle could recover, the fighting man plunged the ten-inch stiletto he retrieved from his left boot into the right eye of the screaming beast. "No!" the parsickle howled as it lunged toward the human that had ruined its eye. The brute lashed out with its sharp claws, intent on slaying the knife-wielding menace before it.

The warrior extracted the KA-BAR from the chest of the parsickle as he blocked and parried every assault the creature attempted. When Angel found the opening he was looking for, the strapping commando propelled his closed fist, still clenching the knife, squarely into the face of the miscreant, knocking the creature to the ground. Never breaking stride, the elite killing machine leaped upon the parsickle, the eleven-inch KA-BAR in both fists and repeatedly stabbed the miscreant in the chest. Blood flew in all directions with every thrust and every slash of the edged weapon. The Angel of Death never relented from his savage attack upon the beast, even as it lay convulsing and dying.

"You…have…killed me. Never…has…a…such…as…you, *human*…slain one…of…of…"

The parsickle lay dead at the commando's knees. He reached out to remove the stiletto from its ruined eye. As he did so, the miscreant…vaporized right before him. On one hand, the legionnaire surmised, that would explain why no trace of these creatures exist. On the other, according to the parsickle, no human had ever slain one before. Making a mental note of the tactic he employed to eliminate the devilish beast, Angel checked the watch on his left wrist, thinking it had grown very dark during the half hour of his confrontation, only to find four hours had passed. Three and a half of those he could not account for. Obviously, the parsickle from another domain possessed the ability to alter space and time. Perhaps, the warrior concluded, he had spent more time in the demon's dimension than he knew. The strange occurrence unnerved him. He was also loath to comprehend what the parsickle had learned about him and his teammates, perhaps his entire species.

Collecting and sheathing his weapons, Angel prayed that the delay did not interfere with his plans of rescuing his team.

Fifteen minutes later, the titan found himself traversing the shallow spillway that would give him access to the west end of the dam. Although it was dark, the warrior made every effort to elude detection in the event someone was patrolling the road deck above. He spent a few minutes surveying the structure and surrounding area with his night vision to ensure there were no surprises awaiting him and to determine the exact location of the maintenance access. When he was satisfied the coast was clear, the battle-hardened vet climbed the west bank and on to the far side of the deck.

Creeping eastward along the road deck, the titan paced the distance to where the westward maintenance access was located. The dam had six access portals located in the lowest section, designated the grout gallery. They were spaced evenly east to west and designed to allow access to the facility in the event of a catastrophe within. Heavy and as shielded and as the main entrance above, they were difficult to access by one man on the end of a rope. Angel chose to enter the farthest from the main entrance, the hub of activity, which normally was the most desolate area of the installation.

The hulking brute secured his rappelling line to a rail support and threw the line out and over. He wasted no time securing his harness and attaching the hardware. Normally, he would descend a line free of the customary safety devices, but given the burden of equipment he was carrying and the fact that he had to manipulate the access controls, the bearded hulk was taking no chances, given the magnitude of the mission.

After rappelling the roughly 210 feet to the maintenance access portal, the goliath tied off his line and began to operate the levers and lock wheel that would allow him access. Initially, the door was tight and difficult to swing outward. It creaked loudly on rusty hinges that probably had not been in service since the dam was constructed. Given that the concrete was three feet thick, it allowed him to squat on the inside ledge in order to close and secure the portal. He hoped the screeching of the door had not given away his entry, although as desolate as the grout gallery was, he was certain it had not.

A steel ladder was secured to the inside wall, but the titan made the six-foot drop to the floor effortlessly. He carefully ascended the six-foot-wide stairwell at the west end of the installation, which exactly mirrored those of the east side. As quietly as possible, Angel made his way to the next level above, the operations gallery. The warrior knew from personal experience and observation that the west staircase saw little use, if any, as evidenced by the deep layer of dust on the handrails.

*****

When Mackenzie finally came around again, she found that meals had been prepared for the captives. She refused to eat the food consisting of some type of beans, civil defense rations, and bottled water. Jim approached the twenty-year-old still lying in her bunk and, after a difficult time, convinced her to eat. Without going into particular detail, he assured her that whatever happened next, she would need to keep her strength up. Jim was concerned about what lay in store for the scantily clad girl. The young blonde assumed Jim was alluding to an impending rescue by her love. Either way, the junior commando was relieved that Mackenzie took his advice.

"Jim, we started to speak about this earlier. Do you see any way out of this?"

"Mac, I just don't know. While you were out, the others and myself put our heads together to determine just that. This is what we determined: as makeshift as it appears, we're locked in a very secure chamber. There are twenty-six guards. That includes Butch and Sam. It would be great if they were stationed in one spot, but we don't know that. They could be scattered throughout the entire dam. That means that any moment in time, we could have multiple battles on our hands. We can be surrounded at any time and attacked from multiple angles. These guys are heavily armed. We know where our weapons are stored, but they are next to impossible to access? Finally, we would have to pull this off with the weight of eleven targets, all civilians except for me, and possibly you given your prior experience. On one hand, I wish the big guy was here. I'm sure he would know what to do. On the other, I'm glad he's not."

"I have to ask you, Jim, how do you mean that?"

"What do you mean? How do you think I *mean* it?"

"Jim, somehow, someway, somewhere, I know Angel is alive!"

"Mac, I think you're—"

"Jim, damn it! I can't explain it. I don't know how I know. But trust me, I know he's alive!"

"Oh, okay, Mac, if that's—"

"Jim! Damn it! Jim! Look at me. Do I look insane?" the beautiful blonde stated with a crazed expression on her face. "I am telling you! Not only is my hero still alive, but I strongly believe he is somewhere in this facility! Jim, I can feel his approach like a fire in my blood!"

The junior combatant carefully listened to the girl's words. He knew she came off as unhinged, but the power of her words tended to convince him. In addition to what the girl in front of him was espousing, no one knew the strapping colossus better than he did. If anyone could have overcome the misfortune of being shot, surviving an impossible dive, vacuum of the water intake, and yes, even a measly old monster, it would be he, the Angel of Death!

As the younger commando was consoling the twenty-year-old girl, one of the soldiers burst into the room, pistol drawn. A nameplate, "Charles," was attached to his uniform. "Get the hell off of that bitch, you dumbass. She's coming with me." The trooper wasted no time in dragging the girl up off her bunk and securing her hands behind her back. "If I find that you have been messing with that," the soldier continued, "I'll toss you into the lake myself!"

"Let me go!" Mackenzie screamed as she struggled against her captor. "Where are you taking me?"

"Not far," Charles replied. "Just up ahead to the detention center."

"The torture chamber, you mean."

"Torture for you, I'm sure. But we're going to have a ball."

The young blonde began shaking and convulsing, knowing what was in store for her. She felt faint and began to crumple.

"Oh no, ya don't, whore! You're not getting out of this by playing sick. Hell, we'll screw that sweet little ass awake or passed out."

Just then, a feeling of calm struck Mackenzie like a lightning bolt. Her love, she could feel his presence nearby. She did not know how or why the commando managed to survive and return to save her but was certain she was not hallucinating. The beautiful captive could feel his loving eyes on her, boring into her soul. *I'm here, my love. Please save me!* she thought to herself. With that, Mackenzie straightened and composed herself. She knew it would not be long until she would be swept up into his muscular arms, pulled into his protective embrace.

"That's my girl," Charles exclaimed. "I can see you are as eager for it as we are to give it to you." The trooper reached out and peeled back the top of the captive's outfit, revealing the entirety of Mackenzie's left breast.

"That's right, shithead! Do your worst because I swear to God, I'm going to watch you die! I will have the biggest smile on my face when it happens. It will be the last thing you will ever see!"

Charles's initial reflex was to punch the girl in the nose. He realized, however, that Hardman would have him killed for destroying her beautiful face, so he opted to kick her in the butt, so hard it brought her to her knees. "Get up, bitch," the soldier spat. "I'm not going to drag you the rest of the way. I'm saving all of my strength for my turn with you."

"Never happen," Mackenzie assured.

"You seem awfully sure of yourself for a stupid piece of ass whore who doesn't mean shit to the world."

"You'll get yours, I promise."

"What? You going to kill all of us? After we're done with you sweet cheeks, you'll be begging us to kill you. Unfortunately, peace for you isn't going to come that easy."

*****

At the top of the landing, the veteran of WWIII crouched low, conforming his body to the steps of the stairs. He listened intently for any sound that would reveal enemy activity. He heard men's cursing, laughter, and vulgar references to female body parts and sex acts. They came across as being very drunk. Angel silently chastised himself for allowing Mackenzie to get caught up in the debauchery and depravity of the place. He was enraged at the thought that it was her second confinement within the hellhole. He would see to it that none of her captors would survive his fury. As he studied the activity, the commando saw a soldier approach some sort of makeshift chamber that had not been there during his last visit, while a larger, similarly constructed room lay beyond. Curious, he continued to watch as the trooper exited the room, pulling something or someone behind him.

Dear Lord, the tribal leader thought to himself. It was Mackenzie. Being taken against her will! The striking beauty, garbed in the most obscene outfit the veteran had ever seen, was dressed in such a way that displayed almost every inch of her feminine anatomy. Angel continued to watch, debating what he should do. His animal instincts dictated that he race over and separate the soldier's head from his shoulders. However, he knew he had to let calm prevail, or else many lives would be in jeopardy. The restraint he demonstrated was one of the most difficult things the warrior ever had to endure. The legionnaire watched helplessly as his girl was taken away, hands bound behind her back, screaming and shouting, while the trooper cursed, pulled, and kicked the young girl along their route.

In order for his mission to be successful, Angel had to first reconnoiter the facility, determine the location of the enemy as well as his teammates, and possibly ascertain the location of their firearms. The commando crept up the next set of steps to arrive at the inspection gallery. Staying low, Angel did not observe movement or sound despite the fact that the barracks were on this level near the east end. The ultimate engine of death quietly dashed toward the barracks using various components and electronic equipment to conceal himself should anyone suddenly venture out of the room unannounced. Sprinting in and out of cover in such fashion, the commando made his way toward the troopers' sleeping quarters. Wishing to avoid a confrontation before he could free his friends, the commando approached the entrance from an acute angle, then checked to ensure no one was near the opening. When all seemed safe, he continued to the east staircase and up to the air vent gallery. Employing the same strategy as before, he conformed to the stair steps until he was certain the floor was safe.

The first thing that caught Angel's attention was a row of gray six-foot-high standard-gear metal lockers. They were twenty-four inches wide, twenty-four inches deep, and seemed a likely place to store his team's firearms and munitions. Starting at the east end of the row, the warrior quietly raised the locking handle and looked inside. Nothing! Knowing that it would require two or three to hold the tribe's equipment, Angel jumped three lockers at a time. In locker number 4, he found a stash of pornography. Locker number 7 revealed three cases of liquor, the top case half empty. Damn! Locker number 10, bingo! The commando recognized his team's weapons and personal effects. Backtracking to lockers 9 and 8, he found the same. Now all that was required was to free his friends.

*****

As Mackenzie was led into the detention center, she realized almost all the troopers were there, if not all of them. She made a quick count as Charles was unbinding her wrists. Twenty-six. That meant if Angel *were* in the facility, he would be free to roam unfettered. The blonde was ushered to the west wall where several tables were arranged together; a folding chair was directly beside one end.

"Okay," came a voice from the back of the room, "up on the chair and onto the stage."

Mackenzie recognized it as Hardman's. "Stage?" The young girl perused the four tables shoved together with disdain. "What do you want with me up there?" Seated in chairs that had been assembled semicircle around the tables were all the soldiers. Another table in the back next to Hardman contained beer and hard liquor. To her horror, the striking blonde also saw a bed, head first against the southern wall.

"We wish you to dance for us, of course."

"I'm sorry. I'm not worth a damn without a pole," the statuesque girl taunted.

"You'll get up on those tables and dance, or I swear I'll slaughter every one of your friends right in front of you," the lieutenant swore.

"All right," the girl agreed, knowing she had little option. "Any music, or is someone going to hum a tune?"

"Procrastination is only going to prolong the inevitable, my dear."

Mackenzie, embarrassed by her near nudity and aware of the exposure the provocative outfit offered, cautiously stepped up onto the chair, then the stage. The soldiers responded with cheers and sexual epithets. The beautiful girl was certain, of the many accomplishments of her young life, dancing to a crowd of perverted drunks was not one of them.

"Now dance," the lieutenant ordered. "Or do I have to send Vincent here up onstage to teach you?"

"Don't you dare put that sick bastard anywhere near me!"

"Then start dancing, you fucking whore," Hardman screamed. "Vidman, bring the prisoners in here one at a time and shoot them in front of this bitch!"

"Okay, okay, I'm dancing." Mackenzie had no clue what she was doing, so she began to shuffle her feet and gyrate. The crowd grew excited.

"So far so good, but I know you can do better," Hardman said before downing several swigs of a brown-colored liquid.

Mackenzie began to undulate and twerk. The throng screamed for more. The blue-eyed blonde remembered an old song of her mother's she used to listen to as a child. She loved the tune and used to sing along with it. Fifteen years later, she had a difficult time remembering all the words, but the song seemed very appropriate now. The scantily clad girl grabbed the material covering her right breast and briefly pulled it away, flashing the crowd as she did so. The soldiers went wild, clamoring for more.

"I need a hero. I'm holding out for a hero till the end of the niiiiiight." Mackenzie then flashed the other breast. The drunken mob went crazy, throwing drinks and charging the stage. "He's gotta be strong, and he's gotta be fast, and he's gotta be fresh from the fiiiiiight."

Suddenly, all the lights within the dam went out.

*****

The titan worked feverishly to sabotage the turbine generator. He had already disabled the backup batteries, so when the generator failed, the entire facility would go dark. Some of the gear he brought with him from the Panther was ten feet of cannon fuse. His plan was to wrap it multiple times around the wire going to the power regulator. The intense heat produced by the burning material would easily cut through the copper wire and crash the system. The remaining nine feet or so would allow him time to run up the one flight of stairs and lie in wait behind the room housing the captives. The fifteen to twenty minutes it would take to restore power would allow the combatant to free his men and, using his night vision, lead them to their weapons. From there it would be a battle to free Mackenzie and the remainder of the captives.

As Angel lit the fuse, he prayed that his actions were timely enough to save his love from misery and death. Once he was certain the fuse was burning properly, the legionnaire ran back up the west staircase and onto the landing. After ensuring no guards were making their rounds, he approached the outside rear panel of the room containing the captives. Curious to learn the disposition of the inhabitants, Angel lightly knocked on the wall. Afraid to press his luck any further, the goliath waited for a reply. Just as he decided no one was in a position to respond, someone whispered, "Who's there?"

Afraid to give away his identity too soon, the seasoned veteran responded, "AD." After a few seconds of muted conversation, he heard someone running to the opposite side of the wall. Angel checked the watch on his left wrist. He had about thirty seconds before the power died.

"AD, it's Jim."

"Not much time. Is there a guard present?"

"Negative. Except for Mac, all accounted for and alone. She was taken to the next room east of here."

"I know! I'm coming in!"

Angel ran to the door and unlocked it. Stepping two feet into the room, he announced, "Listen up! Any second now, the lights are going to go out. It will be as black as a coalmine at night. Everyone, take someone's hand. I have night vision and will lead you to safety. Hurry. Jim, grab the belt of my pistol." Angel began to secure the night vision to his head mount when the lights dimmed, flickered, and then went out. Shouts and curses assailed their ears.

"Now! By the time they realize backup isn't happening, we need to be on that stairwell, going up." As the group made their way toward the west staircase, the warrior added in a low voice, "They won't be able to see us, but they can hear us. Be as quiet as possible. All our lives depend on it! Pass it on."

As they began their ascent, the captives heard more cursing and confusion as the backup power supply failed to engage. Reaching the landing of the inspection gallery, the warrior's night vision incrementally began to go white. Swiveling the device on his head upward and turning it off to prevent damage, Angel realized that one by one, the captors had secured flashlights and were racing toward the staircase. The warrior gathered his charges behind him, his HK at the ready. He again signaled for silence. In a whisper, he instructed, "They are going to go down to the lowest level to investigate the malfunction. When it's clear were going up to the next level, men, that's where your weapons are stored."

When the beams cast by the flashlights disappeared into the grout gallery, the hulking brute redeployed his night vision and led his people up to the air vent gallery, then to the eastern side of the dam where the lockers were emplaced.

"Men, come forth and give me your open hands," Angel stated.

"What's the plan?" Jim asked as his older brother began slamming weapons into their open palms.

"Listen up, everyone! Before long, the power and lights will be back on. When that happens, I want all civilians, other than my people, to climb the next set of stairs and hide in the vestibule area. I want you safe and as far away from the action as possible. Do not—I repeat—do not go outside. There are creatures capable of killing you quicker than these bastards. That's an order!" A quiet mumbling of acknowledgment sanctioned the command.

"What about me?" a voice coming from somewhere behind Hero asked.

"What about you?" the fighting man demanded. Angel had no time or patience for games. "And who *the hell* are you?"

"Name's Jordan. You wanted all civilians upstairs. I'm ex-military. Marines."

"Jordan, welcome to my team. Look, men, the lights will be up shortly. Jordan, I can have Zechariah who's standing to your right loan you the use of his pistol. As we begin to eliminate these sons-a-bitches, we'll see that you get a rifle.

"Yes, sir!" the Marine barked, accompanied by a salute.

The throng remained huddled, waiting for the power to return.

"Listen, men, and be aware, once the lights come on, I expect you'll find these troopers everywhere and anywhere as they scatter to find the person or persons responsible for the sabotage. By now, they must realize their captives have escaped. Some may remain in hiding, hoping to catch one of us as we pass by their position. Also, if we fight our way that deep, be aware of the lowest gallery. It's fraught with hidden crevices."

As soon as Angel spoke those words, the lights came back on. The commando immediately secured his night vision in locker number 10 and began issuing directives. "Civilians, up the stairs and stay there until someone comes for you. Jim, you, Hero, and Mountain Man go to the west staircase and secure your side of this facility. Don't forget, some of them may attempt to ambush you from the vestibule above, so scope it out first. Also, keep track of the body count. We need to account for all twenty-six. As you know, Mac is directly under us. We'll wait at the landing below until you draw the attention of the troopers, then I'll initiate her rescue. Jordan, you stick with me. We will secure our half. Got it?"

Everyone nodded in agreement and embarked upon their mission. As Zechariah passed by the titan, he asked, nodding at the black, odoriferous stain tainting Angel's camo. "What'd ye do, change tha earl in tha 'mergency cars?"

The combatant could not help but laugh despite the urgency of the situation. Mimicking the woodsman's speech, he replied, "Kill't ma sef a Par'see'kle. Tell ye 'bout et later."

Mountain Man's eyes flew as wide as the tribe leader had ever seen them.

Angel held up his and Jordan's launch until the other three were climbing the opposite staircase. "Let's go!" Together they cautiously descended the stairs as quietly as possible, weapons at the ready in case soldiers stumbled into the stairwell.

Angel and Jordan waited several seconds to see if their counterparts ran into trouble before proceeding. Gunfire erupted in what sounded like the west vestibule, although given the size and construction of the facility, it was hard to pinpoint. In any event, the warrior took advantage of the distraction and raced toward the room the girl was in, Jordan in tow. True to his training, the fighting man approached the open doorway at an acute angle to avoid detection. When it was safe, he stealthily entered the room. What he saw made his blood boil.

Lying on her back upon a collection of tables was Mackenzie; a soldier with the nameplate Vincent had her arms pinned down over her head. The garment that had covered her breasts was unzipped and lying under her. The material around her lower torso was raised like a flap and lying on her stomach. A lieutenant, if the stripes on his uniform were correct, was attempting to insert his rigid member into the thrashing, screaming girl. Animalistic rage had replaced the commando's normally scowling visage.

Vincent, who was facing the duo, had been so frenzied over the assault he failed to notice the huge brute with a crazy look in his eye standing just inside the doorway. The strapping warrior performed a feat of magic in that moment. He made the head of the grinning pedophile disappear. In a plume of red and gray, the burst of automatic gunfire vaporized every perverted thought and memory the degenerate ever had.

Lieutenant Hardman turned to determine what had just transpired and found a hulk of a monster, vengeance evident in his demeanor, headed his direction.

"No, hold on, wait! Let me explain!"

The muscular hulking brute that was the Angel of Death strode over to the cowering soldier who was attempting to put his deflating member away, picked him off the ground with his left hand, and threw him against the south wall.

"Watch him," the titan barked to Jordan.

"Yes, sir!" the ex-Marine replied as he raced to the lieutenant who was crumpled helplessly on the floor.

Angel ran to the distraught girl who was struggling to get out of her constraints. When the warrior untied her, she immediately employed her discarded outfit to wipe blood and brains off her upper torso. "And you thought the gruel from that zombie was disgusting," the grinning goliath said, hoping a semblance of levity would bring Mackenzie out of her anguish.

"Funny man," the blue-eyed beauty replied, sitting up. "Come here, you." The young girl slid forward and off the table, wrapping her arms around her rescuer. "Oh, honey, where have you been? I was afraid you wouldn't make it in time."

"Sweetheart, you have no idea what I went through to get here."

"What the hell is that black stinking crap all over your camo?"

"Blood from a parsickle. Had to kill one before I could save you. I'll tell you about it later. Right now, all that matters is we're together." The musclebound commando wrapped his arms around the girl in an encircling embrace and shared a deep and loving kiss. "Look, we need to get you clothed and the hell out of here!"

"My first nude embrace with you, and it had to be here, right?" the girl complained.

Immediately the warrior striped the uniform off what was left of Vincent and handed them to Mackenzie. "A little bloody but beats your previous getup."

"Before we leave here, I intend to burn it."

"Don't blame you," Angel stated as he walked to the door. After looking both directions, he turned to the duo. "Guys, get their weapons. Mac, strip these two of their pistols and stay with me. Jordan, bind and gag that piece of shit. Stay here, stay down, and if it isn't one of the captives or our team, kill it!"

Jordan repeated his predictable, "Yes, sir."

The strapping warrior expected that his gunfire would have drawn attention to their location; however, the sound of automatic weapons above him signified that not to be the case. Rather than take a hit-or-miss approach, the legionnaire decided that the best route was to sweep from the top down. His men were doing so at the western end; he wanted to follow suit on the eastern side to ensure none of the troopers slipped past them. Cautiously scrambling up the staircase, the two made it to the air vent gallery without incident. "Mac, run a spare pistol up to the east vestibule and arm one of the most capable-looking captives. Instruct them to be on the lookout and ensure none of the soldiers get to their level."

When she returned, the combatant instructed her to remain at the landing to ensure their position was not outflanked, while he swept the air vent gallery from east to west.

*****

"Spread out and stay several feet behind me," Jim instructed as they soundlessly crept up the west stairwell toward the vestibule. In battle, a seasoned soldier can sense the enemy's presence if properly trained in the art. The adversary's heart rate rises and pounds harder in his chest. His breathing becomes faster, ragged, and louder. At times, they begin to shift imperceptibly, making tiny fidgeting sounds. Oftentimes, these sounds are not audible to the human ear but are picked up by extrasensory perception. Such was the case for the junior commando.

"Son of a bitch," Jim conceded. "Angel's suspicions were spot on. He certainly knew what he was talking about." The younger brother communicated his concerns to his teammates. Crouching low to the steps, Jim slowly pressed upward, his companions following suit.

Suddenly, one of the soldiers who had lost his nerve jumped up from a squatting position, leveled his rifle, and prepared to fire. He never got the chance. The three tribe members opened up with their automatic weapons a split second sooner and riddled the soldier with ten-millimeter ball. His two comrades jumped into action, intent on joining the fray but never got the chance; a hail of lead decimated the pair. Blood and bits of copper decorated the wall behind them.

Hero and Mountain Man turned and went back down the flight of stairs with Jim in the lead and stopped at the landing. The three scrutinized the top gallery for movement when Mountain Man caught sight of Angel and Mackenzie in the opposite landing. Mountain Man waved his cap in order to gain the titan's attention. Angel waved, acknowledging the action.

Knowing the air vent gallery to be secure, the tribe leader signaled his companions to descend to the next level and to wait for his signal. Once both teams reached the inspection gallery landing, the combatant signaled for two of the triad to advance and the other to monitor the stairwell so as not to be outflanked flanked. Angel left the beautiful blonde with instructions to surveil the steps so they weren't outmaneuvered. As the fighting man swept his end of the facility, he found Jim and Hero doing the same. Their plan was to meet somewhere in the middle.

As they passed a section of wall supporting various maintenance tools and equipment, the goliath watched as Hero selected a short length of chain, careful not to make it rattle. The football player slowly began to swing it over his head. Around and around it went, spinning it faster and faster. When the timing was right, he released the chain so it would sail through the air to land somewhere between their positions, clamoring to the cement floor. Hero's aim was true; however, the chain collapsed and veered to his left, near some tables and equipment.

"The boy was catching on, I'll give him that," the warrior reflected.

The three advancing members stopped and crouched to see if the clatter would flush anyone from hiding. When it seemed as if nothing would become of it, the three began to continue their advance. Suddenly a trooper who was hiding beneath an engineering table on Angel's right accidentally scooted a chair he was using to sight his rifle. Unable to see the sniper for the chairs and other fixtures, Jim and Hero were sitting ducks.

Angel, his keen reflexes ready for any scenario, immediately raised his G3 to his right shoulder and put a three-shot burst into the soldier's back. Fire and smoke belched out of the muzzle of the warrior's weapon. Two chairs screeched along the floor as he was propelled forward by the heavy slugs; the gallery echoed within the confines of the concrete structure.

Thankful for their leader's intervention, Jim and Hero continued to make their way to the midpoint of the gallery, searching and inspecting every object large enough to conceal a person. The titan performed a search of the barracks, finding no one there. As the four met in the center of the gallery, confident that level was clear, they stopped to take a count.

"How many were in the vestibule?" Angel asked of no one in particular.

"Three, you were spot on about their intent to take us from behind," Jim stated.

"Okay, that leaves two galleries and twenty soldiers," the combat veteran reasoned. "Prepare for all-out warfare. Jim, try to keep your guys safe and alert. Remember, if we manage to get to the next level unopposed, our greatest risk lies in being overrun from the bottom level. If I were them, I would try to distract us with a firefight from hell while sneaking up from the bottom level and flanking us."

"You got it, bro!"

The team members went back to their respective stairwells and began their descent to the next level.

"Everything okay?" Angel asked as they cautiously took the steps one at a time.

The blonde shook her head in the affirmative.

"Who did you give the pistol to?"

"Guy named Braiden, claims to be a regular target shooter but nothing that has ever shot back at him."

"Honey, in these last two levels, there are twenty armed soldiers. I anticipate a counterattack from below. Please be vigilant. I can't lose you now."

"Same here, sweetheart."

As the duo reached the operations gallery, Angel waited for Jim to give the all-clear signal before proceeding farther. The warrior watched with great satisfaction as his brother directed Mountain Man to lay low and concealed behind the landing. The veteran of WWIII had Mackenzie do the same. When Jim gave the thumbs-up sign, the three proceeded to creep through the operations gallery. Angel realized that of all the other levels, this gallery presented the most danger due to the abundance of equipment and the two enclosed rooms. Jordan was holding Hardman captive in the room up ahead to his left. The room that used to house the captives was farther down.

The warrior first wanted to ensure that things were in order with Jordan, so he angled this path toward that direction. He watched as Hero snaked his way toward the other room. Angel found that Jordan had Hardman gagged and bound and a pistol in his ear. Giving him the thumbs-up, the fighting man signaled for Jordan to accompany him back into the gallery. As they stepped into the main artery, automatic gunfire assailed their ears.

*****

Hero watched the tribe leader duck into the room Mackenzie had been escorted to earlier. He waited for a moment to ensure his friend wouldn't be ambushed from behind, then proceeded to investigate the room in which he and the others had been held. The football player emulated his mentor's style of approaching from a sharp angle. Squatting at the entrance of the room, he employed Jim's tactic of sensing for the presence of intruders. As quarterback for a successful university football team, he had to be intuitive. Knew exactly where to throw the ball even before you knew where your receiver was. Hero found he could employ that same perception to his task. *Son of a bitch*, the quarterback thought to himself. It worked. He could sense the presence of someone hiding in and about the sleeping area. After fifteen seconds without response, Hero fired a short burst toward the suspect area, ready for a deadly response. Sure enough, automatic gunfire burst forth from underneath two of the beds. Because the blind volley was so inaccurate, it missed the quarterback completely. However, it immediately gave away their positions. Almost as soon as their assault quieted, the football player heard a long string of gunfire to his right. Startled at first, he soon realized it was not directed at him. Still squatting, Hero cut loose with two short bursts, immediately killing his attackers beneath the beds.

*****

Jim remained behind cover of some piece of unknown electronic gadgetry as he watched the football player begin his advance into the room. Just as gunfire erupted, three troopers burst forth from concealment, beginning the act of raising their rifles to their shoulders, putting the football player in their crosshairs. The junior commando wasted no time in sending a long burst of automatic fire into the trio, downing them immediately. Blood and guts splattered the gray concrete floor. The blast from the junior commando's weapon was deafening. As he exited the room, Hero immediately put together the pieces of the deadly scenario. Just as he did so, gunfire erupted all around him. It seemed as if it was coming from somewhere above as bullets were raining down upon him. He could feel the blast as bits of cement and the bullet's copper jackets peppered him. The quarterback made a mad dash back into the room he had just exited and was struck in two places before he could find cover. A grazed left leg and left hand summed up most of the damage.

Jim was perplexed as to where the fire was coming from. He felt completely powerless to do anything to help his friend.

*****

Grateful that the gunfire was not directed at them, the hulking titan realized the soldier's plan was unfolding just as he had predicted. More gunfire, coming from the room Hero had just entered. The goliath could only pray that it was return fire. Given the nearly two-thousand-foot length of the installation, his teammate's position was still a long way off. As he and Jordan stalked their way through the gallery, they could hear even more gunfire as three troopers ran from cover toward Hero's position. They did not get far before the three went down like bowling pins. The strapping commando was relieved to see Hero emerge from the room unscathed, only then to see him go down, recoil as if he were hit, and scamper back into the room. This time, however, Angel could see the source of the assault. Due to his distance from the third intake duct that traversed north to south, the fighting man observed someone lying prone atop the farthest cement ductwork, firing at Hero. Immediately, the hulking brute put his scope on the trooper and squeezed the trigger. A fatal scream echoed through the gallery as he fell to the floor.

*****

Mountain Man waited patiently, undistracted by the numerous bursts of automatic gunfire emanating behind him. The knowledge that his teammates had his back and were successful in their mission made him feel secure in the hazardous environment. Just as his leader predicted, an assault designed to catch them off guard was obviously at play.

The woodsman heard the word, "Go!" echo from down below followed by the scuffling of feet. He heard the whisper of "Let's go. Let's go." In an instant, four armed troopers scrambled into the stairwell as if they were certain an opposing force would not be present. Mountain Man was amazed by their intent focus on the steps, evidently trying not to stumble, totally oblivious to any danger from above.

Duplicating his leader's style of stairwell combat, the woods dweller kept the angle of his rifle consistent with that of the risers. Zechariah felt like a murderer, more so than when they gunned down Jack's men. It was either him or them back then. Now he felt it was more like shooting fish in a barrel. He did not abide by those acts, and it gave him pause.

That pause was just long enough for a wary trooper to raise his rifle and host a barrage of automatic fire lightly strafing the woodsman's left arm and torso. Realizing the stupidity of his inaction, Zechariah unleashed a fusellage of his own. He had noticed earlier that the self-shuckers pulled left to right as they fired. So he began his blitzkrieg, focusing his automatic fire starting on the left and let the rifle work itself to the right. The ten-millimeter rifle rapidly boomed in the confines of the landing as it belched fire and lead like a firehose. The impact of the deadly slugs left a gruesome trail of blood and exposed flesh in their wake. The four troopers tumbled backward; blood spurted like showers from a spinning pinwheel as they did so. The screams of the dead and dying haunted the loner. Straining his senses, Mountain Man crept down the staircase toward the grout gallery, wary to any deception.

Shuffling footfalls alerted Mackenzie to an assault from down below. Obviously, Mountain Man's defense made the soldiers painfully aware that the stairs were being monitored by opposing forces. The girl was a crack shot with most military weapons and was eager to demonstrate her prowess. She keenly maintained surveillance of the area around the bottom landing while keeping the rifle solidly pressed into her right shoulder, her left hand steadying the forearm.

Her diligence paid off as she saw the top of a head start to appear around a corner. The assassin never knew what hit him as his head exploded before his eyes cleared the turn. The girl never flinched, never moved a muscle as she awaited the next attack. She didn't have long to wait as another trooper, hoping to take advantage of the shooter's respite, decided to press his luck. He was quickly rewarded for his bravery with a 180-grain bullet to the face, his brains exiting the four-inch-diameter hole in the back of his head.

The blonde beauty waited silently for another assault. After about sixty seconds, she began to wonder if no one else was interested in trying his luck. Evidently, their plan was to lull the shooter into carelessness, the young girl reasoned, as two soldiers burst into view at the same instant. Obviously, these jerks clearly do not appreciate her training with timed active targets, she thought to herself as she placed a bullet into the eye of one of the men and a bullet into the mouth of the other. "Good riddance to bad garbage," she spat under her breath.

Debating if she should continue into the lower gallery by herself, her leader, followed by Jordan, materialized by her side. "How many did you dispatch?"

"I killed all four of them," the beautiful girl announced with vinegar in her voice.

"I checked with the others. We think we have every level cleared except for this last one. Mac, behind me. Jordan, bring up the rear."

The three stalked their way down the steps and onto the landing, knowing that their counterparts were doing the same on the western end. Angel stopped long enough to retrieve a rifle and spare ammo from one of the downed soldiers and handed the munitions to Jordan. From the titan's previous deployment there, he was well familiar with the installation. The grout gallery, in order to increase stability as the dam's base, had legs set intermittently as part of the casting process. Because of that fact, it contained sizable niches and voids that could conceal their adversaries from view. Being the base of the dam and was heavy with cement, large steel tubes twenty-four feet in diameter were employed to give access to other rectangular areas of the gallery. Tread ways created by pouring cement three feet deep along the length of these tubes provided a twelve-foot-wide path that provided access to the entire length of the facility. Unfortunately, that level also contained the electric generator he had disabled earlier. The noise produced by the mechanical and electric devices echoed throughout the structure and would disguise the whereabouts of the enemy.

The only thing that brought the commando solace was that possibly two of the remaining four were Butch and Sam, who more than likely had not been part of the action so far or possessed any military experience.

At the base of the landing, Angel stopped to educate his two companions about the hazards regarding the layout of the gallery as well as the fact that the lighting was dismal since good lighting was not required. Gunfire suddenly erupted at the far side of the level. Every time he heard shooting, he prayed that his team was okay. This time was no exception.

"Okay, team, we're balls deep into this. Spread out and be careful. Keep fifteen feet apart. Watch for the crevices," the veteran warned.

Jordan realized that the crevices the team leader spoke about were voids in the cement where unsupported material shrunk and left man-sized hollows. He watched as his leader alternated between moving and crouching his way down the tread deck, studying the shadows while keeping his attention focused on the unknown. The Marine also got the impression that Angel and the girl were an item, if for no other reason than what he witnessed between the two earlier and the fact that concern for the big guy radiated from her like an LED sign.

*****

As they crept their way along, staying ten feet apart, Jim took his eyes from his reconnaissance to inspect the damage and repair made to the generator controls. Unfortunately, it proved to be extremely bad timing for the junior veteran as a single shot split the placid quietude. Jim felt something slam into his chest. As the younger brother stumbled backward and went down, he was aware that Mountain

Man had returned fire into the second left void, putting the assailant out of commission.

*****

As shots rang out from the other end of the facility, Ange, Jordan, and Mackenzie redoubled their effort to seek out and destroy the three remaining adversaries. They did not have to wait long as a weapon rolled out of one of the nooks on the right. Before the shooter could raise his weapon, Jordan cut loose with a three-shot burst, placing all three in the assassin's chest. As the man fell to the ground, even in the subdued lighting, it was plainly obvious that it was Butch he had killed.

Angel turned and gave the ex-Marine the thumbs-up. "Only two more left," the titan deduced. "Only so many places they could hide." Closing in on the center of the gallery, the strapping commando could see his teammates approaching far up ahead. *Dear Lord*, he thought. *One is missing. Judging by their similar heights, my brother...my brother's missing. Put out of action by some son of a bitch!*

It was at that moment Sam popped out of his place of concealment on Angel's left and opened fire. Angel immediately responded with a long burst of automatic fire that decimated the hapless trader. Infuriated over the loss of his brother, the fighting man intended to shred Sam to pieces.

In that exact same instant, the last of their quarry sprang out of a nook on the right, intending to make the most of the distraction created by his comrade. Mackenzie recognized the gunman as Wooten and wasted no time in firing on the dirty bastard that had called her a cunt. The one who had threatened to rape her, even with several rounds in her arm.

For a number of seconds, the grout gallery was consumed with ricocheting bullets, smoke, and explosion as four fully automatic rifles spewed potential death and destruction. Each combatant was fighting the effects of jackhammering weapons, blinded vision, and acoustic bombardment. When it was all over, and the smoke had cleared, two dead and one seriously wounded were lying on the cold cement floor. The sound of Mountain Man and Hero running toward them broke the eerie silence.

Sam was dead, unrecognizable due to the devastating effects of a dozen 180-grain hollow-point bullets out of the elite killing machine's rifle. Also gone was Jordan, the ex-Marine who proved himself to be most valuable, shot in the head and chest. Also wounded were Angel and Mackenzie. Grazes to various limbs and torsos, nothing that medical aid and time would not mend.

Finally, there was Woten, crying and thrashing on the gray concrete tread way.

"I give up! I surrender!" The soldier cried like a baby. "I don't want to do this anymore."

Angel approached the blonde who was standing over the crying fellow, a glazed, faraway look in her eyes. "This presents a problem," The titan stated.

"Please help me! I don't want to die—"

"So you wanted to rape me, did you?"

"No, I didn't mean anything. I was just—"

"Even with a few bullets in my arm, did you?" The girl planted a slug in each arm.

"Mac," Angel warned.

"No!" Wooten screamed like a little girl.

"Then you were going to rape me, were you?" The enraged beauty placed a slug in his crotch.

"Aaaiiieee," the soldier screamed. Please no. I… I still want to live.

"Mackenzie," the titan shouted.

"Filthy piece of shit!" Mackenzie then emptied the remainder of the magazine into the pleading man. She then spat in his face.

As stone-cold a killer as he was, the elite killing machine was astounded by the abhorrent actions of the girl. Was not sure he could ever love her again, so despicable were her actions. However, he placed himself inside her head. The psychology of it was that she was getting even for every abominable, repulsive act done to her by every soldier in the facility. The warrior decided that as repulsive as it was, it was probably good therapy. He might have done the same. Perhaps he had.

Angel and Mackenzie found themselves reunited by the woodsman and football player. The two men looked from what was left of Wooten, and the girl who had butchered him, stark revulsion in their faces.

Angel finally steeled himself to ask the question. "How did my brother die?" His inquiry was loud and filled with adrenaline as it echoed through the acoustic confines of the gallery.

"Don't get your hopes up just yet, big brother. I'm almost as hard to take down as you are," Angel's younger brother declared as he sauntered up to his team members.

"Jim! You're alive," Angel accused as he took his brother into his arms.

"Last time I checked, anyway."

"What happened to you?" the older sibling demanded.

"I was shot dead center in the heart. However, as I had my rifle angled across my chest, the bullet struck the receiver of my rifle just where the magazine attaches. It had to penetrate the outer receiver, magazine, several bullets within it, out the other side of the mag, and inner receiver." Unzipping his camo as he spoke, he said, "It barely drew much blood, but it knocked the wind out of my lungs so hard that I passed out for a while."

"Come on, guys," the titan announced, putting his right arm around Mackenzie and his left around his brother. "Let's go check on the captives and do some celebrating."

CHAPTER 10

Angel and Mackenzie were in the barracks discussing their next move while seated at a white folding table, sitting on gray metal folding chairs. It had been three days since the battle with the soldiers. They had used that time to accomplish a number of much-needed tasks such as minister to wounds, give Jordan a proper burial, and rid the facility of dead soldiers. They collected and stored all weapons and ammunition other than what they would carry away with them. Steve, Braiden, and Jason accompanied Hero to retrieve the Panther and both ambulances. Mackenzie, true to her word, unceremoniously burned the revealing attire crafted for her by her captors and stuffed the ashes into Hardman's front pockets.

Angel was getting sick from the smell of the parsickle blood-soaked attire. Even though he showered and washed the garment, he still smelled of a rotting pile of garbage. As none of the troopers wore a uniform his size, he had to wait for the Panther to return so he could obtain a spare. Before they left, he recounted his experience with the devilish monstrosity and advised the team, if attacked, how they might defeat it.

While Hero and company were on assignment, Mountain Man stayed busy attending to Lieutenant Hardman in the hostage room, keeping him fed and under surveillance. Hardman, who was unrelenting in his attack on the woods dweller, referred to Zechariah as a dumb hillbilly. The woodsman would retort that at least he did not get himself captured with his rooster in his hand. The two never stopped. It seemed as if the woodsman reveled in making Hardman's captivity as miserable as possible.

Angel contacted Trish by radio and advised her of their situation and condition while bringing her up to speed on the parsickles that were running rampant throughout their dimension. He learned that their brother Rick, while holding his own to a lesser degree, was gradually succumbing to green disease. Also, Princess was turning into an excellent watchdog as they discovered that someone, or something, was stalking the ledge floor in front of their lair during the night.

"Where do we go from here?" Mackenzie inquired.

"As near as I can determine, given the crazy variables, we are dealing with four issues. First, your father. His rescue is still part of our mission, both for your sake and that of my brother. In fact, for all our lives.

"Second. Transportation. No matter what option we chose—going back to the cave or pressing on—we'll transfer all the fuel from Sam's truck to fill the Panther. We'll use the rest to equally fill the ambulances. We'll restock and resupply medical supplies to the Panther from both ambulances.

"Third. This facility. This structure is a safe stronghold, secure from just about anything out there. Should anything happen to our cave, or should our tribe grow in numbers, this place would be an ideal fortification with plenty of surrounding forest for hunting. When we rescue your father, perhaps he can find a way to purify the lake water. Can you imagine an inexhaustible supply of clean drinking and bathing water? In order to preserve this installation, when we leave, I'm going to lock both vestibules from the inside, then go out and lock the emergency access, climb the rope, and collect my equipment. Should we need to reenter, I can do the reverse.

"Finally, the others. We have three men, two women, and a child who is going to have a child of her own. Then there's Hardman. A viscous rapist bastard whom I would never turn loose upon the world."

"Give the son of a bitch to me!" Mackenzie demanded, grasping the titan's right forearm as she spoke.

"Mac, it's one thing to kill unmercifully and unrepentant in the heat of battle. Please do not act on whatever it is you are planning. It changes a person forever. There is no coming back from that. Trust me, I know."

The young blonde turned away from her hero and shook her head. "I don't know what I'm going to do. I just know that I have to have my revenge, or I'll never be right again. Sorry. Just make one promise. Whatever I decide to do about his fate, you won't interfere."

The commando considered her request for several seconds. "I promise. But I hope you will make the right decision when the time comes."

*****

The next morning, with everyone outside the east vestibule and both doors locked, Angel descended to the grout gallery to exit and lock the maintenance access. After much discussion, it was decided that his team would continue their quest to find Mackenzie's father. That the three men would take one ambulance and look for their family while the three females would do so in the other. What would happen to Hardman, his arms bound behind his back, was anyone's guess.

Angel collected his gear and began his climb up the rope toward the top of the west road deck. As he topped the dam, a loud chorus of shouts, followed by even louder screams assailed his ears. Throwing rope and gear over his shoulders, the fighting man raced to the east bulkhead to see about the commotion. Hero met him three-quarters of the way there.

"Angel…it's…the women. Quick. Come see. Hurry!" the football player divulged.

Racing at full speed, side by side, the veteran asked, "What about the women?" praying that his girl's deepest, darkest thoughts had not come to fruition.

"Come. We don't know what to do!"

"What is it?"

"You'll see!"

As the duo were within sight, the warrior heard Mackenzie screaming, "No, no, no, he was mine. God, he was mine!" as she pounded her fists deep onto Mountain Man's broad chest. Angel found no sight of little Mandy, Stacy, or Hardman.

"What the hell is going on? And where the hell are the others?" the strapping commando demanded.

Mountain Man tried to respond but found it impossible to speak given the literal beating he was suffering at the hands of Mackenzie and the inability to be understood over her constant screaming. He threw up his arms in defeat.

"Someone tell me what the fuck is going on," the tribal leader insisted.

Melissa was the first to attempt an explanation as she tried to hold back tears. "We...we were standing here waiting...waiting for you to return when poor Mandy got sick. Morning sickness... I suppose. Anyway, the poor kid, she...she couldn't help it. She began throwing up something bad. Just so happens she was standing next to that *fucking lieutenant* and ended up vomiting all over him. His clothes, his face and hands...all over."

At that, Mackenzie began to wail, burying her face in the woodsman's barrel chest.

Melissa finally broke down as she continued. "So that *fucking lieutenant*, oh...what did that son of a bitch...son of a bitch do? Auuuggghhh!"

"The bastard kicked her hard...really hard! Oh, no, noooo. So hard that he knocked her over, and she stumbled and fell. Little baby stumbled and fell. Because...she...she was so small, she fell beneath the handrail and...and...auuugghhh...and tumbled into the lake."

Makenzie began screaming, "He was mine. Damn it, he was supposed to be mine!"

The fighting man was stunned to his very core by the revelation. "But...what happened to the other two?"

Melissa took several moments to catch her breath. "You...you can imagine how Stacy felt, you know, watching her little angel fall into the lake. I don't think that was the butcher's intent...didn' meant to do that, but then the son of a bitch said...just had to say... 'Good riddance to the little whore.' You can only imagine what must have been going on in the head of her mother. It was like she turned into some kind of wild woman. The...the look in her eyes. Angel... sir, she would have rivaled you. You could tell she had this animal strength, like…like a mother bear or something. Stacy wove her right arm in through Hardman's bindings and left arm and jumped off the dam, taking the dirty bastard with her."

Mackenzie pulled her face away from the woods dweller's chest. "He was supposed to be *mine*. He…was…supposed…to…*be mine. Mine!*"

The commando's reaction was to race to the rail and search for any sign of life.

"It's not like we didn't want to jump in and save them, the mom and daughter, anyway. We discussed it briefly," Jim reasoned, "but after the story you told about being lucky to get away with your life, well, we were afraid to chance it."

Still peering into the turbulent brackish water, Angel spoke very low, so low that his words almost escaped the others. "No, you did the right thing. There was no hope for any of them. You would have given your lives for nothing." Before turning to face the others, the ultimate engine of death stopped to wipe the tears from his eyes.

The titan knew his next challenge was to reassure Mackenzie. As he walked over and took her into his embrace, it seemed as though Zechariah had been uncomfortable with his circumstance and eager to give her up.

"Honey, I know how you feel. I have felt the same about lost quarry. But look, Hardman met his demise, a very appropriate and vicious one at that. Even more than that, the revenge of blood isn't on your hands."

Continuing to shed tears, the young girl nodded her head in silence.

*****

After briefly mourning the loss of mother and child, the four civilians decided that they would travel together in one ambulance and seek out surviving family members, if still alive. They determined that traveling two up in two different directions would be too risky. Steve agreed to hide one ambulance in the maintenance garage and place the key in the tailpipe before continuing on their journey.

Angel watched their departing friends drive off until they were out of sight before firing up the Panther.

"Something on your mind?" Jim asked from the seat to his brother's right.

"Just thinking," the titan said.

"About what?" the junior commando asked.

"Life. This crazy world we inherited. Wondering if we will ever see those people again, alive. Wondering what lies ahead of us and—"

"And…what, dear?" Mackenzie asked from the center of the back seat.

"Me."

"You sound as if you have some special mission all of your own. You know that we will always be together. If no one else, you will always have me. I will never leave you, and you will never leave me, the Lord willing…"

As the Angel of Death put the transmission into gear, he gently nodded his head so his friends could not see. As Mackenzie's words began to fade inaudibly into oblivion, he wondered why he had a strange feeling regarding the last two discernable words of Mackenzie's statement.

ABOUT THE AUTHOR

John D. Belcastro works as a marketing consultant, owns numerous businesses, and has written professionally for business publications. He has won awards for his various business and philanthropic endeavors.

A product of the cold war of the fifties and sixties, John D. Belcastro vividly remembers the test pattern of the emergency broadcast system blaring over the TV screen while frightening words advised everyone within earshot to seek shelter. As home construction skyrocketed during the post-WWII era, many urban and suburban residents either incorporated bomb shelters into their floor plan or constructed them in their backyard. Most government facilities were strategically hardened and stocked with civil defense rations and water to serve as makeshift shelters.

It was little wonder that, as a young boy with a great imagination, John wondered about the implications of such an attack. Subscribing to the survivalist discipline as a young man, he continued to ask the question, What if? As time went on and nuclear devices grew in magnitude, the development of biochemical weapons added to the fear of what all-out warfare could bring.

John writes about such a world where only the strongest and best prepared would survive. He envisioned a world where a bio-nuclear fusillade would not only destroy most life on the planet but would drastically alter the men and beasts that had the misfortune to survive it. He visualized a civilization that would descend to a frontier society. A culture not only comprised of hunters, gatherers, and pillagers but strong, domineering men who unfortunately would subjugate and enslave their fellow man. Where the strong long for death and the weak sought it. A civilization where the wicked urges of men reign unchecked.

John reveals a world where dangerous creatures roam the earth seeking to rid themselves of mankind's dominion. Where the earth itself rebels to exterminate the parasite that is humanity.